A treasure far greater than gold...

Keelan has awakened from a deep slumber, in another time, in another place, and still haunted by the demons of his past. Determined to recover the Treasure that caused his family's downfall, he arrives at the sweeping Scottish countryside ... and discovers the magic of a gentle, healing touch from a lass who stokes passion's fire in this Highlander's breast.

The mysterious appearance of the Scottish warrior nearly causes Charity to abandon her plans, but she'd been playing the part of a dutiful maid for too long to let someone else walk away with the prize--even if Keelan *is* as great a temptation as the Treasure. Yet when they are forced on the run, Charity discovers that the Highlander may be too irresistible, and to deny him would be impossible ... for love's glorious promise awaits her in his powerful embrace and sensuous kiss.

By Lois Greiman

BEWITCHING THE HIGHLANDER
TEMPTING THE WOLF • TAMING THE BARBARIAN
SEDUCING A PRINCESS • THE PRINCESS MASQUERADE
THE PRINCESS AND HER PIRATE • THE WARRIOR BRIDE
THE MacGOWAN BETROTHAL • THE FRASER BRIDE
HIGHLAND HAWK • HIGHLAND ENCHANTMENT
HIGHLAND SCOUNDREL

*If You've Enjoyed This Book,
Be Sure to Read These Other*
AVON ROMANTIC TREASURES

AND THEN HE KISSED HER *by Laura Lee Guhrke*
CLAIMING THE COURTESAN *by Anna Campbell*
THE DUKE'S INDISCRETION *by Adele Ashworth*
HOW TO ENGAGE AN EARL *by Kathryn Caskie*
THE VISCOUNT IN HER BEDROOM *by Gayle Callen*

Coming Soon

JUST WICKED ENOUGH *by Lorraine Heath*

BEWITCHING THE HIGHLANDER

Lois Greiman

An Avon Romantic Treasure

AVON

An Imprint of HarperCollinsPublishers

AVON BOOKS
An Imprint of HarperCollins*Publishers*
10 East 53rd Street
New York, New York 10022-5299

Copyright © 2007 by Lois Greiman
ISBN: 978-0-06-119134-3
ISBN-10: 0-06-119134-5
www.avonromance.com

First Avon Books paperback printing: August 2007

Avon Trademark Reg. U.S. Pat. Off. and in Other Countries, Marca Registrada, Hecho en U.S.A.
HarperCollins® is a registered trademark of HarperCollins Publishers.

Printed in the U.S.A.

10 9 8 7 6 5 4 3 2 1

Bewitching
The
Highlander

Prologue

1653

"I should have been here," Keelan gritted. He tried to be strong, but his voice sounded pale and spidery amid the wails of Old Bailey's unseen inhabitants.

His mother reached between the rusty squares of the dungeon's enclosure. Her arms were thin and pale, smeared with dirt. He took her hands, felt the bones, sharp and narrow beneath her chilled skin.

"Ye had na way of knowing of our troubles, Ange."

'Twas true. They hadn't informed him, after all. Had sent him no missives. There were only the dreams to suggest there might be troubles at home. Only the dreams.

"Who did this to ye?" His voice sounded

stronger now, the voice of the man he had come to be, the man they had raised him to become.

Iona shook her head. "It matters not."

He gritted his teeth, tasting death on his tongue, feeling bile curdle his stomach. "I heard . . . I was told . . ." His voice broke. "They killed Da."

She tightened her grip, holding him hard, ragged nails digging into his hands. "Nay. Nay, lad, they did na kill him," she said, but there was fear in her voice, tears in her bonny eyes. "He died of his wounds, luv. Na one was to blame."

Anger mingled with a dozen roiling emotions, making his skin clammy, his head light. "Where is Mr. Kirksted? Why is he na here, defending yer name?"

"He was, of course, but as your da's first mate, he too sustained wounds while at sea. Still, he tried to convince them of me innocence."

"Innocence!" His voice cracked like an untried lad's. "This is madness. Ye are na . . ." For a moment he could not push the word past his frozen lips.

"Dunna worry on it, Ange. All will be well. Go back to Paris. Back to your studies."

"Go back!" Was she mad? Had this hideous place pushed her past the brink of sanity? "I canna leave ye here in this . . . this . . ." For a moment he feared he might cry. Might wail like the terrified creature he was.

Her hands tightened. Her voice did the same. "'Tis madness, just as ye have said. Thus, they will surely free me."

"They accused ye of witchcraft." He whispered the words, as if he might keep it secret, as if all hadn't heard the horrible lies. "When all ye did was try to save him."

"I ken, luv. I ken, but 'tis all a mistake. Naught else. They will set me free, sure."

He wanted to believe, was desperate to do so, but there was a quiver in her voice, a terror in her eyes that galvanized his resolve. "I'll see ye released, Mum." His words were a solemn vow spoken hushed and reverent. "I'll speak to Mr. Kirksted. He will still have influence with the—"

"Nay!" Her voice was strident suddenly. "Ye mustn't. Go back to yer university. Go back."

He shook his head. "But surely Kirksted—"

"Ye will stay clear of him," she hissed. "Stay clear. Do ye hear what I say?"

Keelan shook his head, trying to sift through his murky fear to the truth beneath. "Is he responsible for—"

"Nay! Of course na. But if ye make trouble they may well think we be in league, ye and I." Tears made tracks through the grime on her face.

3

"Ye're na a witch!"

"Na," she whispered. "But they dunna care."

"Why are they doing this?"

She shook her head.

"What do they hope to gain? Is it coin? Might they think Da somehow salvaged the great treasure he spoke of? That it was na lost back to the sea as—"

"It does na matter."

He drew himself up. Fear was yet there, but dim now, receding. "Nay, it does na. For I will stop them. This I swear."

"Nay! Please." She seemed so small now, so pale and fragile behind the vile bars. "Promise me ye will na."

He squeezed her hand and held her gaze with his own. "Do ye think me such a coward?"

"A coward . . ." She said the words slowly, her voice calm and unbroken for the first time since his arrival there. "Nay, me luv. Never that." She released his hand and set her palm to his cheek. Her fingertips felt dry and cold. "The blood of the Black Celt flows strong in yer veins. I knew it from the first moment I held ye in me arms. From the moment I loved ye with the whole of me heart."

His throat constricted. "I will see ye free, Mum. This I swear."

Her dark, Gypsy eyes bored into his, and then she nodded, face solemn, eyes bright.

"Verra well," she said. "I will show ye a way. But ye must swear on yer father's grave that ye will follow me every word."

"I dunna need—"

"Swear to me!" she ordered, eyes gleaming in the dimness, and there was naught he could do but obey.

Chapter 1

1819

"**C**older than a sea witch's arse," Keelan muttered and stumbled again, nearly falling face first in the sodden bog. A cold north-westerly drove rain, hard and fast, into his face, soaking the tunic beneath the threadbare waist-coat he held bunched tight at his throat. "And I would be knowing," he added, then snorted at his own wit, dubious though it was. But whose humor would not be a bit stale given the circum-stances? It had been raining since well before dusk. His last meal was little more than a cher-ished memory, and he was still mourning the loss of the small fortune he'd left the three gentlemen with whom he'd been gaming some days past. But the term *gentlemen* was loosely used indeed. Not one of them had cracked a grin the entire evening. On the other hand . . . He tripped again, righted himself, stumbled on. What they lacked in frolicking good natures they more than made up for in coin . . . and size. Arms as big around as Keelan's legs. Necks the size of . . . The toe of his saturated boot caught on something unseen in the darkness. He lurched forward, stopping his fall with his hands and feeling sheep droppings squish between his frigid fingers.

"Ahh," he said, rolling onto his back and laughing into the hard-driving rain. Where there were sheep droppings there were sheep, as ol' Toft was wont to say, Keelan thought, and grinned into the stinging deluge before struggling to his feet. Shuttling up a slippery incline, he gazed into the little dale that fell sharply away. It was as dark as the devil's broom closet below him, but dotted here and there among the sweeping hillocks were clumps of woolly gray. Sheep. Better known to the wayward Scotsman as dinner on the hoof.

Slipping back down the hill a scant few inches, Keelan fumbled with the ancestral sporran that hung from his waist. Opening it was no simple task, for his fingers had gone numb and stupid with the cold. His muscles were cramped and aching, but his night vision did not fail him. Still, dipping a dart into the corked vial was an onerous chore. Neither was it simple to fit the tiny weapon into its wooden tube. Yet he managed.

And voilà! Less than an hour later, the world seemed a brighter place. Quite literally in fact, for Keelan of the Forbes was squatting on his haunches before a small but optimistic fire. There was even a roof of sorts above his head. Granted, that roof was supported by slightly less than three walls and might well tumble in on him with any careless move. But 'twas daft luck that had led him to this dubious shelter in the first place, and he would ever greet good fortune with a merry "good day" when he happened upon it.

His ancient kinsmen had been entirely wrong. This was his path, despite their dire warnings. Who were they to warn him anyway? Their own lives had been fraught with dangers. Hiltsglen—the Black Celt. O'Banyon—the Irish Hound. And Toft—the Wanderer. They had tried to pretend they were naught but ordinary Highlanders, but he knew better from the moment he first met them. Saw the eerie strangeness in them just as he saw it in himself. But while their gifts were astounding—Hiltsglen's granite courage, O'Banyon's bestial strength, Toft's inexplicable abilities—Keelan's own talents seemed to be somewhat more humble. Sleeping, for instance.

He was first-rate at sleeping. Well, that and chicanery. The Irish Hound had headed north looking for a healer and found naught but Keelan, a scheming Highlander just up from a lengthy nap.

Oh aye, Keelan had descended from these men of the mist, but he had somehow failed to inherit their talents. Thus, in the two years since his awakening, he had learned to make his own luck, to do without the creature comforts he had known in his former life. And now, after months of laborious scheming, circumstances were fast improving.

Eyeing the lamb that lay motionless at his feet, he grinned. Unless he was dreadfully mistaken, naught but good would come of this night's—

"Hello," said a towering shadow, and stepped inside the shelter. Firelight flickered on the bare arms that stuck like bulging sausages from holes in a sleeveless tunic.

Keelan scrambled madly to his feet. "Mary and Joseph!" he rasped, scurrying backward and crashing into the crumbling wall behind him.

"Actually . . ." said another, and stepped from the darkness, "my name is Roland." He was as slim as the other was stout, as small as the giant was huge. His round face looked angelic in the flickering glow of the firelight, and his golden hair gleamed like a polished halo. "And yonder gentleman is called Frankie."

Keelan shifted his gaze. Frankie was the approximate size of a draft horse and fisted his plowshare hands with impatient slowness.

"I dunna mind telling ye lads, ye scared the living blazes outta me," Keelan breathed. Always good to tell the truth if it suited his needs.

Roland smiled, but despite his angelic good looks, the expression did nothing to warm one's cockles even if one happened to know what the hell cockles were. "And who might you be, friend?"

Keelan skipped his gaze to the lamb near Frankie's mammoth feet and lied for all he was worth. "Me name be Bruce." His mind was racing like a cheating Englishman, skittering over well-laid schemes. Perhaps, after all, this was not his wisest plan to date. "Of the Highland MacLeods." Stepping forward, he reached for Roland's hand. They shook. "'Tis glad I am to meet ye." He shook Frankie's hand next, relieved when his own average-sized mitt emerged unscathed. "I be Lord Seafirth's lad."

"Seafirth?"

"Aye. Sure ye know him," Keelan said. "Deaf ol' bugger he be, but with a good heart. He lives over yonder." He gave his head a tilt in no particular direction. "Past Learloch Hills."

Roland's eyes gleamed as though anticipating some unspoken pleasure. "The bald old gaffer in the thatched cottage?"

"Aye." Keelan laughed. Perhaps he should have been relieved by the other's seeming jocularity, but his scalp was tingling. Still, it was not a premonition. He didn't believe in premonitions.

"That's the one. Hairless as a hen's egg he be. And near as toothless." Glancing to his right, Keelan calculated his chances of escape. Not bad really. One in ten at least. "Makes him look like a withered ol' apple." He nodded, biding his time. His mind was ever faster than his feet. "I see to his sheep, I do. He's been worried sick aboot poor wee blighter there," he said, and cast his gaze sadly toward the lamb.

Roland's gaze flickered to the inert little body. "Looks rather dead, does it not?"

"Aye." Keelan shook his head. "I fear so. 'Tis a terrible shame, it is. Me master will cry himself to sleep for a week." Keelan's stomach twisted up hard. No, he didn't believe in premonitions, but he was a strong advocate of saving his own hide. "Silly wee lambkin wandered off some days past after the lightning storm and—"

"I don't know any Lord Seafirth," said Roland and took a step forward.

11

Keelan resisted crowding back. It would do no good. The wall was behind him. The roof, such as it was, slanted overhead, and the lamb lay in accusatory silence off to his left. But he straightened his back and fixed a scowl of disappointed surprise on his reputedly handsome face. "I hope ye're na thinking *I* killed this poor beastie."

Roland's bland expression changed naught a whit. "Killed it? Certainly not. We wouldn't be thinking something so uncharitable as all that, would we, Frankie?"

Frankie, Keelan noticed, didn't answer, but shuffled a few steps closer. He also noticed that a good-sized branch drooped from the rotting thatch roof not far above his own head.

"Unfortunately for you, boy, the question is not whether we believe you, but whether Lord Chetfield is in a kindly mood," Roland said.

Chetfield! A sharp vision of pain seared Keelan like a flame, freezing his breath in his chest. He'd come to the right place after all, only to find himself outmanned. "Lord Chetfield?" he repeated blithely.

Roland smiled. His teeth were perfect. His soul was not. "Lord Chetfield is the gentleman whose animal you recently poached, boy."

"Poached!" Keelan puffed out his chest, employing his best expression of offended indignation, but not without once again assessing his chances of escape. If Frankie took but a few more steps, there might just be room to nip between him and the wall. Once he was outside, the devil himself would have a time finding him in the lovely darkness. "As I said afore, this be me master's sheep."

"Seafirth's."

"Aye," Keelan agreed. "*Lad*, he said, tears in his rheumy ol' eyes." Keelan sincerely wished he could conjure up a few tears of his own, but his eyes remained disappointingly dry. "*Me wee lambkin has gone missing. The one with the two-toned face and the speckle of black in his bobbling tail. Fetch him back for me if ever you can.*"

Roland grinned. "Looks to be a ewe lamb."

Frankie had shuffled forward another step.

Keelan shifted his gaze back to the smaller of the two. "What's that ye say?"

"The dead lamb." Roland nodded toward the small beast. "Looks to be the wrong sex, according to your master's pitiable plea."

Keelan quickly perused the lamb's hindquarters and resisted cursing out loud, but fook it all, since when had angelic-looking villains become so damned concerned with the gender of livestock? And supposedly dead livestock at that.

"Aye, well . . ." Keelan said, plotting madly, "Firth's eyesight be na what it once was."

Roland laughed. "Deaf, bald, and blind. Are you certain old Seafirth is still breathing?"

Come on, Frankie lad, Keelan thought. Just a few steps closer, and he would be hotfooting it back toward his kinsmen, such as they were. Empty-handed, true, but neither the Black Celt nor ol' Toft was likely to complain. They'd thought this a fool's errand at the outset. "Aye, well, he's had his share of troubles but—"

"But you're lying like a French whore?"

Keelan cocked his head, actually hoping for an instant that his ears were playing tricks on him. "What's that?"

"This is what I think . . ." Roland's tone was casual, his mouth tilted up at the corner. "You are a miscreant." He shrugged. "Perhaps a daring bandit, but more likely a petty thief. There was trouble in a nearby village. You . . . aggravated the wrong people. Threats were issued. You managed to escape with your life. And . . ." He lifted perfectly manicured hands. "Here you are, slaughtering my lord's prize lambs."

"Slaughtering! Nay. I assure ye—"

"But perhaps I am wrong. Perhaps there is something more sinister at work here." He paused, maybe for thought, maybe to scare the

14

bloody wits out of Keelan, but there was hardly a need for that. The giant was all but breathing down his neck. "Either way, Chetfield will learn the truth before dawn." He smiled, eyes bright as he nodded sideways. "Frankie, let us take our young friend home."

Frankie took one final step forward.

"I'd love to oblige, but I fear I canna," Keelan said, and in that instant leapt for the drooping timber half hidden in the thatch. There was a crack. It came away in his hands . . . no more than twelve inches long. He stared at his would-be weapon, then glanced up in wild horror. A blade appeared like magic in Roland's fist. Frankie grinned and bunched his bovine neck. Fook it! "Let's na be hasty, lads," he suggested, and then the roof came tumbling in.

Keelan sprang forward. Blunt fingers brushed his arm, but he was almost free. Hunching his shoulders, he flashed a grin as he sprinted past. "Sorry to leave ye, lads," he rasped, but something swung suddenly toward his face. Pain exploded in his head like Chinese fireworks, and instantly he was lying on his back while the world spun by in hazy confusion. A thousand thoughts mumbled foggily in his head. A dozen voices chanted and cajoled. Above him, Roland stood against the inky sky.

"Sorry . . . lad," he said, fingering his blade. "Perhaps I forgot to tell you about Bear here."

Keelan shifted his slippery attention to the right. A third man stood there, big as a boulder, blocking out the night. "Bad luck," Keelan rasped, and slid silently into the darkness of his mind.

Chapter 2

Keelan awoke to a scream, only to realize with jolting clarity that it was his own. Pain seared him like a hot brand. Blood streamed down his chest, hot and sticky. His shirt was gone. He was standing with his back against a timber, but his hands were tied. A man the size of a carnival was holding a red-tipped knife not two feet away. What was his name? Brute? Beast? Maybe, it didn't matter. They probably wouldn't be playing crickets together anytime soon.

"So you are awake." The voice that spoke sounded vaguely familiar.

Keelan yanked his attention toward the speaker, but a stranger stood before him. An ordinary man of sixty years or so. Ordinary, yet there was something about him, something odd, something slightly off-kilter.

"I am Lord Chetfield, peer of the realm and master of Crevan House." He smiled. "Mr. Roland here tells me your name is MacLeod." The voice was deep and melodic, yet the lips that spoke it seemed strangely soft, almost feminine.

Keelan blinked, trying to see clearly, but the man's features remained askew. One hand rested on a thick, craggy staff. Its misshapen metal head flowed seamlessly into the dark twisted wood that poked into the chaff beneath the fine leather of his black slippers.

Where the hell were they? Not outside. Some sort of stable. Lanterns hung from pegs on rough-hewn walls. Fodder covered the floor. A dark steed circled its stall restlessly, and near the door, two half-starved wolfhounds watched with gleaming eyes, tethers stretched tight. Keelan's wrists were throbbing. And merciful Mary, his chest hurt like hell.

"Is this true?" asked Chetfield.

Not to mention his poor back. It had been scraped raw and screamed in a thousand pinpoints of agony against the harsh timber behind him. Had they dragged him there? Had they—

The giant with the knife shifted impatiently. Sometime earlier, that same fellow had swung a tree limb in Keelan's direction. He remembered the startling pain with a jolt. Come to think of it, his head hurt like the very devil too.

"Bear," said the old lord. "Our young friend's mind seems to be wandering. Can you help him concentrate on the matter at hand?"

The knife wielder shuffled closer.

"Aye," Keelan snapped, shifting his gaze rapidly from the weapon to the baron. Lord Chetfield! God save him! He'd expected someone different, someone younger perhaps, like the man in his most distant memories. "Aye, MacLeod I be." What had he said about his given name? He couldn't remember. Possibly because he'd been hit in the head by a man the size of a mountain. A furry mountain. Holy fook, the brute had hair everywhere, even on the backs of his hands. If ye sheared him, ye could make a fine coat. Which would be nice, for Keelan was as cold as a winter's morn. Yet he was hot too. Odd, that.

The lord nodded. He wore a stiff, snowy white cravat beneath the long curls of his mutton-chopped jowls. His eyes looked bored. Maybe he was sleepy. Maybe he wouldn't ask about Keelan's given name. Maybe—

Chetfield stepped closer, his movements curiously graceful, silent as a cat upon the chaff beneath him. "And your Christian name, Mr. MacLeod?"

Fook. "Listen," Keelan said, watching Bear from the corner of his eye. Roland and Frankie were also present, but seemed content to observe from some small distance. He'd have to remember to be thankful for that later. "Methinks there may be a bit of a misunderstanding here."

"Oh?" Chetfield lifted the staff, swinging it rhythmically as he paced closer. "And what is it you misunderstand?"

For a moment Keelan was mesmerized by the staff's movement. It was a solid-looking piece, gnarled and knotted, a formidable weapon if need be. He swallowed.

"Mr. MacLeod?"

Keelan jerked his attention back to Chetfield. "Perhaps it seemed to these good gentlemen . . ." He nodded toward the two near the door and tested his bonds. Roland was smoking a narrow cigar, looking smug and relaxed, with a shoulder resting against a weathered wall. "That I had been poaching. But that was na the case."

"Are you saying my employees fabricated the truth, Mr. MacLeod?"

Roland shifted away from the wall. Frankie bunched his mammoth fists, making his biceps coil like serpents.

"Nay. Nay indeed," Keelan argued hurriedly.

What the devil did *fabricated* mean? "I merely meant to say that things are na always as they seem and—"

"The lamb seems to be dead," said the lord, voice smooth, demeanor the same.

"Well there ye have it," Keelan countered. "'Tis naught but a bit of confusion. For ye see, the wee beastie was most probably asleep. 'Tis a chill night. Mayhap he had himself a difficult day, wandering aboot alone in the hillocks as it were. Might it not be that—"

Roland bent. Keelan shifted his attention to the right, saw the man reach down to lift the heretofore unseen lamb by a hind leg. It dangled there like a bad apple from a rain-soaked stem.

"Fie me!" he muttered, knees almost giving way. He should have listened to his elders. This was a fool's errand.

"It seems quite dead, does it not, Mr. MacLeod?"

Fook it all. It really did. Maybe he'd soaked the dart too long in his potent potion. Then again, perhaps the lamb had expired while he was unconscious. Lady Colline had said to wait no more than an hour before waking it with the powder from his sporran. "Aye, aye, now that I see it again, it does indeed look as if it has departed," he agreed, "but ... surely ye dunna think that the poor wee blighter was killed by the likes of meself."

The barn echoed in silence. Light flickered eerily across the lord's haphazard face, illuminating his almost-yellow eyes in the winking firelight. "In fact, that is just what I think."

"Nay! Nay," Keelan said. "As I told yer lads here, I be a shepherd by trade."

"For Lord Seafirth, I believe you said."

Dammit, he shouldn't have been so specific. Lie, aye. But be vague about it. He'd learned that lesson long years past. "Aye. Me master was sore distressed to be missing yon wee lambkin here and—"

"I do not know a Lord Seafirth, Mr. MacLeod."

Bear lumbered closer. The blood on his knife was turning dark. The sight of it made Keelan's guts twist up painfully. He'd never been terrible fond of blood. Had rather hoped to see none during this little adventure. Oh aye, he'd planned for them to catch him poaching. Had expected them to take him to their master. But 'twas a new century—a civilized age, or so he'd been told.

"In point of fact, there is no Lord Seafirth, is there?" asked Chetfield.

"Now ye dunna ken that!" Keelan rasped,

tearing his gaze from the knife. Sweat trickled down his neck.

"Are you calling me a liar?"

"Nay. Nay." The knife was drawing closer. "I would na dream—"

"What is your true name, boy?"

"As I told yer—" he began, but the sentence was cut short by a slice of pain. He screamed. Blood sprayed from his right side. His head swam dizzily. Holy God, the bear man was as quick as a fox. Keelan dropped his head back against the rough post behind him.

"I want you to think carefully before next you speak," said Chetfield. "There is little point in lying."

"Nay." Keelan rolled his head across the timber, making a negative motion.

"Fabrications will save you no pain."

Sweet Mother of Mercy, he had to learn what the hell a fabrication was. Preferably before he was as dead as the lambkin.

"I meant no harm," he rasped. "Me master said I must find the lamb or I would sure lose me job. I have a wife, me lord. And a daughter. Such a wee sweet face she has. I could na bear to—"

The barn echoed with his shriek. Blood streamed over the ribs beneath his left arm. The acrid smell of fading life filled his nostrils.

"Holy God," he said, fighting for conscious-ness. "Ye must believe me."

"Must I?" asked Chetfield. "What think you, Mr. Roland?"

The angelic fellow removed his cheroot and shrugged lazily. "He's lying."

Keelan gave him a disappointed stare. He felt strangely disembodied, as if he were gazing down on himself. He didn't look good. Blood was smeared across his face and torso. A dark bruise was blooming on his forehead. His left eye was swollen nearly shut. His hands were tied behind his back. He couldn't feel them, but he could see them, even though they were hid-den behind his body. Strange.

"Then who is he, I wonder," mused the baron.

Roland smiled. A golden angel gone bad. "I am certain he will tell us."

"Are you?" Chetfield paced to the left. Keelan watched him, turning his eyes but not his head.

"He's nothing but a weakling coward," said Roland.

"Perhaps he was not so weak before you were loosed upon him," Chetfield suggested, lifting his staff and jabbing Keelan in the side. Pain erupted. Unconsciousness loomed. "I believe you broke his ribs. Did I not tell you to leave our guests undamaged, Mr. Roland?"

"He tried to escape."

"Indeed." Chetfield chuckled. The sound roiled eerily in the dimly lit barn.

"I assure you, my lord, he is nothing but a thief."

"Must I remind you that things are not always as they seem?"

Roland watched him with hooded eyes. "No, my lord, but this little dung heap is no more than a waste of time."

"Growing soft, are you, Mr. Roland?"

"You know I'm not."

"Do I, I wonder. Or do I think you plan to kill this boy quickly in the hopes of returning to your own cozy bed?"

"I have done—"

"Your bed," he continued, "where you clutch yourself and dream of a charitable maid to do the same in your stead."

Roland gritted his teeth.

"Your bed," continued the other, "where the maid refuses to accompany you, little caring what you offer as a bribe for her favors."

Roland made a strangled noise deep in his throat, but Keelan couldn't drag his attention from Chetfield, for the power in him was mesmerizing. Who was he? Not the soft heir he had expected to find.

Something touched Keelan's neck. He jerked, forgetting for an instant that he was tied. Pain seared him, burning through the haze of agony and uncertainty. Roland was holding his cigar to his throat. The smell of charred flesh filled the stable.

Roland watched him eye to eye, face expressionless as he pulled the cheroot away.

"Tell us about yourself, boy," he said pleasantly.

"Mary and Joseph!" The pain was insurmountable, all consuming. The cheroot drew closer. "I've already said—"

White-hot pain again, burning all thought.

"I'm nothing!" His voice was shattered. "Ye were right."

Roland gave him a satisfied nod and sucked on his cheroot, watching from inches away.

"I'm naught but a thief," Keelan gasped. "A thief and a cheat."

"A cheat?" Roland said, removing his cigar and rolling it between his fingers. Keelan watched the movement, transfixed, horrified. The smell of his own ruined flesh made his stomach churn. He was lucky indeed there was nothing in it.

"'Twas naught but a friendly game of dice between meself and three others."

"Dice?" Chetfield scowled.

Fook! His mind was muddled, scrambling back to ancient times, happier times. "Hazard!" Keelan corrected.

"I haven't heard it called dice in some long years." Chetfield smiled. "Please, continue."

"We be playing hazard," Keelan said. "Big large lads they were. And well-to-do." He shifted his gaze to Roland and back. "It weren't na terrible deed. I but wanted enough to get a decent meal in me poor shriveled belly."

"How much did you fleece them for?" Roland asked, still watching the tip of his cheroot flare.

"Three pence. Enough for a pint and a bowl of stew. Na more."

Roland glanced up, brows raised, so close every speck in his dark-angel's eyes was clear and bold.

"A few shillings," he corrected quickly. "Truly. But in the end I felt shamed and freely left the lot of it—"

Pain again, but low now, below his navel, charring the blood that clung to his flesh. Keelan gritted his teeth, struggling for lucidness.

"They learned the truth," he rasped through the pain. "Knew I was cheating and threatened me life, they did. Ye were right. 'Twas just as ye suspected."

"Let me venture a guess. They planned to use your hide to make themselves a fine belt?"

"Hang me." The cheroot moved. Keelan watched it. There was no need to pretend panic. No way to gracefully deliver the carefully polished lies he had planned to insinuate himself into Chetfield's presence. If the truth would save him, he would gladly use it, but it would not. That much he knew. Thus he would play the cards dealt him. "They were to hang me, but I got me hands on a nearby chair and swung with all me might."

"Kill someone, did you?"

"Nay! Nay, I but—"

Roland grinned. Chetfield only stared, face devoid of emotion, slanted eyes bright.

"I dunna think him dead," Keelan corrected, "but I canna be certain. I dashed out as soon as I could. 'Twas dark. I slipped into the hills."

"And found yourself on Lord Chetfield's property."

"I did na ken what I was doing." And that was the bloody truth. "I swear to the saints. I did na ken. And I was hungry. 'Twas three days since I had so much as a bite. I saw a meadow filled with sheep and thought sure a man of such astounding wealth would na miss one small lambkin."

Roland turned his smug gaze to his master.

There was a momentary pause from Chetfield, then: "There is nothing to salvage here. Let me know when it's finished," he said, and turned stiffly away.

Chapter 3

Clarity speared through Keelan's muzzy system. Death rushed at him, dark maw wide.

"Nay! Nay, me lord!" he rasped. "Dunna do this. I can be of service to ye. I swear it."

"Oh?" Chetfield stopped, turned slowly back, golden eyes blank, face unconcerned. "What is it you can do?"

Keelan wet his lips with a tongue as dry as a severed stump. "I've a fair voice," he said. "I can sing a—"

"Kill him before he shames himself completely," Chetfield said, and turned toward the door. But in that instant Keelan felt the deep burn of the old man's pain in his own loins. Felt it and did not deny it, though it was not the pain his informant had told him to expect. Not the goring of an enraged bull, but something else. Something far more sinister.

"Heal ye," Keelan said. His words were no more than a whisper, yet they echoed in the sudden silence, dragged from the bottom of his questionable soul.

The world stood still.

Chetfield turned back. "What say you?"

"I can heal ye," Keelan said. 'Twas a lie. Perhaps.

"Of what?"

He caught the other's gaze. "Of that which ye dare na speak."

The baron smiled. "I fear you are confused, my boy, for I dare all. Have, in fact, for more years than you can count."

"Ye lie," murmured Keelan.

"Shut your mouth, boy," Roland snarled, but Chetfield raised his hand, holding him at bay, head tilted, eyes almost closed.

"You have powers, Highlander?"

"Aye," he said.

"Powers!" Roland laughed. Bear grinned, a slice of evil in the midst of his matted beard. But Keelan was only interested in Chetfield, focused on the glowing eyes that watched him like a hunting wolf's.

"What sort of powers?"

A cold draft of liquid fear washed through Keelan, but he was too tired, too sober to care. "There be magic in me hands."

"You're gifted?"

"Aye."

Roland scoffed. "Surely you don't believe—"

"Quiet," hissed the master, and turning stiffly, stepped close. Fear came with him, an aura of unexpected evil. "Heal me then," he said.

Keelan tilted his head against the timber, watching, solemn, as terrified of his own words as of the man before him. "Nay."

He was never certain who struck him. His head rang with the pain of it. Blood pooled in his mouth, dripped from his cracked lips.

His mother's face floated into view, bonny eyes laughing. She didn't chide like the others who came in his dreams. Did not blame him. Though she should.

"Who are you?" Chetfield rasped, and Keelan grinned.

"Ange," he said and his mother smiled from his memory. He had inherited her Gypsy looks, the dark, untamed hair, the walnut-hued skin. Only his eyes were different, silvery blue where hers were as black as midnight, shifting from anger to laughter with the beat of her heart. He smiled at her.

"He's gone to the other side," Frankie rasped.

"Ye were healthy afore," Keelan intoned. The image was clear now, as clear as river water.

Chetfield in the bull's enclosure, eyes shining, staff raised as he stood over a cowering servant. "Until Mead's untimely death."

Chetfield stepped closer, voice quiet, body still. "You know of Mead?"

"Aye." Two pence had bought him much information in a nearby hamlet. He had been told of an accident, but he had not been told the truth. Poor Mead must have fought back. Must have gotten in one good blow, for the master was wounded.

"What clan are you?"

Keelan rested his head against the pillar behind him. By the light of a tallow candle, his mother had told him tales. Stories of warriors of stone, of gifted maids, of dark-haired Irishmen with magic in their hands. Perhaps long ago he had believed he descended from such heroes. "Me ancestors come from the far Highlands and stretch back to the Druids." Exhaustion was settling in like a black cloud, heavy and cool, almost soothing.

The old man struck him this time, but Keelan was beyond pain, beyond caring, in the vague hinterlands at the far side of lucid.

"You lie," Chetfield hissed.

"Often," Keelan muttered, and grinned through the blood. The expression hurt far more than

Chetfield's blow. "But I be a bit too weary to do so just now."

"What is your surname?"

"I canna say."

"I could kill you with a word," hissed Chetfield, but the lies came easy now, borne on the wings of hovering unconsciousness.

"I think ye may have already," Keelan murmured. "Still, I dunna ken me true name for I had na da."

The old man's eyes were narrow, slits with the merest spark of excitement in their depths. "I do not believe you."

The world seemed hazy, peaceful. He couldn't feel his limbs. "Verra well."

"Who raised you?"

"They called her Sorciere."

"She was a witch?" Chetfield rasped, eyes alight.

"Some said as much." Keelan laughed. The noise echoed eerily in the dark space. He rather liked the sound of it. "But never to her face."

"She could heal?"

Keelan smiled. "And kill."

"Kill!" Roland growled. "This is rubbish, Master—"

"Prove yourself," Chetfield said.

Keelan shook his head. This was the moment he had planned for, the moment he would prove his worth, make himself indispensable, gain the treasure that was rightfully his. But it was too late now. His plans had been laid waste. "It does na work such, as I think ye ken."

Chetfield smiled, a soft expression of evil. "Then make your peace," he said.

Keelan nodded, or tried to, but he did not turn his attention from the other. Could not. "There will be no peace for ye. Only pain."

Chetfield stood absolutely still, staring, thinking things unspoken. "Cut him free," he said finally.

"My lord—"

"Do as I say!" he hissed.

Roland moved like a shadow, slipping behind the timber. There was a grating sensation, and then Keelan's arms spilled to his sides. He pulled them numbly forward. His fingers refused to move.

The baron stood very still, both hands on the head of his craggy staff. "I shall give you one last chance, boy."

Keelan shook his head. His pate wobbled as he eyed his own torso. The skin was ripped and bloodied, burned and bruised. "I am sore weakened," he said, and glanced up. Evil stood before him. "'Twould take me whole strength to touch the likes of ye."

Chetfield narrowed his golden eyes. "Because you think me powerful or because you think me evil?"

"Both."

"Bloody bastard!" Roland cursed, but Chetfield lifted a graceful hand and smiled.

"The lamb," he said, and shifted his gaze with malevolent slowness to the beast's still form. "Bring breath to the lamb and I shall spare your life, Highlander."

Keelan laughed. His plans had come to fruition. But too late. Too damned late. His powders were gone. His magic with them. "It canna be done," he said. "Na without the Lord God himself."

"Then I suggest you pray."

The world was a hazy plane, gray with mist and uncertainty. "God and I have na spoke for some years," Keelan said. "Indeed—"

"You are running short on time, boy," said Chetfield. Roland grinned and tightened his grip on the knife.

Keelan watched the light play across the lamb's flaccid form, then stumbled toward it. His legs trembled, scraped raw beneath the tattered remains of his tartan. He dropped to his knees. The movement jarred him like a blow, threatening his consciousness, bobbing his head. The others followed him, circled round.

He glanced up. Even now he was not beyond fear. He had neither the courage of the Celt, nor the cleverness of the Irishman. As his mother well knew. "My lord," he said, "I beg ye, let me rest this night so that I might—"

"As you may have guessed, Highlander, I am not a patient man. Give the lamb life or forfeit your own."

Keelan settled back on his haunches. A prayer came to his mind, long forgotten and ill-used, but it was there nonetheless, chanting through his chilled brain. He let it hum along, then, reaching forward, set his hands on the tiny lamb's barrel. Its ribs were distinct beneath the wet woolen curls, the droopy black ears lax, one crushed beneath the tiny head, one soft and limp against its mottled face. Its shoulder felt as cold as chilled meat.

Closing his eyes halfway, Keelan rolled them back in his head. Then, lifting his hands a fraction of an inch from the tiny body, Keelan ran his fingers along the coarse wool and began to hum.

The brute squad was close, leaning in, watching. But mayhap he could yet best them. They thought him beaten.

Keelan passed his hands over the lamb's head.

Roland's touch was a caress on the hilt of his knife. Changing the rhythm of the chant, Keelan raised the volume high, then let it fall abruptly. The bastard shifted nervously back. So he was not comfortable with the supernatural . . . or the faux supernatural. Keelan would have laughed if the door wasn't so damnably far away.

He didn't glance in that direction, but imagined it in his mind. Twenty strides. It might just as well have been a mile.

Then again, mayhap he could grab Chetfield. He was a powerful adversary, aye, but would that not make him a powerful tool?

"I am becoming bored, Highlander," said the baron.

Keelan continued his chant, trilling his hands along the woolly neck, over the tiny nostrils.

"Let me alleviate your boredom, my lord," Roland said.

Keelan didn't glance up, though he recognized the threat. 'Twas death that entertained this crew. Death and pain, the acrid smell of some hapless stranger's lifeblood.

"And Mr. Roland is becoming impatient," Chetfield added.

Keelan shut out the sound of his words. Aye, he'd failed when called to action those many years ago, but he was yet a Scot. His antecedents had lived with naught but hope for years beyond time. Had fought the odds and won. Liam the Irishman, the Black Celt, Sir Stanton Hallaway. Bold men all. Men who would not die easy. Who would not lie down and—

"Kill him," Chetfield said, but in that moment Keelan lurched to his feet with a roar.

"Take me then!" he shouted, but the foursome fell back, eyes wide with terror. Frankie hit his knees like a loosed boulder, blubbering for mercy.

Keelan stared in confusion. Then, from behind him, he heard a pitiable bleat. He turned like one in a trance . . . just in time to see the lambkin wobble to its feet.

"Merciful Mary—" he rasped, and stumbled backward.

Frankie was still muttering. Bear's eyes were limned with white.

"It's a trick," snarled Roland.

"Perhaps," Chetfield said. "But it's a very good trick. Make certain our young friend remains with us through the night, won't you?"

"A pleasure," said the bastard, but when he stepped forward, Keelan saw that his hands trembled.

Chapter 4

"What happened to him?" The maid's voice was soft and breathy, imbued with an earthy cockney accent.

"What happened?" Someone chuckled. Or maybe it was the grating sound of iron-shod wheels against gravel. "'Tis a dangerous world, Cherie. Perhaps a wild animal got to him."

Keelan let lucidness filter slowly through him, cataloguing the aches and pains as he did so. He was lying on his back. He knew as much, for every piece of misplaced fodder prodded him like the devil's pitchfork. But that was the least of his worries, for it felt as if his very heart was exposed, beating through the tattered remains of his chest and throbbing with shattering intensity in the inflamed agony of his ribs. His lips were stiff with crusted blood, and the left side of his face felt strangely lifeless and mis-

40

shapen. Truth to tell, his entire body thrummed with pain. But wait. No. His right ear seemed surprisingly unscathed. Glory be, it barely hurt at all. And he wasn't freezing. Cold yes. Freezing no. In fact, there was a spot on his right side just above his hip that was relatively warm. Perhaps that was because he was bleeding again. He tried to glance down. Only one eye opened. Still, it was enough to see that it was not blood that warmed him, but the bicolored lambkin.

Memories of his own unnatural acts stormed in. In the sober light of day they seemed all the more insane.

"Hold still."

Keelan glanced up. The maid with the honey-eyed voice was kneeling beside him. Her face was sprinkled with delicate freckles and was as bonny as the month of May.

"Who are ye?" he asked. The words croaked rustily from his throat, but she shushed him. The lamb remained where it was, curled against his side like a slumbering puppy.

"Quiet now. You've been hurt."

Someone laughed, but Keelan doubted if it was he, since his ribs remained intact, such as they were.

"Perhaps it was wolves." Roland, the bastard, stood but a few feet away.

"Wolves?" The girl scrunched her sunny face. Her hand, where it lay against his arm, was as soft and tentative as a sigh. "Naw." She blinked, looking worried. "This late in the year?"

"As I said, the world's a dangerous place." Roland smirked. "Isn't that right, boy?"

It took Keelan a moment to realize he was being spoken to, for the girl was very near. Like a tiny wild rose in a scratchy field of brambles, she had captured his attention.

"I said, there are dangers aplenty, aren't there, Highlander?"

"Aye." Keelan's voice was little more than a croak. "There are indeed."

"Tell me," Roland continued. His tone was conversational but for a smattering of humor. Oh aye, he was enjoying this new sport. "Were you attacked by a beast?" There was a veiled threat in his voice, but there was no need. Keelan knew the rules of this game, had learned them in his youth, when bullies roamed aplenty.

"Aye," he said, resting his head on the mound of fodder behind him. He'd been left to rest after the lamb's resurrection, but sleep had done him little good. "Three of them."

"Wolves, you think?" asked the girl and shuddered.

"'Twas dark," said Keelan. "I could na be

certain what manner of beastie they be."

"You needn't worry, Cherie," said Roland, "so long as you're with me."

Her eyes were wide, heavily lashed, and the color of fine Irish whisky. Or mayhap cheap Irish whisky. Truth be told, Keelan was fond of both and could dearly use some just about then. "So he was like this when you found him?" she asked.

Roland tsked. "'Tis a terrible thing," said he, but his words lacked conviction. He would not survive long on the stage. Or by the power of his wits alone. "You're fortunate I came along, aren't you, Scotsman?"

Keelan's head hurt like the very devil, throbbing to the beat of his heart. "I've always been lucky," he rasped.

Roland chuckled.

"Lucky?" The girl's voice was wispy, her eyes bright, as though she might weep for the injuries done him. "You poor, dear thing. You must have fought like a lion." Her hand trembled a little against his side. She blinked, shifted her gaze, wrinkled her fair brow. "But the lamb . . . Wherever did the lamb come from? Why did the beasts not devour it?"

Silence fell over the place. Keelan turned his one good eye toward Roland, who glanced uncomfortably toward the tiny creature. Had Keelan not ached in every fiber of his bludgeoned body, he would have enjoyed the moment.

"'Tis me master's," Keelan said through swollen lips. "I was but hoping to return it to the fold when I was set upon."

The girl's lips parted. Her eyes widened. "You mean to say you fought off the beasties . . ." She paused. "For naught but a mere small lamb?"

The words tripped off her rose-petal lips like magic. As if he were a revered hero of old. A valiant knight instead of a battered fool far out of his own time and place. Still, he tried to give her a demure glance, but it was no simple feat with only one functioning eye. "You make me sound verra brave, lass," he countered shyly, "when in truth—"

"No." She touched his lips. The feel of her fingertips against his skin seemed to draw out the pain. Or maybe it was naught but the look of worry in her dewy eyes. Either way, she was a balm to body and soul. "Don't speak. I shall fetch some salves and tonics." She rose to her feet. Her skirt swished, skimming his bare skin. "And milk for your precious lamb."

He tried to object, but his lips were too broken, his mind too slow. In a moment she was gone, and he was left alone . . . with Roland.

The bastard moved closer, like a cold wind blowing from a frigid shore, sweeping aside the curtain of hope and showing the darkness behind.

"Pretty little piece, isn't she?" he crooned. The threat would have been obvious to a deaf man. Keelan wasn't deaf. Almost blind, true enough, but his right ear was in damned fine condition.

"Is she?" Keelan asked. "I could na tell, what with me eye having been beat shut by . . . the beasties."

Roland said nothing for a moment, then chuckled and stepped closer. He was smoking again. Fresh waves of remembered pain coursed through Keelan at the scent. "I see you are wiser than you look, Scotsman. Of course . . ." He twirled the cheroot. "You look just short of dead."

"Aye, well . . ." Keelan shifted slightly, nudging the lamb gently with his hip. It tottled to its little trotters. Near the door, a hound rose with a growl. "Looks can be deceiving."

Perhaps Roland intended some sort of nasty rejoinder, but just then the lamb bleated. The bastard stepped back, eyeing it cautiously, and Keelan almost smiled. But he *was* smarter than he looked, and now seemed a likely time to prove it. Thus he kept his expression solemn.

45

"What kind of game are you playing, Highlander?"

Keelan shifted, trying to find comfort, only to discover there was no such place. "If 'tis a game, it be a terrible painful one."

Rounding Keelan's outstretched feet, Roland approached him from the opposite side and squatted, holding the tip of his glowing cigar close to the other's tattered skin. "It would be wise of you to remember that . . . lad."

Every wound throbbed with unrelenting zeal. "I am na likely to forget."

"That is good to hear for—" But in that moment the maid hurried noisily back in. The second hound rose, pulling its tether tight, watching with head lowered, eyes gleaming.

"What is good?" she asked.

Roland rose to his feet, eyes shining much like the hound's. "The Celt here said he won't be needing your ministrations after all, Cherie."

"Won't be needing me?" She approached with quick steps, sturdy, scuffed shoes rapping intermittently against straw and hard-packed dirt. "What nonsense is this then? He is simply being brave again." Squatting beside him, she set a carved wooden tray next to a pile of chaff. It was laden with bottles and bags and one hollowed basin that boasted steaming contents. The scent of figwort wafted cozily into the air. She was staring at him with soft, troubled eyes. "'Twould be best to get you to the house, but I dare not without the master's permission." She paused, shook her head, then brightened rapidly. "But never mind that, I fear the pain of moving you would be too great if we do not make you more comfortable first." Her lovely brow creased. "Thus I will treat you here."

"Ye needn't bother," Keelan said. "'Tis certain I will mend on me own."

She shook her head. "You must be famished."

He managed a brave smile though his stomach was knotted up like a sailor's finest. "'Tis the lamb which worries me most," he demurred. "I fear it lost its mum and will na last much longer without sustenance."

"Of course," she said and stood abruptly. "Mr. Roland, might I ask you to feed the poor thing whilst I—"

But the bastard was already backing away, eyes narrowed, expression tense as he sprinted his gaze to the lamb and back. "I've more important tasks than to play nursemaid to a bit of mutton," he said, and giving the lamb one last fleeting glance, disappeared like a fleeing banshee, slamming the door behind him.

Chapter 5

The girl made a small mewl of surprise as the door banged shut. "Well now, where do you suppose he's hurrying off to?"

Keelan shifted, trying to ease a newfound ache. "To torture butterflies mayhap?"

"What's that?"

He glanced up. Her perfect brows were arched high above her velveteen eyes. Was she in love with the bastard? The idea sent a jagged shard of pain spurring through Keelan's system, though he knew better than to care.

"I am certain Master Chetfield has more important duties for him to see to than to tend to the likes of me and one wee small lambkin," Keelan said.

"Aye, the master keeps him quite . . ." She paused, scrunched her pretty face. "When did you meet Lord Chetfield?"

Fook. He was going to have to be more careful what he said. True, the girl looked as sinister as a song thrush, but now was not the time for foolish mistakes. He'd planned too long, learned too much. Now was the time to become sinfully wealthy. "In truth, I've na had the honor," he said.

"Then how do you know of him?" she asked, but he shifted, closed his eyes, and moaned softly.

She had dropped sympathetically to her knees before next he glanced up.

"My apologies." Her small, fairy-soft hand lay gently on an unscathed portion of his abdomen, surprisingly near one of his favorite anatomical parts. "Here I am yammering on while you're one step short of heaven's door."

"Nay. Na a'tall, lass. Dunna feel ye have to—" he began, and interrupted himself with yet another low moan.

"What shall I see to first?" she asked, voice atremble.

"The lambkin," he gritted. Mayhap it was a ploy in part to gain her admiration. He himself could no longer separate artifice from fact, but certainly he could ill-afford to let the little creature perish. Not this late into such a perilous game. "If ye could help me with the poor wee lamb, I would be forever in yer debt."

"But your chest." Her gaze skimmed him. "And your arms. And your . . ." Her voice broke as her attention settled on his face. The catch in her words did complicated things to his battered system, firing up a strange ache in the deepest part of him. The only part, seemingly, that didn't already hurt.

"There now, lass," he said, shushing the confusing mix of unwanted feelings. "Ye needn't worry. I come from a long line of tetchy Scots and will be right as rain in no time a'tall. But I must see to me master's lamb."

He gave her a grin. She drew back, looking terrified by the effects. It did not bode well. Mayhap he'd best find himself a looking glass before next he dared a smile.

"I've brought some milk for the poor babe," she said, and lifted a wine bottle from the tray. "Perhaps I can convince him to drink a bit. I've seen it done with the miller's colt."

"'Tis kind of ye, lass," Keelan said, and shifted to launch into a sitting position. Pain shot through him like a thousand loosed arrows, striking with unerring accuracy.

She hissed in unison with his agony and pressed him carefully back onto the fodder. "What are you thinking, luv? You mustn't move."

Luv. The word tasted like nectar from her lips.

"But the lamb—" he croaked, and wondered if she would be increasingly impressed if he added passing out to the morning's performance.

"Don't you be worrying about the lamb, now." She tsked. "You must rest."

"Ye are kindness itself, lass, but—" Keelan said, and bracing against the coming pain, forced himself into an upright position. He didn't have to fake dizziness. Indeed, the world went momentarily black, then was shot with sparkling stars that burst in his head like black powder. He felt himself slipping sideways.

"Careful!" Her hands were surprisingly strong against his arm. Her breath was warm upon his cheek. Clarity swam slowly back in, surprising him almost as much as the sharp feelings of arousal. Her bonny brown curls caressed his chest like a tender flirtation. Her lashes framed her whisky, troubled eyes, and her bosoms ... Sweet Mary, her bosoms, bunched together like a bouquet of posies! "You must be more careful with yourself."

He gave her a brave smile, though in truth, the most courageous part of his performance involved keeping his gaze from slipping into the depths of her simple décolletage. She was beautifully crafted, lovingly endowed. "Ye are wondrous kind," he said, "but truly I can tend to meself."

51

"There'll be none of that talk now," she said. "I'll be caring for you, whether you like it or nay."

He did like it—the way her hands felt against his skin, the way her voice fell on his ears. The resurrected lamb, on the other hand, was butting him painfully with its pointy little nose.

She glanced down at the tiny creature. "It does look hungry. But are you certain you're up to the task?"

Despite the night just past, he was definitely *up*. Which was rather surprising, for while he enjoyed a bonny lass as much as the next wandering rogue, he found himself most attracted to those who could engage his intellect as well as his more bestial parts. Still, it had been a long while since he had enjoyed the full pleasures of a woman's charms. Several months certainly. He shifted, fully aware he had lost the horsehair sporran so effective in hiding his appreciation of the fairer sex. Pain ripped through him.

"Don't move, luv," she murmured.

"Ange," he corrected, remembering his mother's name for him.

She blinked. "I barely speak the King's English. French . . ." She shook her head, causing her bonny locks to brush her shoulders.

"Some call me Angel, but in truth, lass, the

name be better suited to yer unearthly beauty."

"Please," she said, "you must lie still or you'll break open your wounds." Her voice was as soft as a dream, her face pixie perfect.

Keelan pulled himself from her eyes. This was hardly the time to be distracted by a comely lass, regardless of how sweet her temperament or alluring her bosom, for Chetfield was not the rich but innocuous fool he had hoped him to be. "And yer name be Cherie?"

She shook her head and scowled a bit as she retrieved the wine bottle. The opening was fitted with a little dome of cloth bound tight with a strip of leather to the glass lip. "'Tis simply what Mr. Roland calls me from time to time."

"And Mr. Roland be . . . a friend of yers?"

"A friend?" she said, and wiped the bottle on her apron. "Sure. I suppose he is that. A nice enough bloke. Like a brother to me in a manner of speaking."

Keelan's seared skin suggested otherwise, but he nodded amicably. "Hand me the bottle, will ye, lass?"

She did so with a scowl of protest.

"Then what do the others call ye?" he asked.

She gave a little shrug. Her gown was a delicate green. Gathered gently across her bosom, it slipped half an inch to kindly display one bonny shoulder. It was snowy white with just a smattering of intriguing freckles. How far, Keelan wondered, did those delightful little spots continue? "Me kin call me Charity," she said.

Their gazes met, hers warm and soft, his gritty and one-eyed. Fie. She'd probably be even prettier with the aid of binocular vision.

She cleared her throat and dropped her gaze to the bottle.

"'Tis our nanny goat's finest," she explained softly.

Pulling himself from her gaze, he refused to fall into her cleavage as he lifted the wine bottle. Even that small feat sent tendrils of pain slicing through his back and arms, but milk dripped from the tip of the cloth, apparently just as intended. "Clever lass," he said, indicating the makeshift nipple.

"Clever? Me?" she said, and laughed a little. "Nay. 'Tis simply a trick I've seen done before, as I've said. And since Glory was all but bursting with milk . . ." She shrugged again. Another freckle appeared, but Keelan carefully turned his gaze toward the lamb, offering the nipple as he did so. Smelling the milk, the lambkin butted impatiently at his arm. He managed to remain lucid.

"Mayhap it would be wiser to simply bring ol'

Glory in here and have her do the task herself," Keelan suggested, but the girl shook her head.

"She'll have none of it. We tried to give her one of Horny's twins, seein' as how she's so well endowed, but she'd have nothing to do with him, cute little beggar though he was."

"Horny?" Keelan asked, offering the nipple again.

"Aye," she said, gently guiding the lamb toward the milk source. "On account of her one misshapen horn."

"Ahh," Keelan said, and stifled a chuckle as much for her charming naïveté as for the sake of his own battered ribs. "Perhaps if you hold the wee one's head steady, we might manage this better."

She did so, straddling the animal and cradling its face so that it was all but hidden beneath her generous hem. Lucky little blighter.

Keelan nudged the nipple into its mouth. The lamb promptly spit it out. He tried again with the same results, but finally, when his arms were atremble with fatigue, the lambkin took hold and suckled. There were a few tentative slurps before the tiny tail began to wriggle merrily.

"Look at that, will you?" Charity whispered, and Keelan had to admit that even with pain slicing him like rusty knives, there was some earthy magic in seeing the tiny creature's happy wiggle. "You saved her from hunger just as sure as you saved her from the beasts." There was admiration in her voice . . . and maybe more, but Keelan was hardly a fool for sentimentality. 'Twas just that kind of rubbish that could find a lad on the wrong end of an angry husband's sword. Besides, he was hardly in a position to fall for this lass, though resisting temptation had never been his forte. Chicanery, on the other hand . . .

"Methinks *ye* saved her with this clever bottle," he said, and winced as Lambkin slurped the bottle dry and bumped his arm.

"Here now, don't you be doing that," Charity scolded, and lifting the lamb, set it aside. After doing the same with the bottle, she retrieved the basin and placed it carefully by his scraped elbow. "'Fraid I can't take credit for the bottle, 'cuz like me uncle Brawley was fond of saying, *Our little Charity, she may not be the brightest star in the heavens.*"

"But?"

She dipped a cloth into the water, then wrung it out and touched it to his brow. "What?"

"Brawley's statement must surely have been followed by a *but*."

She tilted her head, washing carefully. "No. Why?"

Because otherwise Uncle Brawley was an ass, he thought, but she interrupted his musings.

"I loved him something fierce," she said. "He used to give me horseback rides on his shoulders. Him so tall and me just a little nipper."

Keelan scowled, for suddenly the image was so clear in his mind, he could all but reach out and touch her sable curls as she bounced along. Her chubby cheeks were dimpled and her hands splayed across the man's dark head as she giggled with glee. But the picture unfurled with languid clarity until he saw that he himself was the child's mount while Charity stood some feet away, eyes gleaming with laughter as he galloped past—past the roses that climbed the thatched cottage behind him, past the sheep that ceased their grazing to watch.

"Mr. Angel!"

He felt her hand snag his arm and was yanked back to reality.

"Mr. Angel, ye looked pale as a turnip for a minute there. I thought you might faint dead away. Are you well?"

Of course he wasn't well. The pain was making him delusional. There could be no other explanation, but he gave her a smile to prove his normalcy. "Mayhap I can forgive yer uncle, then, since he made ye laugh," he intoned.

She tilted her head, studying him. "How did you know I laughed?"

The child's eyes were shining like diamonds as she bent over her bearer's head, bare toes curled, and giggles echoing like music in the fragrant garden.

"Mr. Angel?" she said, touching his arm and snatching him back once again.

Holy God, he had to quit doing that. He wasn't a witch. Couldn't see the future, no matter—

"Perhaps I'd best fetch Lord Chetfield," Charity said, half rising, but he grabbed her arm.

"Nay!" he rasped, nearly passing out for his trouble. "Nay," he repeated, but softer, finding his senses. "Stay. Please. Tell me of yer childhood."

She settled uncertainly back onto the fodder. The miraculous little lambkin wandered toward him, then dropped to her knobby knees and curled up once again at Keelan's side.

"They must have spoiled ye something fierce," he said.

She had dipped the rag back into the water, but stopped her swishing as her mesmerizing gaze shot to his. "And how'd you know that?"

"Because ye are sure the bonniest lass I've yet to lay me eyes upon."

She canted her head at him, silent for a moment. "Me mum was fond of saying that flirting with a Scotsman was like teasing a caged bear. It may be safe, but it weren't never wise."

"I never flirt, lass," he said, resting his head on the straw behind him. "Unless I can see the maid out of both of me eyes."

She stared at him for a moment, then laughed out loud, and suddenly the world stopped, for it was the exact sound of the little girl's giggle. The sound of unfettered joy. The sound of goodness. A gentle testimony that the world was not overcome by evil, but dotted here and there with islands of kindness and light. And quite unexpectedly, Keelan longed to be different. Better. Stronger.

"There are some who might be feeling sorry for themselves if they was you," she said.

"I'll have plenty of time for that once ye've returned to heaven," he said.

"Still not flirting?" she asked, setting the cloth aside and reaching for a dark glass jar. The contents smelled of lavender and something he couldn't quite identify. Dipping her fingers inside, she gently smeared the unctuous lotion into the swelling above his eye.

"Vervain," he said, immediately feeling the effects.

"You know herbage?" she asked, surprise brightening her luminous face.

Lady Colline, the Irish Hound's bride, had been an attentive tutor, despite her husband's rather carnivorous nature. "Na more than yer average bullock."

"Your chest and arms are sore inflamed." She plied the cloth again, smoothing it around the open wounds. It was amazingly soothing. Relaxing, even. He sighed. She rinsed the cloth and returned to her ministrations, cleansing carefully, fingers gently probing a gash on his arm. He turned his head to catch her worried gaze.

"Perhaps this ought to be stitched," she suggested.

The world felt right and good. "Do what ye must, lass."

"Me?" She shook her head. "I fear I'm not up to the task. But Frankie has been known to right the worst—"

"Frankie!"

Her eyes widened at his reaction. "He be in Lord Chetfield's employ."

Dark memories swarmed in. "I'm certain I'll mend without his help. Just do what ye can, lass. All will be well."

Her scowl deepened as she skimmed her hand down his midline, washing gently. The muscles tingled beneath her touch. Her brow wrinkled into a thoughtful frown. "This be the strangest wound yet," she said, cleansing gently.

Mother Mary, she was a bonny bit of fluff. Just past the silky crest of her head, he could see the lovely soft mounds of her bosoms, making him light-headed again.

"However did you get burned?" she asked, and blinked up at him.

Yanked back to reality, he snagged his gaze from her cleavage. "Burned? Nay, lass, I'm certain ye're wrong. 'Twas the beasties."

She shook her head. "I've not seen the likes of these wounds." Her fingers trilled gently about the edges of the circular lesion. "Not in all me days." She gasped, looking up. "Do you suppose the beasts were bewitched? Do you think your wounds were caused by . . . Lucifer?"

Aye, in a manner of speaking they were. He remained absolutely still as ancient memories stormed through him. Betrayal. Pain. Shame so deep it seared him to the core of his very soul. He was a coward. But because of that cowardice, he yet lived. And because of her courage, she had died. 'Twas what bravery gave you. What love had to offer. "Nay, lass," he said. "They were but ordinary beasties. I'm certain of it."

She shook her head, staring at his wounds. "The devil is tricky," she said, and raised her gaze to his. "But you bested him." Her eyes were soft with adoration.

"Lass . . ." he murmured, dubious conscience scorching him. "Mayhap I be na what ye think I be."

She flitted her gaze to the lambkin. "You are bravery." Her voice trembled a little. "And kindness."

Oh, aye, he was all of that. So brave and kind that he had come to lie and steal, then creep into the night and leave her to fend for herself.

"'Twould be best, lass," he said softly, "if ye did na venture out alone at night."

She nodded, lips parted. "I shall stay close to Mr. Roland if ever I—"

He cursed under his breath.

She raised her brows, eyes wide and wondering. "What's that?"

Keelan cursed again, but silently now. He was, if nothing else, the master of his emotions. Indeed, he had abolished feelings many long years past. But the thought of the bastard with such a sweet maid curdled his entrails. "I'm certain Roland be a fine, upstanding chap," he said, barely able to force the lie past his battered lips, "yet ye must surely ken the effect ye have on a man, lass."

She stared at him for a moment, then dropped

her gaze and blushed. The color seeped from her cheeks over the tiny swirl of her ears. And suddenly he wanted quite desperately to reach out and caress her cheek, to kiss the smooth loveliness of her neck. To lay her down in the straw beneath them and feel her heart beat through the luscious skin of her bonny bosom. But he would not; he must keep his head. Literally and figuratively.

"Tell me," he said, admiring the way her lashes swept dark and full against the tender skin of her lively cheeks. "How did a comely lass like yerself end up so far afield?"

She cleared her throat and turned to wring out the rag again. When she smoothed it against his wrist, it felt warm and soothing, though he longed for her touch elsewhere. "I don't know what you mean."

She had lifted his hand in hers and turned it to lave the palm. The sensation was shockingly erotic, and even more so when she curled the cloth around his digits to wash each finger. Beneath his tattered tartan, his manhood reared to attention. Good thing he'd been dragged on his back instead of the reverse. He'd have to remember to thank the bastards for that, after he stole their master blind and made them all look like fools.

She glanced up, cleavage perfectly centered beneath the pointed peak of her adorable little chin. His erection bucked beneath the rucked wool.

"I would venture to guess ye were raised in London," he explained.

"Oh, me cockney," she said, retrieving more salve and easing it carefully into his scraped knuckles. Keelan was quite certain such simple ministrations couldn't be the least bit arousing. "Aye. I was born just off Soho Square. Me father be a hatter, but he keeps a Jersey cow and a couple a laying hens. Mum leads ol' Myrtle down to Drury Lane each afternoon. The fashionable folk pay extra for a spritz of fresh milk in their syllabubs, you know."

Keelan had no idea what a syllabub was, but a man's appreciation for a pretty woman would not change in a thousand years. And her mother was surely a beauty.

"It seems as if that would have been a fine job for ye, then, lass," he said, but she shrugged.

"Myrtle had her favorites and I wasn't amongst them. Was wont to give me a swift kick to the shins when I took to the stool. 'Sides, I always hoped to become a lady's maid," she said, and grinned. "I know it's unlikely, but I thought maybe if I got me a position at a fine house, I might find a way. 'Twas naught but luck that brought me here. Me cousin Edgar was traveling through and just happened to learn the master was in need of help."

"So ye ventured all this way on yer own?"

She blushed again. The color fascinated him no end. "I wasn't particular happy with me current master."

He watched her. It was no hard chore. Well, it was hard . . . but not difficult. "He was pressing ye," he said.

She lifted her gaze. "What's that?"

"He made . . . ungentlemanly advances," he guessed.

She blinked, blushed, glanced down, hiding her lovely bosom. "How did you know?"

Because he still had one good eye. "'Twas naught but a guess. So ye've felt safe here?"

She cleared her throat, avoiding his gaze. "Master Chetfield don't let no one bother me much."

And why was that? The baron was an animal. No better than his horrid antecedent. Indeed, perhaps he was just as bloodthirsty as Kirksted had been more than a hundred years before. So why would he protect the girl unless . . . The truth struck Keelan with a fresh rush of pain. The devious bastard was saving her for himself, keeping the others at bay so she was his alone. Chetfield had sustained an injury that would make that impossible, however. An informant had told him as much, but the truth was somehow different. An image struck his mind like a blow, confusing, horrifying. He thrust it aside.

"So ye and the master are . . ." He waited for her to finish the sentence. She didn't. "Ye are . . . betrothed?" he guessed.

Her laughter bubbled forth like loosed champagne, spilling the festering images from his mind, setting him free. "Betrothed! You jest, sure."

He allowed himself a careful breath. "In truth, lass, I am usually quite amusing, but with these broken ribs and whatnot—"

"He's like a father to me."

And like a brutal bastard with murderous ancestors and dark secrets barely hidden, to Keelan. "And Roland be yer brother," he said, voice level.

She washed a bit of blood from his side. "Like a brother, aye."

He nodded. It hurt. "How long have ye been residing here at Crevan House, lass?"

She winced at the sight of his wounds. "Going on half a year."

Six months with these bastards? "And they

haven't . . ." He calmed himself. Took a breath. "And still ye feel safe in their midst?"

"Oh aye, I know some of them look terrible dangerous." Reaching to the side, she greased up her fingers and eased them carefully over the burn above his tartan. "But in truth, they're as peaceful as your Lambkin there."

His back felt as if it had been peeled raw from his trip through the field to the stable. He glanced at the lamb. It slept like a rocked bairn. "Truly?"

"Oh aye, Master Chetfield seems gruff, I won't be lying to you, but in his own way, he looks after me."

All the while wishing to hell he could do more than look.

"He's good-hearted and sweet as honeyed yams but . . ."

"But?"

"He ain't been entirely healthy ever since he was mauled by that bull, I'm told."

"The bull?" he asked, scalp tingling.

"Oh sure, I suspect you haven't heard the story. 'Tis said they had a terrible mean beast here at Crevan House. Sometimes the gardener, Mr. Mead, would feed it turnips and whatnot that was left over. Only one day he ventured into the pen for some reason that'll never be knowed, and the bull charged him. Master Chetfield, he tried to save him. Climbed into the pen himself, he did."

Images screamed through Keelan's soul. Terror and pain, yes. But no charging bull. Nothing so innocent.

"He tried to save him, and got mauled hisself. But it was too late. Mead was already gone. Cook says the master was covered in blood when he finally reached the house."

Blood, but not his own. So how had he become injured? An untamed image struck Keelan, jolting him to the core.

Charity leaned in close. "Is something amiss, Mr. Angel? Are you quite well? You're pale as a ghost."

"Yes, Mr. MacLeod, are you quite well?" asked another.

Keelan jerked his gaze upward just as Charity turned with a gasp.

Chetfield stood before them, eyes gleaming like a wolf's, the staff that killed Mead held tight in his hand.

Chapter 6

"**M**aster," said Charity, "I didn't hear you come in."

Chetfield smiled at her, soft mouth quirking while his eyes gleamed in his peculiar face. From his vantage point, he could probably see straight down her gown to her shoe ribbons. But the girl remained blissfully unaware.

Keelan forced himself to relax. He was, after all, no one's protector. None but his own.

"So you are patching up our poor battered visitor, I see," Chetfield said, and leaned both hands on the head of his knobby staff.

"I am doing me best, me lord, but he be sore wounded." Charity gave Keelan a quick, worried glance from limpid eyes. "Something did terrible damage."

"That I can see."

"What do you think it might have been?"

"I believe our guest would be the one to answer that," Chetfield said, and smiled again. Evil shone in his eyes.

"It was dark," Keelan said.

Charity scowled. "I think his ribs may well be broke. He be clawed and scraped everywhere, and I fear I can do little out here in the stable."

The old man raised a brow. "Then what would you suggest?"

"I been wondering if we might bring him into the manor house so that I could better tend his injuries?"

"Nay," said Keelan, sudden panic spurring up inside him.

They turned to him in surprised unison.

"That is to say," Keelan continued, "I've na wish to be a burden."

"A burden. You'd be no such thing," crooned the girl. "We'd be more than happy to see to you until you mend. Wouldn't we, me lord?"

Chetfield stared at her for several seconds, then smiled dotingly. "Take a look at her, Mr. MacLeod," he said, "for you may never again see the face of kindness itself."

She gave Keelan's hand a squeeze in silent hope. "Surely it is not safe out here," she said. "We don't even know what did this to him at the outset."

The old man's eyes burned Keelan's soul. "It is indeed a troublesome mystery," he said, his voice so strangely familiar.

He had heard that voice before, but the pages of his memory were fogged by time beyond end.

"And what if I should agree, little Charity?"

"Oh, me lord." Her voice was barely audible. "You would be the best master ever to live, and I would be eternally in your debt."

Keelan's mind shunted back to the present. He hardly needed another black mark on his soul. Did not want her indebted on his behalf. "I am certain I will be perfectly safe out here in the—" he began, but Chetfield stopped him with the graceful wave of an elegant hand.

"But our little Charity wants you inside," Chetfield said, "and nothing makes an old man's heart so light as seeing a smile upon the face of a pretty maid."

Charity sprang to her feet. Grasping the old man's hand, she kissed his cheek.

Keelan actually recoiled at the sight.

"Thank you ever so much, me lord," she murmured. "Your reward shall surely be in heaven."

"But not too soon I hope," he said, and patted her cheek. "Go now, little miss, and make a room ready for your patient."

"As you wish, me lord," she said, and sparing Keelan one quick, happy glance, she hurried past the hounds and from the stable. Her footfalls rushed away. The barn dropped into silence.

"So you have met my Charity," Chetfield intoned, yellow eyes half hidden behind heavy lids.

"I didn't touch her," Keelan said, and Chetfield laughed.

"No, I don't suppose you did. Shattered bones do make the act more difficult, though not impossible. I can tell you this from experience," he said, and smiled as he paced.

Keelan watched, breath held. "I'm not interested in her, if that be what worries ye," he lied.

"Tell me, my young friend . . ." Chetfield paced closer, full lips smirked into a smile. "Do I look worried to you?"

Nay. He looked smug and misshapen and deadly. Keelan's muscles ached with the tension and torture.

"What I am is eager," Chetfield said. "Eager for you to fulfill your promise, Mr. MacLeod." He circled slowly, eyes alight with something Keelan could neither define nor understand. "So that I may return to the pleasures of my youth. You *can* heal me, can you not?"

Fear curled tight around Keelan's heart. The

lamb cowered against his side. He put a battered hand on the woolly little back. "There be powers I canna explain," he said.

"Indeed there are, Mr. MacLeod. But do you possess such powers?"

"Na until I am healed meself."

The eerie eyes stared. Tension built like a gathering storm, then Chetfield smiled. "And so I allow you into my home, Mr. MacLeod. Under my roof, with my most cherished servant."

Keelan tried to remain silent, for time and pain had taught him the penalties of acting the fool, but the words ventured out on their own. "What be yer plans for her?"

One thin eyebrow rose. "Would you be her protector?" The old man's tone was mild, but there was something in the eyes. Something beyond deadly that very closely matched the untamed gleam of the bristly hounds behind him.

"I but wonder," Keelan said. The conversation was nearly as wearing as the torture had been.

"Wondering can be a very dangerous thing."

"As I was told earlier, 'tis a dangerous world."

Chetfield laughed. "It is indeed, young man, but I tell you this . . ." He stepped closer, casually lifted his stick, and thrust it into the burn on Keelan's abdomen.

White-hot pain scoured Keelan, searing his senses. He would have scrambled away, but agony, or something akin to it, kept him writhing beneath the old man's surprising strength.

"It will become far more dangerous if you try to take her from me. I can kill you in ways you cannot yet imagine," Chetfield hissed. "If you put a hand to her, you may well hope for any one of them."

"Merciful God—" he rasped.

The staff was removed. The old man canted his head as if in curiosity. "Prayer will not help you, boy. Nothing will help you." He sounded matter-of-fact now, as if he were not evil personified, as if they but shared an everyday conversation. "Should you betray me, you will die with a plea on your tongue," he added pleasantly. "And you will die forever."

Every inch of Keelan screamed in agony, but perhaps it was that agony that brought the devil to life in him. "Forever?" he rasped, fighting the pain. "How can—"

Chetfield speared him again. Pain clawed through Keelan like a wild beast.

"I'll na touch her," he gasped.

"Good. That is good," Chetfield murmured, and drew the staff away. "Rest now, Mr. Mac-Leod. And heal. I want you in full strength as soon as possible." He canted his head at a noise from outside.

The door opened. The hounds rose threateningly, but Charity blew merrily inside, seemingly unconcerned by any of the beasts. Bear and Frankie trundled in after her, steps slow, faces troubled as their gazes skipped to Lambkin.

"You must be gentle," she said, addressing the giants. "Do you understand?"

Frankie, apparently the genius of the two, nodded. Bear remained silent and unmoving, gaze shifting nervously from the lamb to his master.

"Mr. Angel . . ." She hurried to Keelan's side. "These two gents have come to help you to the house."

Reality dawned with pain-induced slowness. Terror came on its dragging heels. "Truly, I will be fine here in this lovely stable."

"Nonsense," Charity said, and squatting again, curled her fingers around his. He was tempted to pull his away lest her master get the wrong impression and kill him with a glare. "They shall carry you by your arms and legs . . . to save your ribs."

He felt the blood leave his face in a clammy rush. "Fie me, lass, could ye na just stab me in the heart and be done with it?"

"It may hurt a bit."

"A bit! The beating hurt a bit."

She scowled as if bemused . . . or aggravated, but her tone remained breathy. "Beating?"

"Mauling," he corrected, not daring to dart his gaze from one giant to the next. "The mauling . . . by the unknown beasties."

"Perhaps Bear could carry you on his back."

"Mother Mary full of grace," he murmured, and actually thought he might faint. In fact, he rather hoped he would.

"Or on a blanket?"

And of all those present, she was the only one who had *not* intended to kill him.

She scrunched her freckled face. "Frankie," she said, rising quickly. "Run up to the house and ask Mrs. Graves to fetch a good, strong blanket."

The giant shambled gratefully away. Charity turned to Keelan with doe-bright eyes. "You'll feel much improved once you are placed upon a proper pallet."

He very much doubted it. He would be under the unearthly eye of the master. Far better to be left to his devices in the stable where he could move about at will . . . well, once he could move around a'tall, at any rate.

"I'm grateful to ye, sure," Keelan said, "but I have na desire to cause any problems with—"

"Problems? Naw," corrected Charity. "'Tis an honor to tend such a brave shepherd, is it not, me lord?"

Chetfield's tone was dry as death. "An honor."

"But . . . what of Lambkin?" The question flew out on the wings of a brainstorm. "She will need tending."

Charity smiled. "I shall see to her myself."

"But . . ." He curled his fingers into the lamb's wool, feeling frantic.

"Never fear, young Scot," said Chetfield, smiling ghoulishly. "We shall send the lamb with you if it makes my Charity happy."

The door opened and Frankie reappeared, carrying a gray blanket in his plowshare hands.

"You are too kind, me lord," Charity breathed, taking the woolen and spreading it on the ground next to Keelan, who eyed it as one might a serpent. "Very well then," she said. "Now we must shift him carefully onto the blanket."

"Holy God," Keelan breathed.

"Come along," she said, waving them over. They came reluctantly. She sent Bear to the far side. Lambkin clambered unceremoniously onto Keelan's chest. The sharp little hooves hurt like hell as they dug into his bare skin, but he held her close.

"I think it best if I stay in the barn," he tried again, but the giants were already bending over him. "Truly, I dunna—"

But at that moment they grasped his arms and legs in meaty claws, and suddenly he was being torn in two. He felt himself leave the painful comfort of the dirt floor, felt each laceration scream as it was ripped open afresh. Perhaps they set him gently as a babe onto the blanket, but it felt as if he were drop-kicked against the wall. He jerked against the agony.

"Gently. Gently," someone said, but the words were mingled with wolfish growls as they shuffled him through the door and into the shattering light of day.

The journey to the house was a nightmarish trek through hell. Every muscle shrieked, lungs screaming for air beneath throbbing ribs. His foot struck something immobile, sending shards of shivery agony through his body like slivers of steel. But it was the stairs that were nearly his undoing. Every jolting step tore him in twain. They turned a corner. He felt himself tilt off balance before the blanket was jerked upright, and his head, having slipped off the edge, rapped the wall with resounding finality. The room swam by in vivid hues. And then he was dropped, falling, thrashing, until he landed in blackness.

Chapter 7

*T*he graveyard was dark, its silence broken by naught but the haunting query of a tawny owl. Silver shrouds of mist coiled silently skyward, seeming to merge with the tilted stones themselves.

But three small boys stood hunched before a shadowed sepulcher.

"Nay, ye touch it," hissed the smallest of the three. His fair head was gilded by moonlight, his blue eyes limned with white.

"Ye're scared," accused the darkest of the three. "Scared of something what's been dead a hundred years."

"I am na," said the first, and fisted narrow hands beside his shivering body.

"Then do it."

He bit his lip, steeled his scrawny form, and reached out with a trembling hand.

"I'm scared," said an ancient voice.

The three gasped and spun about to face the speaker.

An old man stood beside a wind-tortured tree, his gnarled hands fisted on the top of his oaken cane.

"Who are ye?" asked the oldest of the trio. His shaky voice was filled with bravado, but he did not seem to mind that his companions were huddled close to his side.

"I am of na concern, lads, but he that rests yonder . . ." He shook his head and limped forward, a bent old man with hard years behind him. "Him I'd leave be if I cared to live out me life in peace."

The threesome glanced toward the sepulcher and back. "But he's dead."

The old man eased himself onto a crooked stump. "Sure of that, are ye?"

The tallest lad scrunched his face. "He's been in there since afore I was born."

Humor shone on the gaffer's lined visage. "So long as that?"

The boy scowled. "Who are ye, ol' man?"

The ancient visitor eased back a mite, saving his back. "Them that know me call me Toft."

"Toft?" the three whispered in unison and huddled still closer together.

"So ye've heard of me." The old man nodded, happy. "'Tis good to know. 'Tis good indeed."

"Ye are the Wanderer," whispered the littlest lad.

"The last remaining of the Black Celt's unearthly line."

"Mayhap na the last."

The youngest boy had curled a tight fist into his brother's oversized tunic. "Ye're here," he whispered, gaze never roaming from the old man's face. "But where else be ye?"

"Hush," warned the eldest, but dared not turn toward the small one. "'Tis naught but rumor."

Toft shuffled his hands on the smooth curve of his cane. "What rumor is that, lad?"

Eyes shifted back and forth. The scrawny boy was scowling. "'Tis said ye have . . . a gift."

"A gift, aye? Well, truth be told, we all have gifts, lads. When ye be me own venerable age, ye may well see that it be a gift simply to awake in the morn." A frog croaked. The smallest boy jumped and squeezed close to his brother's side. "Or to hear the call of a—"

"'Tis said ye can be two places at once," rasped the grubby, dark-haired lad.

"Ahh." The old man nodded slowly, as if he were very nearly asleep. "That be a fine gift indeed, but—" He rose to his feet. The boys crowded back. "'Tis naught compared to the gifts of the lad what lies beneath that stone."

The small boy's knuckles twisted hard in his brother's shirt. "Be he truly the Black Celt's son?"

"His son?" The gaffer shook his head. "A rumor, lad, naught more."

"Just as I said," hissed the dark boy, and poked the blond lad with a bony elbow. "The Celt was na wed."

"Wed?" The old man's eyes sparkled in the uncertain light. "Nay. He was na. Na back when the world was new." He sighed, heavy and deep. "But there was a maid." He seemed to be looking back, remembering a time long before his own. "A bonny, enchanting woman na man could resist."

"The Golden Lady," whispered the small one. "She was a witch."

"A witch?" Toft nodded slowly. "Aye, I suspect that is what we would call her in this age. A witch, an enchantress. The most beautiful of women. And deadly. None could resist her. Not the Celt nor the Irish Hound who befriended him. But when the Celt learned of her betrayal, he rejected her. Her fury knew na bounds, for never had she been turned aside."

"She cast a spell," whispered the tiny lad.

"Aye, she did that," agreed Toft. "She turned the warriors to granite until the day they could right the wrongs. 'Tis much the same with yon hero," he said, and nodded toward the sepulcher. "He sleeps until he must rise to set things right regarding his kin."

Silence echoed in the misty vale, then: "How will it happen?"

"Magic!" said Toft, and his voice was suddenly

loud in the darkness. The boys cowered away in a clump.

All mouths were open, all eyes wide.

"There be a curse on that sepulcher," Toft warned, striding forward. "A curse that will strike you down if you bother its keeper. Now go. Go!" he ordered. "And do not disturb the dark Angel again."

Released from their trance, the boys scattered like chaff in a windstorm, racing between the markers and away.

Silence fell on the night again. The old man turned . . . and gasped.

A shadow stepped from shadow.

"So that's the way of it." Keelan's voice was quiet in the darkness.

"Keelan, I did na ken ye were aboot."

"I am cursed."

"Nay, lad. 'Twas just the tale of a silly old man who but hopes to keep the lads from defiling the resting place of their elders."

For a moment Keelan almost allowed himself to believe, but he had been doing so for too long already, for many months now since the day he awoke, bewildered and alone. Toft had come to his aid, sheltered him, comforted him. Lied to him. "I have dreamed," he said.

The old man's face looked broken. "Naught but dreams, brought on by the blow to yer pate most like."

"The blow. How did it happen?"

"I canna say for certain. 'Twas most likely when yer boat turned and yer poor dear parents were lost. Na one can say for sure. Ye were still addled when I found ye, as ye well ken."

"Me mum." He felt the pain in his soul. *"She wore flowers in her hair."*

The old man nodded slowly.

"Yellow flowers, nestled in her sable curls." His voice was singsong. *"I thought her the most beautiful woman that lived."*

"She was bonny beyond words."

"Aye," Keelan said. *"Aye, but she killed me."*

Tears shone in the old man's eyes.

"And I her," he added.

"Angel."

Keelan awoke to the sound of Charity's voice. She was seated on the edge of his mattress, eyes wide with worry.

"Are you well?"

"Nay," he mumbled. His head throbbed. He felt parched and broken and disoriented. "I've been beat like a bleeding rug, and I hurt like the verra . . ." He remembered Chetfield suddenly and flinched inwardly. "What be ye doing in me chamber?"

"I came down to see what I might do to make you more comfortable."

The room was dark but for one flickering flame. It tossed its light upon her seal-dark hair, shadowed her whisky eyes, caressed the mounded ivory skin above her bodice. The edges of her simple auburn gown melded with the shadows, making her seem disconnected to any earthly ties, alone in her perfect beauty.

He shifted uncomfortably and pulled his gaze away, searching for reality. "Where am I?"

She touched his forehead with gentle fingers, smoothing back his hair, before slipping her hand down his arm. "Surely you remember? You're at Crevan House. Safe within its walls."

He glanced down, marveling at the euphoria of her touch, and found that his chest was bare, his lower extremities lost beneath the softness of a pearly blanket.

"Am I naked?"

She laughed. The sound was light and sweet. She took his hand in hers and caressed his scraped knuckles. "Tell me, Highlander, what brought you here to us?"

Titillating sensations shivered up his arm. "Am I dreaming?"

"Perhaps," she said, and smiled.

He nodded and rested his head back against the downy pillow. "Ye are beauty itself, lass."

Lifting his hand, she kissed his knuckles, watching him all the while. Desire quivered through him. "Why have you come here?" she asked again, and turning his hand over, kissed his palm.

"Mary and Joseph," he rasped, unnerved by the quivering sensations, "ye should visit me dreams more often."

She laughed. The sound was husky, shivering through his battered system like mulled wine. "Perhaps I would if you would answer my questions."

His eyes had fallen closed, but then, he was dreaming. It only seemed right. "I came for what is mine," he said.

"What?"

He opened his eyes at the sharp tone, but she drew a breath, loosened her grip, smiled. Candlelight flickered across her pixie-bright features. "What is yours?"

The world was foggy, tired. "The lambkin," he murmured. Old memories flittered through him. "The lambkin and mayhap more."

"More what?"

"Should na a dream kiss more and talk less, lass?"

"Where do you hurt?"

He thought of the hours gone by. His head ached foggily, but the wracking pain almost seemed like naught but a distant dream frayed by time. Nevertheless, he put his fingers to his brow.

Reaching up, she smoothed back his hair. Her touch was feather soft, a sweet caress of hope against his skin. Her kiss was warm magic upon his forehead. Her hair brushed the bare skin of his chest. Contentment washed over him in lulling waves.

"Where else?"

He touched his arm. She kissed it. Tingling sensations sailed smoothly through him. He put his hand to his chest. She trailed liquid fingers across his skin, lighting a path, healing with touch, then kissed him where his heart beat heavy against his ribs.

Raising her amber gaze to his, she whispered, "Where now?" in a voice so soft he but felt it in his soul.

He lowered his hand to the burn on his belly, and she bent, letting her hair lap gently against his injured side. He drifted away on the sweet sensations. Her lips were a balm against his wound, kissing gently, easing the pain, heightening his senses until she drew slowly away.

Her tawny eyes were heavy-lidded now, her lips ruddy and plump. "Where?" she murmured.

Reaching down, he pulled the gray blanket

aside. He was indeed naked, and hopelessly ready, as hard and ripe as a gourd.

She shifted her eyes to it, then tilted back her head and stood up.

Not until that moment did he realize he'd been entirely wrong about her gown. It was not auburn at all, but pale and sheer. It flowed from her alabaster shoulders like gossamer magic. Candlelight shone through the gauzy fabric, kissing her sweet curves with light, brushing her straining nipples with dusky color.

He rose to his elbows. Against his belly, his engorged desire danced with need. She watched it, nostrils flared, then reached up and untied the single lace that held the magical gown in place. It slipped off one shoulder, and with that simple movement, Keelan felt the lingering remnants of pain recede like a wayward dream.

The gown dipped lower, revealing her breasts. Bright capped and lovely, they were as firm and round as ripe melons.

Desire washed over him, pulling him tight.

She smiled and let the gown dip toward her navel. It was a perfect hollow in the center of her being. He reached for her and she came. Her skin was velvet soft beneath his fingertips. He slipped his hand around her back and pulled her close beside the bed.

Her skin smelled like earthy magic when he kissed her hip. He slipped his hand along her spine. She dipped her head back and moaned as he slid his fingers between the firm round hillocks of her succulent bottom, and then the gown fell away, revealing delicate curls at the apex of her thighs. He kissed them. She shuddered and lifted one knee, placing it on the bed, opening to him. He caressed the inner softness of her thigh, and she moaned. The husky, midnight sound was almost his undoing. He slipped his hand along her leg. Feeling the liquid heat of her desire against his fingers, he rasped a prayer to a generous God even as she mounted the bed. He made room for her, eager beyond words. But she did not stretch out beside him. Instead, propped on hands and knees, she turned and straddled him.

Her buttocks shone in the flickering light, and he could do nothing but smooth his fingers over the satin curves. She wriggled beneath his touch. He slipped his hand lower, ready to reach between her thighs, but in that moment she kissed his aching shaft.

Lightning struck him. He jerked his head back into the pillow a moment before she sucked him into the velvety heaven of her mouth. Keelan gasped at the glorious torture and clawed the sheet beneath him. She was liquid heat around him, wet and fierce and demanding.

He groaned, beyond pain, beyond euphoria, gripping the bedsheets in fingers like talons, wanting more, needing more. But she drew away and lapped her tongue along the length of his straining desire. He shuddered beneath her ministrations, but she was already turning toward him, bare limbs brushing his flesh as she straddled him once again.

Her eyes gleamed with mischievous pleasure when she faced him. Her lips were swollen and bright. And her breasts! Holy fook, her breasts, dangling warm and heavy above his face like ripened fruit.

"Take me," she breathed.

"I believe he's coming to," said a voice. The harsh sound rasped against Keelan's raw senses.

"Wake for me," repeated a softer voice.

His mind churned like a wobbly mill. He opened swollen eyes. Lord Chetfield stood not two feet away. Keelan jerked. Pain roared through him at the motion.

Near the middle of the bed, Lambkin wobbled to her feet and stumbled off her master's nether parts. Keelan blinked, trying to find his bearings in the roiling mists of unreality. The last dream had seemed more real than this. And far more pleasant. Or had it been a dream a'tall?

"Careful, luv. Careful."

He cut his gaze to the left. Charity stood on the other side of his mattress, but she wasn't gazing at him with lust-filled eyes and kiss-swollen lips. Neither was she naked. Instead, she was wearing the simple auburn gown from his dreams. Confused, he glanced down, but he couldn't be certain whether he was naked or not, for his lower regions were covered with blankets.

So there was a God, but he had a damned strange sense of humor.

"Where am I?" His voice was nothing more than a croak.

Charity shifted her worried eyes toward the ghoul and back. "You are at Crevan House with me and Lord Chetfield. Don't you remember?"

Memories rushed at him like winged bats. Torture, lies, pain. Yes, he remembered. But the dream had seemed so real.

He tried to prop himself on his elbows but it hurt like hell, and she still wasn't naked, so there seemed little point to the effort. He eased back onto the mattress, head swimming miserably, and let his eyes fall closed.

"How long have I been unawares?" It felt as if the words were dragged from his throat with a garden rake.

"Through a day and a night," she murmured.

"Our Charity was quite concerned for your well-being," Chetfield said.

He felt like death come to visit, and yet he had no wish to hear worry in her sweet voice, little matter how he felt.

"You were talking in your sleep," Chetfield added, but his voice seemed to come from a great distance, and Keelan's attention had slipped away.

It was not the girl's fault that he was— His thoughts slammed to a halt as the old man's words came home to him. "I did na mean what I said!" he rasped.

The room went silent. The wolf-eyed ghoul was watching him from close proximity. "And what is it exactly that you didn't mean, Mr. Mac-Leod?"

Keelan glanced at Charity and back. She looked tense, and still fully dressed. Maybe that was best. "I was but dreaming," he croaked.

The old man's expression was unchanged. Keelan forced himself to relax. He was, after all, still alive.

"Here then," said the girl, and settled carefully onto his mattress. Her position brought back flaming memories of the vivid dreams just past, pumping up his heart rate, hardening his desire. Still, she was modestly clothed. He informed his erection, but it remained stubbornly engorged. "You must be drier than cinders, you poor thing."

Aye, his throat hurt. But what didn't? She was holding a goblet, he realized, and suddenly felt rather giddy at the sight of it.

"You will have to sit up to drink," she said.

His ability to do so seemed unlikely . . . rather tantamount to flying.

"Perhaps we could ask Bear and Frankie to assist again," Chetfield suggested.

"Nay," Keelan rasped, grasping the bedsheet in a white-knuckled hand, and yanking himself upright. Every inch of him gasped in protest. His head bobbled back in silent agony, but he gritted his teeth against the pain and held on to consciousness with a fierce grip.

"Are you all right?" she murmured. There was worry in her tender tone. Worry that he was loath to cause, but fook it all, he wasn't all right. He was going to pass out. Again.

"Angel?"

"I'm foine," he lied. "Just give me . . ." He concentrated on breathing, on living. He was damned good at living, had proved that if nothing else a thousand times over. "A moment."

She touched her hand to his brow. "I am so sorry, luv. Where does it hurt?"

Keelan stared at her through pain-narrowed eyes, but despite his good sense he could not hold back the dreams. Erotic memories rolled in like darkling clouds—sweet unfettered Charity, kissing his brow, his chest, his . . . He jerked his gaze past her to Chetfield, who stood watching with unbending attention.

"Nowhere," he rasped.

"But surely—"

"I be well. Completely healed." His tone was scratchy. "'Tis a bleeding miracle."

She looked at him as if he were daft. Which might very well have been the case. He was daft and starving and very possibly naked. He'd always hoped he'd die naked, but there had been other stipulations. Such as not sharing the room with a ghoulish lord who wanted to tear the very life from his chest.

"Drink this," Charity said, and put the goblet to his lips. Keelan didn't try to resist. Instead he sucked in the watered wine, then sputtered, gasping and choking.

She drew the glass away. "You must take it slow."

94

He nodded, still seeing her as she'd been in his dreams. Taking a deep breath, he chanced another long sip.

She watched him, lips slightly parted, then: "I long to take you inside of me," she said.

Chapter 8

Wine sputtered down Keelan's windpipe. He coughed, hacked, and yanked his streaming gaze to the ghoul. But Chetfield's mismatched features remained calm.

Charity waited, looking worried until the sputtering subsided. "Are you well now?"

Keelan tried to clear his throat, coughed again, glanced at the soft-lipped ghoul, then back at the girl. "What say ye?" he croaked.

"I but asked if you were well—"

"Afore that."

She blinked, thinking, then: "I said, I long to get some food inside of you."

He dropped his head back against the pillows, feeling old even beyond his irrational years. Old and beaten and hopeless.

"Mr. Angel?"

He rolled his eyes toward her. Still fully dressed. "Aye?"

"You must eat if you are ever to get me on my back."

He snapped his head toward her. "What?" he croaked.

She jerked away a half an inch. "You have to eat," she said, "to get your strength back."

Keelan speared Chetfield with a frantic gaze. The other's eyes gleamed like a wary wolf's. Did he know? Did he realize what Keelan was thinking, dreaming? Or was it more diabolical than that? Perhaps the two of them were in league. Perhaps sweet Charity truly was spouting the lewd propositions he imagined and they were but watching his reactions and chortling at him behind his back. Or . . . perhaps he was going mad.

He nodded dismally at the thought.

"You can eat?" she asked.

He turned his gaze to the girl's. Good God, he was tired, exhausted really. He felt himself drift into oblivion.

"I need you," she whispered.

He jerked awake. But Chetfield still wasn't trying to kill him. Which probably meant he was hallucinating again. Father God, he couldn't take much more of this. He dropped his head back, hoping to find the dreams again.

"Mr. MacLeod." Chetfield's voice was smooth, almost soothing. "I fear the maid is correct. You must eat soon or you will be of no use to me."

Keelan opened his eyes, caught the baron's gaze. They seemed to be alone in this broken span of time.

Chetfield smiled. "Might you be able to guess what I do with those who do not please me?"

"I be starving," he intoned, and Chetfield laughed just as the girl reentered the room. Once again she held a tray in her hands. Once again something steamed from a bowl. Or was it all still a dream?

"Did I hear him right?" she murmured.

Chetfield nodded sagaciously. "Our young friend appears to be rather famished."

She settled back onto the bed, setting the tray beside Keelan's hip. A ceramic bowl was filled with a thin soup that curled tentative tendrils of fragrance toward his nostrils. Keelan felt his battered system twitch lethargically to life. True, some areas had previously shown interest when Charity entered the room. But he was quite certain those parts would react long after they put him in his grave. In fact, he had some evidence to support that theory.

"Oxtail soup," she said, and lifted a spoon toward his mouth. Fatigue lay like a millstone upon his shoulders. Nevertheless, he shifted his gaze to the ghoul and opened his mouth.

Charity spooned in the broth, and with it, his indolent system jerked to life. The bread she offered tasted like ambrosia. He finished the bowl, ate the bread from her fingers, and watched her lively face as she smiled and set the spoon back on the tray.

"Very good, Mr. Angel. Very good."

"Yes," added the old man. Keelan had almost forgotten his existence. What a pity he must remember. "I'm certain you'll be up and doing what you do in no time at all." He turned toward the girl. "Shall we leave him sleep now, my dear?"

She nodded and touched Keelan's hand. Feelings spurred quietly through him. "Sleep now, luv. And if you've a need, I shall come."

He did have needs, he thought, but before he could figure out exactly what they were, sleep took him in its hard grasp.

Dreams came again. Not pleasant now, but harsh and old, still raw after a hundred plus years—his mother's pleading eyes, the taste of death on his tongue, and the knowledge . . . the unending certainty of his own cowardice.

* * *

"Mr. Angel." An apple-bright face stared down at him. "Mr. Angel," Charity said, "you're scaring your lamb."

He glanced down. Lambkin stood, knobby-kneed and befuddled beside him, dark ears drooping.

Ragged memories stormed through him, leaving a bitter aftertaste. "What did I say?" His voice was a harsh croak.

"I couldn't understand a word of it," she said, and handed him Lambkin's bottle. He turned it toward the little ewe, who took it without hesitation, bobbling her tail at the first taste. "But you seemed terrible distraught."

Distraught. He almost laughed at the word.

"Are you feeling any better?"

He took inventory. His left foot hardly hurt a'tall. "Aye, lass," he said, and searched hopelessly for some hope, but the ancient dreams made him melancholy. "I be fit as a milch maid."

"You know what it is you need?"

He took a stab in the dark. "A pint o' whisky?"

"To return to your master's house, to sleep in your own bed."

He didn't answer. The dream was still close, hovering like a dark wraith, ready to devour him, for he knew the truth, had known it all along—his mother's potion was not meant to make him brave. It would only make him safe.

"Mr. Angel . . ." Charity said.

He drew his mind back from his grim thoughts and gave her a weak smile. "Something tells me yer lord might take it amiss if I tried to leave without his permission," he said.

"Lord Chetfield?" Her satiny brows rose. "Naw. He wouldn't be bothered a'tall. He only wants what's best for you. Besides . . ." She shrugged a bonny shoulder, eyes wide and bright. "He's not here today."

"What's that?" Keelan asked, perking up.

"The master," she said. "He had errands to see to in the village. Took Frankie and some of the others with him."

His mind was spinning suddenly, giving him hope, reason. "Where's Roland?"

"With the master."

"And Beast?"

Her brows knit together, then: "You mean Bear?" she asked, and picked up Lambkin, who had just sucked the bottle dry.

"Aye."

"I believe he's in the barn," she said, and opened the window, bending double to deposit the little creature on the ground. "But truth be told, 'tis more likely he's having hisself a nap."

Keelan shifted his gaze toward the door, considering chances, options. Aye, he was hurting, but he wasn't dead. Not yet at any rate. "Tell me, lass, does your master spend most of his year here at Crevan House?"

"Aye. Ever since I've been here leastways. So there's no reason you can't leave now and come back later to—"

"And afore that?"

She scowled a little, but brightened quickly and shrugged a pretty shoulder. "I don't rightly know. He only come here after his father was killed."

Keelan's scalp tingled. "The old master was killed?"

She nodded, watching him. "Robbed, I'm told. And beat. 'Twas a terrible thing. Cook says you couldn't even recognize his face. "

"Did they catch the murderer?"

"I wouldn't be knowing for certain." She canted her bonny head. "Why do you ask?"

Gritting his teeth, he forced himself to a sitting position. "Yer master has been . . ." His head spun like a child's toy. He put his hand to it, trying to hold it in place. His brow was tight with grime and inflammation. "He's been verra good to me. I would but ken more aboot him. He thinks a good deal of ye, lass," he said, watching her face from the corner of his eye.

"He must have told ye something of himself."

She was frowning. "You don't look so good, luv."

He felt his face with tentative fingers. His left eye had opened a bit, but he could see little through the tender slit. "I'm certain ye're wrong, lass. I've heard from those who know that I be a bonny lad," he said, and tried a grin.

She gave him a stricken glance. "Maybe a good warm soaking is what you're needing before you leave. Cook has some herbs what will help ease the pain."

"Aye well . . ." He prodded the bruise on his forehead. It hurt like a son of a witch. And he should know. "That and a keg o' ale might well do the trick."

"There's a lovely tub in the next room." She paused, watching him. "Bear could carry you if you like."

He shot his gaze sideways, waiting for her to grin, but her expression remained absolutely earnest. "Naked, I suppose," he said.

Her blush started at her ears this time. "Well . . ." She glanced at the mattress. "If that's what you prefer."

He didn't bother to stifle his laughter, though it hurt like hell. "Thank ye kindly, lass, but me own tastes dunna run toward slavering beasties.

But if *ye* wished to assist with me bath, I am sure it would do me naught but good."

Her eyes opened wide. Her sweet lips parted. She was already shaking her head.

"Nay. Of course na," he corrected quickly. "I dunna ken what I be thinking. Certain I am that I can make me own way . . ." He lifted his arm in an attempt to sweep the blankets aside and gasped in pain.

"There now. Leave off." She was hovering over him in an instant, her hands tender on his exposed shoulder. "Ye mustn't break open your . . . Oh! Your poor back. It's all a-tatter . . ." Her voice trembled a little. "Scraped to bits it be." Her face was mere inches from his, her hand like trembling velvet against his shoulder. "With pieces of rocks and such . . . Mr. Angel, maybe Crevan House is simply ill luck for you."

Or maybe Chetfield was a murderous lecher and his henchmen bastards of the first water. "Ill luck?"

"Perhaps you should leave," she whispered, "before you're hurt again, only worse."

He felt himself pale. Did she know more than she admitted? Should he leave now while he could? But nay, this one thing he would see through to the end. "Na to worry, lass, I'm certain me luck's taken a turn for the better."

She was watching him closely. "So you still don't remember what happened?"

He shook his head. It hurt.

"Well ain't that a whistle?" she murmured, then brightened. "But mayhap 'tis best you don't recall. The bad, it'll find you in its own time. No need to go looking for it, as me mum was fond a saying."

"I suspect ye're right, lass."

She nodded, her small face solemn and set. "I shall help you with your bath."

He watched her from close proximity. She was as soft as a sigh. As pretty as a comforting angel. "There's something I must tell ye, lass." Angelic enough to make him wish to admit his sins, both real and imagined.

She leaned in, eyes wide, breath held. "What's that?" Angelic enough to make him want to confess all. Almost.

"I most usually bathe in the nude," he said.

She drew back abruptly, and he chuckled. "Have ye any notion how bonny ye are when ye blush, lass?"

She raised her wide amber gaze to his. "Maybe it would be best to wait for help."

"Ye're probably right," he admitted, and shifting slightly, groaned at the effects.

"There now. You must be careful," she said,

then, thinking hard, added, "You stay still. I'll fetch the water."

"I've na wish for ye to go to all that trouble for the likes of me," he lied, but she was already hurrying away.

He smiled to himself, and in a matter of minutes she was back, directing a young man who scurried after her, a bucket in each hand. Pimples plagued his cheeks. He darted a glance toward Charity and away, blushing furiously.

So, Keelan thought, he wasn't the only one who imagined her naked.

Footsteps rustled in the hallway, and then a woman waddled in. "So you finally wake." Her voice was all but a roar. Keelan drew back at the barrage on his senses and blinked his one good eye. She was the fattest person he had seen in all his considerable years, with not one chin but three. The apron wrapped about her middle barely tied at her spine and her feet were invisible beneath the hem of her mammoth skirt. "Land sakes, but he's an ugly beggar, ain't he?"

"Cook," Charity hissed. "Please."

"Well it don't matter none. Ain't like I'm a songbird myself, aye? But I was once. Skinny as our Cherry here. And just as pretty." She shook her head. Body parts jiggled and continued to do so long after she turned to wander toward the adjoining room. "Suitors come from far away as Lincolnshire just for a glimpse of me." Keelan could hear water splash into a receptacle. In a moment she was back, handing the boy her buckets, then shooing him out ahead of her. He gave Charity another glance and ducked into the hallway. "Randy as a bunch of wild hounds they were. Handsome ones. Ugly ones. Rich ones." She turned, wiping her hands on an apron the size of a wheat field. "I was once courted by a lord. Had a face that looked like a tattie gone bad, but he was a baron just the same. Would you believe that?"

Keelan opened his mouth.

"Had a manor house big as a castle." She propped her meaty knuckles on what might have been her hips and stared at him. "What you need is to steep in a good basil bath with maybe a bit of borage. Cherry honey, you help him to his feet. I'll fetch my things," she said and was gone, leaving them to stare at each other in unblinking stupefaction.

Charity cleared her throat. She wasn't as brazen as the girl who had appeared in his so real dreams, but she was every bit as bonny. Her lips were like summer magic, and though a thousand aches plagued him, he couldn't help but wonder if they would feel as soft as they had during his feverish fantasies. "Here we go then," she said and reaching for the blankets, pulled them aside as he watched her bright face.

She stared for an instant, and then her eyes widened and her mouth opened in soundless horror.

Joseph and Mary! Were his wounds so very grievous? Was he missing a leg? He glanced down, but too late. The blankets had already been whipped back into place.

"On our feet yet, are we?" roared Cook. Coming round the corner, she took one look at Charity's face and stopped. "What happened?" Water sloshed onto the floor.

"His . . . He's . . ."

"What?"

"He's . . ." The girl's face was as bright as an Edinburgh rose, and suddenly Keelan realized the problem. "He's in his altogether," she hissed.

Chapter 9

"Altogeth . . . Oh . . ."** Cook roared and howled with laughter. "Well of course he is. I couldn't hardly let him lie there hour after hour in that filthy rag he come in, could I?"

Keelan remained mute, for despite his usual demeanor, he was almost as embarrassed as the girl. Which was interesting because, truth to tell, he'd always thought modesty was well overrated. He was, in normal circumstances, quite comfortable with nudity. Indeed, it was his favorite state, for himself and, say . . . half the rest of the population. But it seemed he was at something of a disadvantage here. For one thing, he was fully aroused, and his embarrassment seemed to be doing nothing to diminish his size.

"Cherry luv," said Cook, still chuckling, "why don't you fetch the potions I left on the table. I'll get the boy here settled safely into the tub."

Despite the girl's obvious consternation, she didn't faint. Instead she skittered her gaze to his, to Cook's, then fled like a hunted bunny.

Silence settled over the room, broken by Cook's chuckle. "Our little Charity ain't been around much. Cook, on the other hand . . ." she began, and reaching out, snapped the blankets aside. The words died on her lips. Her eyes went wide in the folds of her face. "Well now," she said, still staring. "Is that for me, lad?" They stared at each other for a full five seconds, and then she roared in glee. "I jest, boy," she said, grabbing his arm and hoisting him to his feet.

He was almost too stunned to feel the pain. Almost. But his first jarring step changed that. Agony stabbed through every inch of him. And yet his erection bobbled merrily, leading them toward the tub.

"There now, laddie luv, you're doing good. Just keep going. That's right. One foot in front of the other. So you got a thing for our Cherry, do you?" Cook shouted.

Keelan's skin felt as if it were being peeled off his back with a paring knife. But they'd finally reached the tub.

"Well done," said the fat lady. "Now all you

got to do is step inside. Won't be no big task for a hero like yourself. Just one little step. Then you'll feel better."

He could feel his knees giving way, but his member was holding up nicely under the pressure.

"Unless that thing is too heavy for you. I could lift it for you, if you're in need of assist."

Keelan never remembered stepping over the rim. Didn't remember drawing his second foot inside. But he wasn't likely to forget how she chuckled as she eased him down into the gentle waves. The water felt like an odd mixture of fire and satin, soothing and burning all at once.

"Cook?" Charity's voice was uncertain from the bedchamber.

"Just a moment, lass," she called, then to Keelan, "we don't want her fainting dead away, do we now." She glanced around. "So maybe we'd best cover up your finer features." Picking up a towel from a nearby commode, she draped it across his nether parts. "There now. How are you feeling?"

"Am I in hell?" Keelan asked.

The big woman chuckled. "Come on in, lass. He's 'bout as decent as a Scotsman can be."

Charity came on timid feet, carrying the notorious tray of bags and vials. She was already blushing. Or maybe she was still blushing.

"Here now," Cook said, reached for the tray, and set it on the nearby commode. "Much as I hate to leave you here with a naked Celt, I can't hardly let Mrs. Graves alone for a blink without her burning down the kitchens. So listen pert, Cherry luv. You must wash his wounds with this." She held up a fat brown bottle. "And wash them thorough. It's going to hurt some, but not so much as if they start to fester. Leave the ointment on while he soaks, else . . ." Her voice droned on, but Keelan was beyond listening. Holding the tub's rim in aching fingers, he eased himself carefully against the slanted back. The contact didn't make him pass out. He closed his eyes, settled more firmly against the smooth metal, and let out a cautious sigh.

". . . and call me if he causes you any trouble," Cook was saying.

"Trouble?" The girl's voice was breathy with sympathy. "The poor bloke can't hardly sit up."

"Aye well," said Cook, tone dark. "Sitting up ain't necessary for some things. I'll be in the kitchen sharpening the cutlery," she said, and waddled away.

Keelan opened his eye just in time to see Charity's gaze dash from the towel to a point just above his left shoulder. She cleared her throat

and refused to look him in the eye. In fact, everything else in the room seemed absolutely fascinating, but finally she planted her gaze firmly on
his right ear, as if challenging him to say something about her wayward glance. "Is the water
warm enough?"

"Aye, lass," Keelan assured her. "Dunna trouble yerself. In fact, I am certain I can handle what
needs doing with the ointments and such."

She tilted her head, seeming to momentarily
forget the uncomfortable fact that she was sitting
beside a battered man covered in naught but a
towel. "You know something of medicines?"

"Na a thing, but I've na wish to see ye faint
dead away."

His ear seemed all the more fascinating.

"Perhaps ye might shift the tonics close beside
the tub that I can—"

"I ain't a little girl, you know."

He couldn't help but notice how her bosom
swelled above the edge of her simple bodice.

"I mean, I ain't as innocent as I seem." She had
settled her bottom on the tub's rim, blocking the
door from his view as she sat staring at him. Her
chin was raised in defiance, and somehow he
couldn't quite stop himself from imagining her
doing the same thing without a stitch of clothes
to cover her glory. "I've seen men in the . . . in

113

the altogether before." She was slanted slightly toward him, the rim of the tub nestled firmly in the cleft between her legs. "Well . . ." She fumbled the fat brown jar from the tray. "I've seen . . . *a* man in the altogether . . . before." She cleared her throat and unstopped the jar. The smell of mint filled the room. "I've been down to Gray's Mill, you know."

"Oh?" He had no idea where she was going with her current train of thought, but so long as she was sitting on his bathtub it hardly mattered.

She dipped her fingers into the ointment and leaned forward. Her bosom swelled toward him, but he managed to refrain from doing anything that was likely to get him killed. Her fingers were unsteady against his cheek, but the ointment was soothing, her voice the same. He closed his eyes and tried not to imagine her nipples.

"Gray's Mill?"

"'Tis a favored place when the summer days grow long. Brady Cushing could swim like a merman." She gently dabbed a bit of ointment into a cut above his left eye. The pain eased a little.

"Was he?"

She gave him a scowl, dipped out more stuff, and smoothed it into the wound on his neck. "Was he what?"

"A merman."

"He was the miller's son," she said, and winced as she smoothed ointment into the oozing wound on his arm.

"So Brady and ye were . . ." Naked? "Friends?" he asked.

That scowl again, cute as an inchworm. "Sure. I mean . . . I didn't know him real good being as I lived some good distance away. Me father used to say handsome boys was all well and good, but they was more trustworthy if you kept a couple miles betweenst them and yer daughter. Still . . ." She tried to look worldly-wise, but only managed adorable. "I got to see him now and again.

"If you lean forward I can have at your back."

He couldn't fight down the grin, even though leaning forward made every muscle groan in agony. After all, in his mind she was naked.

"Oooh your poor, tattered skin. The terrible beast must have dragged you half a league by the look of things."

"Aye," he said distractedly. "So ye and Brady were . . . swimming mates?"

"Well we—" she began, then her eyes went wide. "Naw! I mean . . . naw. *I* didn't . . . That is to say, I've never been . . ." She flashed her gaze to him and away. "Swimming."

But blessed Mary, she would be beautiful. Floating on her back with her bonny brown hair sweeping silken free across her lovely breasts. He could imagine it well.

"So ye remained on the shore," he said, "waiting for yer love to come to ye?"

"He was not my love . . ." Her eyes were beyond expressive, her fingers fidgety. "Exactly."

Against all likelihood, her hand felt like heaven against his skin, easing away the pain. "So just a dalliance then?" he asked.

She cleared her throat and gently doused his back with a steady stream of water. "Friends more like. Like you said early on."

"Tell me, lass," He couldn't help but smile into her eyes. "Do you always treat yer friends so well?"

"Why sure I—" she began, then jerked away. "I never . . . I didn't mean to say I . . . We was only friends."

"Naked friends be the verra best sort."

Her mouth opened and shut, her face red as a berry. "*He* was in the altogether. Not me."

"Ahh." Keelan couldn't help but notice that she didn't quite manage to force herself to say the word *naked*. If he weren't aroused to the point of explosion, that might be terribly sweet. "And he did na mind ye watching?"

"Well he . . . he . . . ."

"Didn't ken ye were there?" he finished quietly.

She opened her mouth and gave him a peeved glance "Scooch down in the water so's I can wash your shoulders."

He did so. It hurt. When he eased back up, the towel slipped lower, but Keelan pulled the shield resolutely into place.

Charity swallowed and raised her gaze back to his.

"Tell me, lass, how old was Master Brady when ye last saw him . . . in the altogether?"

She bunched her brows over liquid eyes. "I don't see how that matters none." She cleared her throat. "There's blood in your hair."

"How old were ye then, lass?"

She was avoiding his gaze again. "Close your eyes. I'll wash it for you."

He did so. After all, his imagination was ever as clear as his vision . . . and twice as lurid.

The water felt soothing on his scalp, her fingers magic against his skin. The scent of lavender mingled with thyme, easing his battered senses. Her thumb brushed his ear with tender slowness. His hair washed against his shoulders, slick as a seal.

"You need a trim," she said, but her voice was

as soft as a sigh. He opened his eyes to find hers. "I can cut it for you if you like."

He imagined that . . . alone with her, her hands soft as a dream against his skin. She'd laugh at his jests. And of course . . . they'd be naked.

He cleared his throat. "Mayhap that would na be a good idea, lass."

"We might wait until you're feeling better," she said, dipping into the brown jar again and reaching down to rub ointment in the wound above the towel.

Keelan tensed beneath her ministrations and gritted his teeth against the titillating agony. She eased her fingers over the aching muscles of his abdomen. He was but a sigh's distance from ecstasy. She was a towel from fainting.

"I'm a fair hand with a scissors," she murmured, and dropped her hand with breathtaking slowness to the next wound.

He caught her fingers before he knew what he was doing. "I'm certain ye're a fair hand at a host of things, lass," Keelan rasped, "but . . ." He paused, remembering to breathe. "I fear the experience might be more than me poor system can handle just aboot now."

She scowled. Kissing her would be so simple, so pleasant, so deadly.

He cleared his throat and tried to do the

same with his thoughts. "Mayhap I was entirely wrong, lass. Mayhap ye've na idea what ye do to a man."

Her lips moved prettily. "If I've hurt you I—"

"Nay," he breathed. "Nay, lass. Yer touch is naught but magic."

Her scowl deepened. Her lips were but inches away, teasing, tempting, begging.

"Tell me, lass, if this Brady resisted ye I would ken his trick." Her scent, as light as a morning breeze, tantalized him. Her fingers felt soft and fragile. He drew them near and kissed the tips.

Her lips parted. No sound escaped.

He raised his gaze slowly to hers. "Did he resist?"

She nodded.

"And what of the others?"

"What others?" Her words were barely a whisper.

"The other men who be smitten by yer merest glance. Who follow ye like lambkins on a string. Have they resisted also?" He brushed her knuckles with his thumb and held his breath, not certain whether he hoped she would confirm or deny. Innocence, after all, was its own guardian.

Her nod was more thoughtful this time, her eyes wider still. She licked her lips with seductive slowness.

"So ye are . . ." He searched for the proper words, trying to remember that he had not come here to lose himself in a bonny maid's sweet embrace. "Ye are untried?"

Her lips parted the slightest degree. He kissed her wrist and was rewarded with a puffed exhalation. When she spoke, her words were breathy. "I'm not certain I take your meaning, Mr. Angel."

He kissed her arm. "Have ye never been loved, lass?"

"Loved? Oh aye, me mum loved me something—"

"Nay." He shook his head and touched her face. She shivered beneath his hand, and with that physical proof of her arousal, he couldn't resist slipping his hand behind the weight of her fragrant hair and pulling her down for a kiss.

Her lips touched his, as soft as a sigh, as tempting as sin itself, but suddenly the world exploded.

"What the hell is this!" Roland snarled and stepped into view.

Chapter 10

"**R**oland!" Charity's tone was breathy, her eyes wide as she leapt to her feet. "I didn't expect you back so soon."

"I guess time moves right along when you're with our patient here," Roland said, and took a strutting step forward. "Thought I'd come on in and see how he's doing, but it looks to me that you're doing quite well, aye Highlander?"

Merciful God, so Chetfield wasn't the only bastard who hoped to bed the girl. "The lass here was kind enough to see to me wounds," Keelan said, fighting to keep his tone level.

Roland smiled, but it was carnivorous at best. "It looks like she's seen a good deal, all right. Cherie luv, why don't you run along to the kitchen. Cook's been asking about you."

She fidgeted. "But Mr. Angel here needs my assist."

Roland turned toward her, eyes flat. "We'll manage on our own."

"I don't think—"

"And it's just as well you don't start now." For a moment rage twisted Roland's face, transforming it from angelic to satanic, but he drew a calming breath. His features relaxed into a semblance of normalcy, but his eyes remained rabid. "Run along to the kitchen before supper is ruined."

"Very well then," she said, "if you're sure you can handle him."

The bastard smiled, his eyes never leaving Keelan. "Quite sure."

"You soak as long as you like then, luv. I'll be back in a bit with your meal," she said, then turned and hurried from the room.

Keelan cleared his throat. "This is na what it looks to be."

"Isn't it?" asked Roland, tone level, eyes insane. "'Cuz it almost looked as if you were kissing my girl."

"Ye see," said Keelan, "'tis just what I was saying. The situation is na a'tall what it seems."

"Then you'd best explain yourself," Roland said, and reached with malevolent slowness into his jacket.

Keelan felt the blood rush from his face as the bastard drew out a cigar. "The lass . . . Charity, is it? She but hopes to see me gone from this place. Said as much, in fact. Wanted to get me healed as soon as possible and thought a bath might bring me quicker toward that end."

"Ahh," Roland said, and twirled the cheroot between his fingers. "And you, Highlander, what were you thinking?"

"Well . . ." Fook it all, he was at a terrible disadvantage, lying nearly prone at the other's feet like a slab of shrinking beef. "I thought the quicker I mend, the quicker I can see to the duties me new master has given me."

"So you weren't planning to bed her."

"Bed her!" Merciful God, he was in trouble. He was as weak as a milk-fed pup, there were no weapons close to hand, and he seemed to be the only one in the room who was naked. God, he hated being the only one naked. On the other hand, having the bastard naked would hardly make the situation any more appealing. If Charity returned, though . . . Roland stepped closer, stopping Keelan's thoughts. "Nay. I hardly know the lass. I would na consider—" he began, but at that moment the bastard yanked a knife from inside his coat and reached down.

"Damn you to hell!" he rasped.

Reaching out frantically, Keelan grabbed the first thing that came to hand. His fingers closed around a bottle. He threw it with all his might. It bounced off Roland's cheek, sloshing liquid in his face.

The bastard screamed and stumbled back, but Keelan was already scrambling out of the tub. His feet slipped on the floor. He bobbled, caught his balance, and prepared to dash for the door, but Roland was already recovering and stood between him and safety, arms outstretched and knife held ready.

"Listen." Keelan glanced through the doorway that seemed a lifetime away. "I can understand yer feelings. She's a bonny lass and no mistake, but this be a bad idea."

"I believe you're wrong there, Highlander."

He was breathing hard. The exertion burned deep in his chest and back, nearly doubling him over. "Leave me be and I'll not tell the lass 'twas ye who wounded me at the start." There was nothing close to hand that could possibly be misconstrued as a weapon. Wrapping his arm about himself, Keelan cradled his lower ribs in his right hand. "But if ye kill me, she'll ken yer true nature."

"Kill you!" The bastard smiled. The expression was strangely beatific. "I don't plan to kill you, boy. Not right away."

Near the door there was a ceramic pitcher. If

he could get that far, maybe he could use it as a shield. Of course, if he could get to the door, it might behoove him to run like bloody hell. He almost laughed out loud at the thought. Run? Sweet Mary, he could barely stand up. Laughing wasn't all that likely either.

And the bastard was stalking him. Keelan sidled sideways. "What would Charity say?"

He smiled again. "If I cut off your balls? She'd probably say, *Look, there's some poor bastard with no balls.*"

Keelan shook his head, still easing sideways, careful not to make any sudden moves . . . or pass out. "Truly, I dunna think she'd use such language."

Roland narrowed his eyes. "Are you laughing at me, boy?"

"Nay!" He chanced another lateral step, stalling, praying. The backs of his legs struck something. He fended it off, worked his way around it. "Nay indeed, but ye must think of the unfairness of the situation."

Roland remained silent, watching, knife outstretched.

"Ye are clever," Keelan said.

The bastard's mouth quirked as he nodded his agreement.

"And strong and hale. While I am . . ." Keelan

made a motion with his hand. "I am sadly weakened and sore wounded."

"It's a terrible truth," said the bastard, and settled himself on the balls of his feet, arms outstretched, eyes laughing, waiting. "But life is rarely fair."

Keelan was, quite literally, backed into a corner, and the lovely pitcher was still some feet away. "Harm me and she will know. There will be na way to make her believe ye are . . ." Human. "The gentle man ye pretend to be."

The bastard grinned. "You think I care what she believes?"

Oddly enough, he did. "She will na come to a coward." He knew the moment the words left his mouth that he had made a mistake.

"Are you calling me a coward, Highlander?"

"Nay." Keelan's heart was pounding like a runaway steed. "But 'tis na me own opinion that matters, is it now? 'Tis hers," Keelan said.

For a moment the world was utterly silent, and then the bastard laughed. The sound echoed eerily in the room

"You think I object to taking her against her wishes?"

Keelan's stomach churned at the thought. "She is sweetness itself," he gritted. "Any man who is a man would care for her wishes."

"So you think I'm not a man."

Fook it all! Keelan clenched his fists, loosened them, tried to force out a soothing rejoinder, but nothing came to mind.

"Maybe you think I'm an animal," Roland said and shifted the knife to his other hand.

"Nay. Nay indeed," Keelan said, every ounce of concentration focused on the blade. "In truth I've always thought rather highly of the beasts of the—"

"Damn you!" Roland snarled and leapt.

Keelan lunged sideways, grabbing the pitcher. It felt as heavy as a horse, but he swept it in front of him. Roland sliced sideways. The blade slashed across the hard-baked ceramic, missing Keelan's thigh by the barest inch.

"Yer master will be sore disappointed to find us like this," he rasped, drawing the pitcher higher.

The bastard laughed. "And you'll be sore disappointed to learn he's still in the village," he said and lunged again.

Keelan just managed to save his throat from the blade that slashed like lightning across the pottery. "You're wrong." His voice sounded raspy. His knees wobbled with fatigue. "He's on his way here even now."

"Let the old fool come. I'll give him the same as—"

"Your wish is my command, Mr. Roland," said a melodious voice.

They jerked toward the doorway in unison. Chetfield stood watching them with an odd smirk, hand lightly holding his staff as if he'd waited there for hours.

"My lord." Roland's voice was weak. "I didn't expect you to return so soon."

Silence echoed in the room, punctuated by tension as tight as a knot.

The baron smiled without humor. "Is that any reason for you to disembowel our Celtic friend?"

A muscle jumped in the bastard's jaw. "I found him with the girl," he said, and Chetfield turned his deadly attention to Keelan.

Chapter 11

"**D**efine *with*," Chetfield said. His voice was low and as deadly as a serpent.

In the hallway, Charity pressed her back to the wall and held her breath in starving lungs.

"She was but assisting with me bath," said the Highlander. "'Twas naught more devious than that."

"So you are not attracted to our Cherry?" Chetfield's staff rapped against the floorboards as he paced inside.

Charity fisted her hands, heart pounding against her ribs. Why hadn't he left? Why?

"Attracted to her! Nay. Of course not," said the Celt, but his tone was off, his denial foolish.

Charity gritted her teeth and cursed in silence. Fool of a Scotsman! Where the hell had he learned to lie?

"So you've no desire to take her to your bed?"

Chetfield asked. His tone was level, devoid of passion, but there was death in the air.

She could wait no longer. Pushing herself from the wall, she pasted on a wide-eyed expression and strode noisily into the bedchamber. "Is everything all right in here?" she called out and stepped unceremoniously into the bathing room just as the Highlander glanced down, apparently checking the strategic placement of the pitcher. Chetfield's eyes were gleaming. Roland made some kind of indescribable noise deep in his throat.

She blinked. "Mr. Angel . . ." she gasped, tone rife with dim dismay, "whatever are you doing up and about?"

The Highlander glanced at Roland, but whatever weapon he'd brandished had already been hidden back inside his coat. "I was just . . ." He cleared his throat. "Me bath was growing chill . . . I thought I might . . ." He glanced at the pitcher, moved it a little. "I thought I might fetch some hot water."

That was the best he could come up with? "By yourself?" she asked, and shifted her wide-eyed gaze from one man to the next. "Mr. Angel, are you feeling right in your head? Have you forgot that you are sore wounded?"

He gave her a grin, looking all the while as if

he might fall flat on his face. Idiot! Short of tying him onto a steed, she'd given him every chance to escape.

"Now that ye mention it, I do remember something aboot pain, lass," he said.

Quips? Now? She should have let the creepy little bastard have him instead of sending Chetfield in to save him. She'd planned to do just that. Would have, in fact, if he hadn't been gazing up at her with those damned soulful eyes just minutes before. "I'm certain Mr. Roland would have been happy to help you. Wouldn't you have, Mr. Roland?"

"Certainly," said the bastard, and Chetfield laughed, jarring the tension like a buffeting wind.

"Charity, my dear," he crooned, "why don't you run and fetch one of my old tunics to save our young friend from any further embarrassment. Unless you wish to spend the rest of the day hiding behind a pitcher, Mr. MacLeod."

"Nay." The Highlander cleared his throat. "Nay, a tunic would be much appreciated."

Charity delayed a moment, but there was nothing for it. She had little choice but to do as ordered. As for the Celt, he would have to learn to survive without her. Still, once out of sight, she raced up the stairs, yanked a garment from the wardrobe, and flew back down the steps. Reaching the bedchamber door, she steadied her breath and strode inside, but despite her rush, the Highlander's face was increasingly pale. Chetfield was just lowering his cane, stepping back, looking smug. She felt herself blanch, but hid the emotion behind a blank expression.

"Ahh, there you are, my dear, and not a moment too soon," Chetfield said. "I'm afraid our young friend is weakening."

For a moment her naïve façade almost crumbled, but her survival instincts were strong. "Mr. Angel," she said, grabbing his arm, steadying him. "Are you quite all right?"

"Aye." Taking the tunic from her, he draped it in front of him and set the pitcher aside, but his hands were unsteady, his gaze caught on the two villains who stood not far away. The burn on his abdomen was oozing again. Bloody bastards. "Aye. I but need a moment."

"Yes, you rest," Chetfield crooned, and turned toward his servant. "Mr. Roland and I have things to discuss," he added, and in a moment they were gone.

The Highlander watched them go, then drew a careful breath and tried to wrap the garment around his waist, but his uncertain fingers lost their hold on the fabric. It slipped to the floor.

"Oh," she breathed, watching it fall. He closed his eyes, looking for all the world as if he might pass out. From embarrassment or fatigue, she couldn't be sure, yet there seemed nothing she could do but retrieve the garment.

Bending, she gave him a glance on the way down and felt her eyes widen. So her weird, lurid dreams hadn't exaggerated his appeal, she thought, and remembered to blush as she cleared her throat and straightened.

His fingers brushed hers as she handed off the garment, but even now his hands could not function properly. The tunic slipped back to their feet. She would have laughed if she'd dared.

"Mary and Joseph," he murmured, but it was no great chore to fetch it back. She straightened, remembering not to smile. He reached to take the tunic once again, but she cleared her throat, averted her gaze, and tightened her grip.

"Perhaps I should hold on to it until you reach your bed," she suggested.

He was, she noticed, starting to sweat. "And mayhap I should don the tunic before Chetfield returns and kills me with a glance," he countered.

"Master Chetfield?" She would never be the actress her mother had been, but this once she would give it her all. "Oh no, you've got him

133

all wrong," she said, and urged him toward the door. "The master, he looks fierce at times, but he wouldn't hurt a fly."

"How about a Scotsman?"

"What's that?" Who was this man? The gentle shepherd with a softness for orphaned lambs or the naked rogue with a hardness for . . . her?

"I dunna believe he is over fond of me," he asserted.

"Oh no." She furrowed her brow. "You've got the wrong impression altogether. It's just the pain that makes him a bit snappish at times."

"Pain," he murmured.

"In his hip." She made certain to drop every "h," to keep her tone girlish, her eyes wide. There were only two things that made a woman less threatening than naïveté. And that was breasts. She happened to display all three. "From the goring, you remember. 'Tis the reason he limps at times." It was a lie, of course. But the truth would do him no good. "Are you all right?" she asked, eyeing him. "Ye look terrible pale again."

"Aye, lass, I be fine," he said, but he didn't look fine. He looked as if he'd seen a ghost. As if he knew the truth of Chetfield's injury.

"You mustn't try to do for yourself again. Not until you're full healed."

"Do for meself?"

134

"Fetching the water," she said. "Roland would have surely got it for you."

"This Roland." He tripped, blanched, took a careful breath. "Ye've known him for some time, ye say."

"Ever since I come to Crevan House."

"Six months ago." He'd reached the bed and closed his eyes as if in silent thanksgiving.

"Aye."

"Which was well after Chetfield's father was killed." Taking the tunic from her hands, he draped it in front of his body and turned carefully. She held his arm lest he fell face first onto the hardwood. "Tell me, lass, the villain what killed the old master, did he steal anything of import?"

She shrugged, mind spinning. Why the devil did he ask? "As I said, I weren't here at the time."

"But ye must have heard. Tales like this . . . they tend to wander."

Wander where? She'd spent a lifetime dredging up those stories. "Master Chetfield is still as rich as the regent," she said.

"So ye didn't hear that he'd lost something terrible precious?"

"Why do you ask?" she inquired, no longer able to hold back the words. She'd gotten little enough out of him when she'd awakened him from his dreams some nights before. Indeed, she had hoped for more, but he had fallen asleep, leaving her with naught but suspicions and her own erotic imaginings.

"I hate to think a thief had taken anything of great value from someone ye care aboot," he said, but he was lying. He had to be. Chetfield had had him beaten. She was sure of it, and no one could forgive that. Not even a Scotsman with angelic eyes and a devilish smile. "I understand why they call you Angel," she said, and touched his brow. "Did Cook's potions ease your pain a'tall?"

"I be still alive." Twisting carefully, he drew his legs onto the bed and let his eyes fall closed. "Thanks to ye," he added, and looked at her.

Charity yanked her gaze from the bunched tunic. He had an unearthly allure, true, but he held no interest for her. Perhaps he was harmless, just an innocent shepherd as he vowed to be, but perhaps he was more . . . or less. Either way, neither his heaven-blue eyes nor his satyr's smile had any bearing on her. She would do as she must, play her part, even if it demanded that she pretend interest, for surely even he would not be so foolish as to stay and incur Chetfield's wrath. Surely even he would realize the eerie old man's obsession with her and get himself gone before it was too late.

"Lass," he murmured. She watched his lips move. It was no great chore. "Mayhap it would be wise if ye did na look at me such."

She blinked and blushed. "I don't know what you're talking about."

His silvery eyes softened. His mouth, lovingly sculpted by a master craftsman, tilted up at the corners. "Yer lord would skin me alive if I so much as touched yer sleeve, Charity."

"You're talking crazy," she said, and reached tentatively for the tunic that hid some of his finer parts.

Perhaps it was thoughts of death that made him tighten his grip on the garment. Perhaps he wasn't as daft as he seemed, but when she tugged, he relented. The fabric slid away, exposing all. It was quite a lot. Nevertheless, she managed not to stare. Instead, she grasped the garment in both hands and opened the neck hole.

"I'm talking about *them*," he said, and tilted his head toward the door.

Her heart clenched. What did he know? How much? "Them?"

"The lot of them. They're bloody—" He stopped himself, gritted his teeth. "They're not what they seem, lass."

Why had he come here, she wondered wildly, but wrinkled her brow and reached up to touch a cool hand to his forehead. "Are you feeling feverish again, luv?"

He grabbed her arm, fingers hard against her skin. "Ye've got to leave this place."

"What are you talking about? Master Chetfield ain't nothing but kindness itself," she said, and wondered if, in the end, he would survive her lies.

Chapter 12

"**S**o ye finally wake, do ye?"

Keelan sat up. The room was dark and silent, but he could see Toft's face as clear as sunlight. The girl was not in his chamber, only in his dreams. He had seen little of her in the past few days. She had left his chamber some nights before without heeding his warning. But now, without her bonny presence to muddle his thoughts, he knew it was for the best. Knew her safe departure would surely cause his death. The idea gnawed at his guts like a greedy hound.

The old man shook his gnarled head. He was smallish and bent, with a face like an ancient gnome. "Ye have followed yer daft plan, then, I see."

Keelan put a hand to his throbbing head. "How did ye find me?"

Toft snorted. "I have a gift. Did ye na ken?"

"Aye, well, it took ye a good while to get here. Yer talents must be wearing thin."

"'Tis seemingly better than ye can do, lad. What have ye done with yer gift?"

"Go back to where ye came from, old man."

"Ye disregarded me warnings, and now ye look like the devil's own."

"It's fine I be."

Toft chuckled. The sound reverberated in the deep shadows of the room, almost soothing. Almost nostalgic, though Keelan would rather take a lashing than admit it. "Yer ribs ache and yer head throbs like a bleeding war drum."

"Stay out of me head."

"Here ye are then," Toft said, and nudged Keelan's elbow.

Glancing up was painful.

"Drink it," Toft said, tilting a fat-bottomed amber bottle at him. The contents smelled of verbena.

But Keelan only laughed. "I think I've taken enough potions from me kin already, gaffer."

The old man's face remained sober. "Ye think yer mum did it to spite ye, lad? Ye think she put ye to sleep because she was evil?" He leaned forward, gritted his crooked teeth. "Nay, she made ye drink to keep ye safe. Sent yer body back to the Highlands so that ye would na suffer the same fate as she. So that ye would sleep until it was safe for ye to rise. She was courage itself, boy. Courage and cleverness. And she did it naught but for love."

The memories pounded in Keelan's head. Failure, cowardice, foolishness. "I need no such love," he rasped.

"Ye dunna ken what ye need," scoffed the other, and touched the bottle to Keelan's arm again. "Drink it. Lady Colline mixed it with ye in mind."

A rivulet of shame washed through Keelan. O'Banyon's bride had taught him much, never knowing why he coveted such herbal knowledge. Never knowing he hoped to trick an old man, to take the treasure his father had lost many long years ago. "She knows where I be?"

Their gazes met. "Nay. Nor her husband or the Celt, na till I deem it best to tell them," he said, and thrust the bottle forward again.

It was a threat of sorts, but Keelan ignored it. "As it happens, I've na wish to sleep for another seven score years, old man."

"If ye dunna get a chance to heal ye will sleep forever, ye daft bugger."

"Daft am I?" Keelan shifted to his feet, the pain

almost unnoticed. "I've found him!" he snarled. "Lord Chetfield's heir."

"Chetfield's—!" Toft began, then snorted. "Is that what ye think he be?"

Keelan narrowed his eyes, thinking. "Aye. I ken he is. A distant relation, true, but me da's blood be on his hands nevertheless."

The old man shook his head. "Sure ye have lived too long to be this foolish, lad."

"What the devil are ye talking aboot?"

"Drink the brew and I'll tell ye."

"Ye'll tell me either way," Keelan said. "Or have ye come all this far distant by yer unearthly means only to stand there and shake yer head at me?"

"The ol' man be dangerous," Toft croaked.

Keelan chuckled sardonically. "Dangerous he is, but who be ye calling *old*, gaffer?"

"So ye truly dunna ken." Toft shook his head. "Can ye be so dense? Have ye na heard him speak?"

Something clicked in Keelan's mind. Something curdled in his belly. "What about his speech?"

"Drink the potion."

Keelan's scalp tingled eerily. "What is it ye ken, ye stubborn ol'—" he began, but Toft stepped forward and pushed the bottle against his hand.

Their fingers brushed. There was a spark of something unknown, almost painful, and then he was gone.

Reality settled around Keelan. He was alone. Memories struck him hard, tearing at his mind, but he eased them back, shutting them in a corner, out of sight, quiet. The old gaffer had claimed kinship when first Keelan had stepped from the shadows. His uncle, he'd said. But it had been a lie. In truth, they were cousins of sorts. Keelan's mother had had a twin sister. A sister with whom she had shared her worries through time and distance. A sister who had traveled from the Highlands to London to retrieve her nephew's body. A sister who had borne a son to watch over Keelan's tomb. It was that son who had sired Toft, who had entrusted him with ancient secrets, who had made him vow to look after his elders.

Keelan drew a deep breath and glanced about. The lambkin lay curled against his side. So the nightmares were true. He was at Crevan House. But so was the maid called Charity. Her image came to him as sweet and gentle as a song. The memory of her skin against his only hours before smote him. Why did she remain there? Surely she could see she was in danger? Surely she realized circumstances were not what they seemed.

143

That her innocence . . . nay, her very *life* might well be forfeit if she stayed.

But no. She was trust itself, open to the world. Soft and warm and loving. To be protected and nurtured and—

He stopped himself with a rasp of disgust. He was no protector. No warrior. That much he had proven a hundred years past. Reaching out, he pulled his blankets aside and pushed his legs over the edge of the mattress. Agony went with him, threatening to drown him in its dark undertow. He waited for the worst of the pain to pass, then forced himself carefully to his feet. He didn't swoon like a flirting debutante. A favorable sign. Instead he took a couple of tentative steps around the room. The lamb watched him from the bed, eyes dark and shiny as beads, little head resting on obsidian hooves. Outside the window, a rook cawed. Lifting his arms, Keelan stretched the muscles in his back and managed to refrain from passing out. Good. Excellent. He would not be speedy, but speed was unlikely to save his tattered hide anyway.

Stealth was what he needed. Stealth and wits.

He had come to the right place. His scalp tingled, but that had nothing to do with the facts. 'Twas logic and inquiries that had brought him here. Chetfield was the man he sought. Chetfield with the oddly familiar voice.

Have ye na heard him speak?

The memory of Toft haunted him. But he turned it aside.

Bending one knee carefully, Keelan tested his muscles. He would be unlikely to beat Lambkin in a battle of brawn, but the past years had made him crafty. Or perhaps it was deeper than that. Perhaps it was his mother's Scottish blood, thick as stew, flowing through his veins. For she had been wily. Oh aye, she had been that.

Keelan put his hand on the door latch. It made not the slightest noise as it opened, yet Lambkin raised her little head with an inquisitive bleat.

"Ye stay," he whispered. She blinked bicolored lashes and settled back down, curling her neck over knobby knees once again.

The hallway was quiet. Keelan's bare feet were just as silent against the wooden floorboards. For he had learned much over the past decades, much about deception and bitterness and heartbreak. But also about caution and self-preservation and planning.

During the daylight hours, he had taken to shuffling carefully about the house, insisting that he must exercise his poor tattered muscles.

But in truth he had felt the need to learn about the manor's sprawling design.

He had come far, and he would not leave until he gained the treasure. The treasure that was rightfully his, that had been taken from his father so many long years past. But what was it exactly? And where? Perhaps not here at all. But Sir Stanton, his father, had spoken eloquently of it in the letters to his beloved Iona. 'Twas not a thing easily set aside, not even for a bold privateer. How difficult, then, for a cowardly bastard like Chetfield to leave it be?

Nay, it would not be found on some distant estate. It would be close to hand, well hidden, mayhap, but near enough to gaze upon, to touch. Thus, Keelan would search the house. He would begin at floor level, avoid Chetfield's upper chambers as long as possible, and search the south rooms where the silvery moon would afford him some light.

The floorboards were blessedly quiet beneath his feet, though each step was more painful than the last. If they found him unconscious on the woolen rug, would they put him from his misery or drag him outside for more torture? 'Twas impossible to guess. Best to stay alert then.

Near the foot of the winding stairs something creaked. Keelan jerked in that direction, heart pounding. The house stretched on forever, cast in shadows of varying darkness. Each was the shape of a baron with a soul as black as Satan's. Keelan waited to die, to be killed with naught more than a glance, but nothing happened.

Finally, unable to bear the torturous immobility, he stepped woodenly into the nearest room and pressed his back to the wall, heart pounding like a hammer against his battered ribs. Reaching to his right, he curled his fingers around a brass candlestick. It felt solid and heavy in his hand. He raised it above his head and waited. Minutes stretched into eternity. Night shifted wearily away until every fiber burned with exhaustion.

Unable to remain motionless another moment, Keelan forced himself to step away from the wall. A dozen unseen eyes watched him, a dozen voices whispered in his head, but he began his search nevertheless.

The room held musical instruments. A pianoforte. A lute. A gracefully arched charsach that looked to be as old as he, but though Keelan examined each piece, none seemed to be of particular value.

He moved silently on. The next chamber was a sitting room that boasted broad windows on each side, but little else. He searched it rapidly, then stepped back into the hall.

But a flicker of movement caught his eye. An apparition floated down from above.

Keelan jerked back in terror. But the ghost failed to notice. Instead it turned at the bottom of the steps and hurried away, clutching its dark skirt in one hand and glancing behind. The face was pale and oval.

Charity? He almost rushed after her, but she was already gone, hidden from sight, vanished into the shadows.

Exhausted and confused, Keelan held his breath, waiting, mind churning, but the apparition did not reappear. Thus he finally crept back to his borrowed room. Easing open the door, he stepped inside. It was not until then that something leapt at him.

Keelan lunged to the right. Pain crashed through his shoulder. He raised his arm to ward off the next blow, but all that greeted him was Lambkin's plaintive bleat. The little ewe had but leapt from the bed to greet her master, who, being the brave soul he was, had slammed his shoulder into the doorjamb.

"Mary and Joseph," Keelan whispered, and picked up the lamb, shutting the door shakily behind him.

* * *

"Time to rise, lad."

Light struck Keelan's eyelids like a well-honed claymore. He raised a hand, moaned at the pain in his skull, and gazed at the shimmering blue square of sky just revealed by Cook's cheery arrival.

"And how is our ugly patient this morning?"

He blinked against the light. "Have I done something to offend ye, Cook?"

She stared at him a moment, then laughed heartily and reached behind him for the pillow. "Here now, what's this?" she asked, and glanced at the floor.

Keelan turned his gaze. A heavy amber bottle sat beside the bed—the bottle from his dream. His blood felt cold, but she was already lumbering toward it. There was nothing he could do but reach down and snatch it up.

"'Tis naught," he rasped. The glass felt cool and smooth against his fingers. "Naught but a bit of something for me parched throat," he said as he gripped the bottle tighter and turned the conversation aside. "It hardly seems worth getting meself torn to shreds if folks be still waking me for na good reason."

She stared at him a moment, then snorted. "'Tis time for breakfast."

The bottle felt heavy in his hand, conjuring up a hundred chilling memories. His stomach twisted. "I dunna want breakfast," he said, but she was already shifting the pillows against the scrolled metal of the headboard.

"Glad I am to hear it for I've brought nothing but a few nuggets of grain and a nip for your lambkin there."

"Mayhap that could wait until—"

"Oh, quit your moping, boy," Cook said, fiddling with the blankets. "You'll not win our little Cherry's heart by whining."

He snapped his gaze toward the door, certain Chetfield would be there, had been there the whole night past. "I've no wish to win her heart."

"What part were you hoping for then?" she asked, closing a fleshy hand around his arm and shifting him back against the pillows. Pain ripped him in twain. Holy hell, there was no need for Chetfield to bother killing him. His cook was doing a fine job of it.

"What say you?" she asked.

He managed to glance up through the circling stars. She was scowling, her chins bunched tight beneath her pursed mouth.

He tried to think through the pain. "What?"

She propped her fists in the region of her

waist. "Listen, lad, you've got some impressive attributes." She nodded toward his nether parts. "That I'll admit, and I'm no prude by any stretch, but Charity's dear to my heart. I'll not see her bruised and tossed aside."

He shifted carefully, trying to breathe. "I dunna think meself able to toss anyone aboot just now."

Her brows lowered. Her voice did the same. "I ain't jesting, boy."

She glared down at him, then waddled away to glance down the hall and shut the door behind her.

Keelan refrained from shifting back as she approached the bed again, but good sense suggested he was a fool. She could tear him limb from limb if she so desired.

"What are your intentions?" she asked.

"Me . . ." Merciful Mother. "Intentions?"

"Toward the girl."

He glanced at the door, doubting he could reach it before her, despite her heft. "Listen . . . Cook, I've only just met—"

"She ain't safe here," she hissed, and thrust the milk bottle into his hand.

Keelan glanced nervously toward the door. Lambkin rose to her feet and stretched. "What do you mean, not—"

"Come now, lad." Cook rested her backside on the bed beside him. He tilted precariously in her direction and turned the makeshift nipple toward Lambkin. "Surely you're not as daft as all that."

His skin felt prickly. "I fear ye may be wrong there."

"I know the master is bent on healing you," she said, leaning close, "but things ain't just as they seem."

He tightened his fingers on both bottles. "How do you mean?"

"Roland." Her mouth pursed. "There's evil in him."

His ribs throbbed in unison with his head. "What makes you think so?"

"Just a feeling, an itching on the skin. Don't get me wrong, the master, he loves Cherry like a daughter and will protect her whilst he can, but that Roland . . ." She shook her head. "He's a bad one. Just waiting around till the master can't control him no more."

His stomach crunched dangerously. His mind was buzzing with a hundred scrambling thoughts. "What happened to Mead?"

Her eyes all but disappeared into the folds of her face when she scowled. "How do you know about him?"

"I heard Lord Chetfield tried to save him . . . that night . . . from the bull."

She shook her head. "Mead, he was always getting himself in trouble. Don't get me wrong. He was a good enough fellow, but he had a weakness for the girls. If they had bosoms he'd make a try for them. Thought himself quite handsome. And clever. Had him a plan to get rich."

His scalp tingled. "What plan?"

"He never said. Whatever it was died with him. But he did say he knew something that someone would pay dear to keep quiet."

The image of Mead beneath Chetfield's staff burned in Keelan's mind. "Maybe he told one of the other women."

She shook her head. "Would have maybe, but things had changed in them last years."

"What things?" he asked, but he knew. Suddenly, with awful clarity, he knew.

"Seems he spent time between the wrong legs," she said.

"He had the clap," Keelan rasped.

She watched him, eyes narrowed. "I thought I was the only one who knowed that."

She was. At least Chetfield hadn't known. Not until after Mead's death, after it was too late and he felt his servant's malady sear his own body.

"Ye tried to heal him," Keelan said. His scalp felt prickly, his head hopelessly clear.

"I couldn't do much for him though." She glanced at the bottle he still held in his hand. "Maybe he needed some of that water of yours. You're looking stronger. Got some color in your cheeks."

"What of yer master?" he asked. "Did ye try to heal him? After he was gored."

"He never wanted no help. The master, he's a proud one."

Answers were lining up like goslings in his mind. "Like his sire?" His voice sounded distant to his own ears. Lambkin slurped at the bottle.

"Similar I suspect. Though the old man was harder. And not so dapper. Nevertheless, he liked his jewels."

"Jewels?" Keelan's heart clenched up tight.

"Aye. He was terrible beat when he was found. Face all but gone. Wouldn't have recognized him but for the ring he always wore."

"They left his ring?" His voice was a monotone.

"Constable must have arrived before he could take it, they said."

He nodded, though it was difficult to manage even that. "But the brigand was never caught?"

"No. Never was. Run off, I'm told."

"So you were here at Crevan House even then."

"Been here for near thirty years. No fatter than you when I first come."

"And Mead?"

"He wasn't fat neither."

Keelan forced a smile. "But he was here, when the old master died. He was here?"

"Sure. Weren't but ten years ago. Old Mead, he was full of vinegar back then, before his . . . misfortune."

"And what was Lord Chetfield like when he was young?"

She shook her head. "I never met the young master. He only came some weeks after the old man's death. He grew up elsewhere."

Lambkin abandoned the bottle and poked Keelan's hand.

"Where did he live before Crevan House?" Keelan asked, voice taut.

"Bottle's empty," Cook said.

"Did ye know his mother a'tall?"

"You ask a mighty lot of questions about the master," she said, "when you should be wondering about Roland. You must have seen the way he looks at our Charity."

"She's a bonny lass. Any man would look."

She narrowed her eyes. "I'm thinking you ain't as daft as you seem."

He leaned his head back against the pillows, trying to resist the thoughts that buzzed through his mind. "Ye might well be surprised."

"I seldom am. You've got a good mind. A good mind and a good heart," she said, and hoisted herself laboriously to her feet.

"Ye're wrong," he said, and turned his back to her and the truth.

Chapter 13

Days passed. Nightmares lingered. Dreams of the past, the present, the future, all muddled together. Iona's eyes, scared, pleading. Iona's grave . . . changing into Charity's. Keelan woke with a start, sweating, breathing hard.

"Charity." He said her name aloud, and suddenly he was out of bed, needing to warn her. To tell her the truth, but in that instant she breezed through the door.

"Angel. Angel luv." She hurried toward him, dark gown rustling. "What's amiss?"

"Ye died," he breathed.

"No. No. All is well." Reaching up, she smoothed his hair gently back from his brow. "'Twas naught but a dream. I am fine. Your lamb is fine." She nodded toward the bed. Lambkin gazed at him with adoring eyes. "As are you. Healing amazing well. See." She raised his hand with her own. The abraded skin looked pink and healthy. She kissed his knuckles. "Soon you'll be as right as rain. Strong as ever you were."

He shook his head. "I was never strong."

Her smile was sweetness itself. "What's this nonsense? You saved Lambkin from the beasties what attacked you. Saved her at your own peril."

Her eyes shone like polished amber. Her smile was like the sun, warm and kindly in her bright fairy's face.

"Leave here," Keelan whispered.

Her expression clouded. "What's that?"

He shook his head, a thousand truths rushing in at once. "Things are na what they seem, lass. Ye are na safe. Ye must—"

"Shh," she hissed, and then he heard the footsteps.

His heart faltered and clenched as Chetfield stepped into the room. "Mr. MacLeod," he said. His tone was level, but his eyes were flat. Flat and dead. "Is there some trouble here?" Malevolence was as heavy as sin, saturating the very air they breathed.

Danger. It was all around him, closing off his air, but Charity squeezed his hand. "I think he was dreaming again, Master," she said.

Keelan stared at her sunny face. Didn't she see

the danger? Couldn't she feel it? She loosened her grip on his fingers, but he held tight for an instant, desperately longing to tell her the truth, to save her from them, from himself, from the world.

The old man nodded. "Indeed."

"'Cuz he spoke of danger and the like." She shook her head and tugged her fingers from his grasp. "You can hardly blame him though, I suspect," she added, and shuddered. "After what he's been through with the beasties and all."

Run, Keelan wanted to say. *Run while you can.* But he couldn't take his gaze from the baron.

As for Chetfield, he stood absolutely still, studying Keelan's face.

"His wounds is healing surprising well, though, don't you think, Master?"

The old man's eyes were narrowed in thought.

"But how about you?" she asked, and reaching out, touched the other's arm. "You're looking a mite peaked yourself. Is your hip hurting you again?"

The intensity of the old man's attention dimmed as he turned toward Charity. Keelan felt relief flood through him.

"Poor thing." She tsked. "Taking care of the lot of us when you're hurting yourself."

159

Chetfield stared at her a moment, eyes narrowed, then lifted his lips in the semblance of a smile. "A man cannot worry about something so mundane as pain when you are in the room, sweet Charity. Indeed, I am certain it was the sound of your dulcet voice and nothing else that has brought our young visitor from the brink of death.

"I am right, am I not, Mr. MacLeod? It is her voice and nothing else?" He turned slowly back toward Keelan, but the girl was speaking again.

"Well, actually, there is more," she said, flickering her gaze toward Keelan and blushing.

Chetfield shifted his attention back to her. The room was as silent as death.

Fie me, Keelan thought, remembering the kiss they'd shared, remembering the healing feel of her skin against his, and realizing that healing might well be the death of him.

"Oh?" The old man's face was set in expressionless lines.

Charity laughed. "Me smile might be passing fair, but it can't hold no candle to Cook's verbena tonic. There now, Master Chetfield . . ." She tsked. "You look as tired as me mum's Myrtle. You'd best lie down. I'll have Cook send something up to ease your pain as soon as ever she can."

He was silent a moment as if searching for some evil in her words, but finally he spoke. "You are too kind, my dear," he said, and turned slowly toward Keelan. "But I've heard our young visitor here has some skill in healing."

Her brows shot up. "Angel?"

"Yes. Did you not hear? He healed the lamb with nothing more than the touch of his hands."

"Lambkin?" She scowled, shifting her gaze toward the bed.

"Marvelous, is it not? I thought, perhaps, he might be able to assist me."

So the true game had begun, Keelan thought. But Chetfield was a far more powerful adversary even than imagined. Darker, crueler, with unspeakable atrocities behind him.

"You're a healer?" she asked.

Keelan turned toward her, finding he had no wish to lie. Strange indeed, for lies had been his faithful companions since the day he stepped from darkness. Yet suddenly he had an urgent need to tell her all, to win her heart on the truth alone. "Some think so," he said instead.

"You doubt?" asked the old man, and there was something in his tone, something low and deadly.

Keelan caught himself, hedged carefully. "I've na wish to brag to the lass," he said.

"Odd," countered the old man, and smiled grimly. "Most do."

"You can heal with your touch?" she asked.

No. 'Twas all a lie, he wanted to say. There were those who truly had been blessed with the gift of healing. Those who had the power of wild beasts in their hands. Those who were as indestructible as granite. As for himself, he received scattered pieces of dreams he could no longer separate from reality. He'd rather have a stick in the eye.

"'Tis a magical gift then," Charity said.

Chetfield chuckled. "I fear I do not believe in magic, but when one becomes as ancient as I, one cannot afford to rule out any possibilities."

"Master," Charity chided, and gently took his arm. "You are hardly ancient."

Keelan closed his eyes, wishing with everything in him that he could believe her words.

"I will expect you in my chamber within the hour. If you've magic in your hands, boy, bring it along," said Chetfield, and turned away, taking the girl with him.

She smiled, hand thrust through the crook in his arm. "I'll have Cook brew your favorite tea, and when you wake you can dine . . ." Her words trailed off.

Keelan sat down. On a chair near the door, Mrs. Graves had left a pile of discarded garments for him, brown breeches, a frayed tunic, and a dark coat. 'Twould hurt like the devil to don them, but there was no time to waste now. His herbs had been lost with his sporran. But the fat-bottomed bottle from his dreams remained beneath his bed. In a moment he held it in his hand.

Perhaps it truly was a healing potion. Or perhaps it would get him killed.

Chetfield's chambers were dark and airless and smelled of things long forgotten. He lay so still upon his scarlet-draped bed that for a moment Keelan thought he might well be dead. He hoped such was the case. But finally he noticed the rise of the old man's chest beneath his silver-shot waistcoat and knew the lecherous baron had defied death one more day and merely slept.

Keelan glanced about the room. Was the treasure here? 'Twould make sense, of course. Keep it close. Keep it safe.

An ancient leather chest stood in the corner. Perhaps it was there. Almost within reach. Maybe now was the time to act. To be bold. No more cowardice. No more doubt. Just action. Vengeance.

"'Tis best not to delay."

Keelan's nerves jumped at the sound of the old man's voice. The teacup bobbled in his hand, but he managed, just barely, to keep his head, to turn slowly toward the bed.

"And what is it I should not delay, me lord?"

Chetfield didn't lift his head, but turned it slightly, golden eyes gleaming in the dimness. "You were thinking of robbing me."

Panic flared in Keelan's soul. But he calmed it. Soothed it. "Old habits," he said, and forced himself to step toward the four-poster bed, though it made his throat ache and his body tremble to do so. "They do indeed die hard."

A smile flickered across the baron's mismatched face. "I suggest you kill them soon, boy," he said, "before they kill *you*."

Keelan took another step forward and grinned, playing his act with desperate care. "I be bludgeoning them even now."

"Tell me, Mr. MacLeod ..." Chetfield said, and sat up, but strangely, as if he were pulled by cords, effortlessly, sitting straight on his bed without bending so much as a knee. "What did you hope to gain here at Crevan House?"

"Not broken ribs and a blinded eye," he said, and dropped onto the mattress, though his muscles quivered as he did so.

Chetfield raised his brows at the audacious

move. "Then perhaps you should have stayed clear of my estate."

"The thought has occurred to me," Keelan admitted, and Chetfield chuckled.

"There is nothing like a few broken bones to clear a man's head, aye?"

Reaching out, Keelan handed over the tea.

Chetfield raised a brow. "Are you hoping to poison me, boy?"

"And be left alone with yon beasties?" Keelan asked, tilting his head toward the world at large.

Chetfield stared for a moment, then took a sip. But if he tasted anything amiss, it did not show in his face. "I believe you have Bear and Frankie quite terrified."

"Roland, on the other hand, may yet eat me alive."

"Oh, don't get me wrong. They all hope to see you dead. 'Tis why I hired the lot of them. They have no morals whatsoever. But your trick with the lamb . . ." He nodded, eyes sharp. "It has them all a bit unnerved, I believe."

Keelan said nothing. Chetfield smiled, teacup held just so, pinky finger raised delicately.

"So you will not disavow your wild tale? You still say you are a healer?"

"As your Charity said," Keelan began, and

shrugged. "'Tis the gift of magic. 'Tis na something I can control."

"Even if your life is forfeit?"

"I think you know something of gifts, Chetfield."

"Oh?" The ancient brows lifted.

Keelan's nerves rattled, but he braced his hands against the mattress and held himself steady. "Ye are well past sixty years, I would guess?" he said, tone casual against the thrumming questions in his head. "Surely in that time ye have learned that gifts are freely given and not taken by force."

"On the contrary, I have found that most everything can be taken by force."

"Not this."

Chetfield narrowed his eyes, watching. "Perhaps," he said as he finished his tea and lay back down. "So we will now see whether you tell the truth . . ." He smiled. "Or whether you will die screaming."

Dark images shrieked through Keelan's mind. His father's torment, his mother's gamble. He had not wanted that kind of love. Had not asked. Had not deserved.

"You remind me of someone," Chetfield said. His voice was soft, his head tilted a little. "What is your true name, boy?"

"I have already told ye."

Chetfield smiled, the expression sweet, or mad. "And now you will tell me the truth."

Keelan forced a shrug. "Ye can rip me piece from piece. It would na change who I be."

"And who is that?"

"A fatherless whelp does na oft come with a pedigree."

"Ahh, I remember now. Your mother was a witch."

Keelan's gut twisted, but he kept his expression carefully bland. "So the village lads said."

Chetfield tsked. "Children can be so cruel."

He shrugged. "Mayhap it's for the best."

The old man raised one brow.

"In truth, yer beasties' ministrations were little more than a Sunday stroll by comparison."

"I'll have to make certain the lads apply more zeal next time."

"I plan to make certain there is na next time."

"Really? And how do you hope to accomplish that?"

Keelan shrugged, held his breath. "By curing you of the clap."

The room went silent for a moment, then: "How did you know?"

"Ye dunna believe I am a seer?"

Chetfield stared, lids heavy over eerie eyes. "It is true that I have seen stranger things, but I rather doubt—"

"Tell me of them," Keelan suggested.

For a moment it almost seemed that he would do just that, but then he smiled knowingly. "So you intend to heal me, do you?"

"Or make you believe as much."

The old man stared at him a moment, then laughed out loud. "You amuse me, lad. Indeed you do. I may actually dislike killing you."

Keelan forced a shrug. "We all must die sometime."

Chetfield tilted his head. The motion was almost coquettish. "Must we?"

Keelan's scalp tingled madly, but he kept his tone casual. "Am I wrong yet again?"

"It seems a bit difficult to believe that a thief is also a healer."

"The Christ was a carpenter."

"Comparing yourself to Jesus Christ, Highlander?"

"Mayhap I should say that Lucifer was once a favored angel."

"So we shall see," he said, "whether you are an angel or the devil himself."

"Which would ye prefer?" Keelan asked, and noticed that the old lord's lids had dropped sleepily. Was it Toft's tonic? Or was it a ploy? Either way, Keelan could delay no longer. Though his skin crawled at the thought of touching the uncanny baron, he raised his hands, palms out, fingers spread.

"I've met the devil," said Chetfield. His tone was muzzy. "Indeed, we got on quite well."

Reaching out, Keelan skimmed his hand slowly above the oddly skewed features.

The old man stared at him, eyes dead. "'Tis my rod that needs healing, boy. Not my head."

"Quiet."

Surprisingly, he did as told. Keelan rocked back, rolled up his eyes, and hummed.

For what seemed a lifetime, the old man stared at him, but finally the eerie eyes fell closed, the head tilted toward the wall, the mouth became lax.

Keelan stopped the motion of his hands. Nothing stirred. He cut his eyes toward the leather chest. 'Twas no more than three strides away, waiting, taunting. And time was running short.

Not daring to breathe, Keelan eased to his feet and turned toward the trunk, but in that instant, he felt Chetfield's eyes flicker toward him.

"I was but hoping to let ye rest," Keelan said, but the old man said nothing. Indeed, he hadn't moved. In fact, his eyes were still closed, his muscles flaccid.

Keelan exhaled carefully and continued. The floor creaked beneath his feet. He glanced back, breath frozen in his throat, but the old man remained as he was, face turned away, body limp. Magic would do that. Magic and a heavy dose of poppy.

Still, his hands shook as he reached for the leather-bound chest. One glance behind him assured him he labored in secret. Taking a careful breath, he lifted the hasp. It made barely a whisper of sound, quieter than his heartbeat against his ribs. He raised the cover slowly.

It was dim inside the box, but he could see that a little of everything resided inside. A woman's lace glove, a scrap of fur, a small book of prayers, a red plume, a ring. A noise whispered behind him. He jerked about, but all was still, the old man's body unmoved.

All was well. All was quiet. And maybe this was it. What he had dreamed of. What he had schemed for. Keelan reached inside. The ring was large. A man's. A ruby adorned the gold band. His heart beat faster. He picked it up, but something was stuck inside, a pale withered stick, odd, jointed . . . like a finger.

Keelan jerked to his feet, loosing the cover.

It dropped downward. But he caught it. Just in time. Just before his own life flashed to a finish. He closed his eyes, trembling, trying to breathe.

The muscles across his back spasmed. His lungs burned in his chest, devouring his ribs.

"What shall I take from you?" Chetfield whispered.

Chapter 14

Keelan spun toward the bed, but the old man was still deep in slumber. Yet his mind was wandering, chuckling, fawning over his mementos. For that's what they were, treasured reminders of the people that he had killed, that he had tortured. Keelan knew it suddenly, felt it in his soul.

The bastard deserved to die. Deserved worse. Keelan was across the distance in an instant. The old man's staff rested against the wall beside his bed. It felt right in his hands, solid, just. Revenge screamed for release.

". . . abed I think." Charity's voice cracked the red haze in his mind.

Someone answered.

Sanity washed in on the memory of pain. Merciful God! 'Twas Roland! Close by. In the hallway.

". . . an old man."

The voices were clearer now. Almost upon him. Keelan's hands trembled with the remnants of rage, but he had not lived so long to act the fool now. Taking two steps forward, he dropped to the edge of the bed, facing Chetfield.

The door creaked open.

But the staff! It was still in his hand, curled against his palm. He tilted it toward the wall. It clattered gently against the plaster and rolled to the corner at an angle just as Roland stepped into the room.

There was a brief moment of silence as the bastard took stock, then: "What the hell are you doing?"

Keelan raised his gaze slowly. "Quiet," he said. "Yer master be sleeping."

"Am I?" The old man's voice was low and lucid.

Keelan turned stiffly toward him, guts twisted in kinks. The old murderer's eyes were as bright and steady as stones. His lips lifted into a parody of a smile.

"Me mistake," Keelan said.

"What mistake is that, boy?" Chetfield crooned.

Keelan managed to keep his gaze from the fallen staff, but he could not quite manage to do the same with his thoughts.

The eerie eyes flickered toward the wall and narrowed.

"You look much improved, Master." Charity's soothing voice sounded otherworldly in the screaming silence. Stepping forward, she perched like a songbird on the far side of the bed. "You must have slept good." She reached out, brushing the old man's hair back from his forehead. His brows lowered, but he turned his gaze toward her.

The shift of his attention felt like an anchor had been lifted from Keelan's chest, like a breath of cool air to starving lungs.

"Could be Angel here be a right good healer, eh?"

Near the corner of the bed, Roland shifted irritably. "If he's a healer, I'm a panting wolfhound."

"I thought I smelled dog," Keelan said.

"What's that?" Roland snarled, but Charity spoke first, her tone thoughtful.

"Me uncle had him a wolfhound."

They turned toward her in unison.

"Thought he was a person. Sat at table next to his youngest daughter, Mavis. They had them the same color eyes." She blinked. "Uncle's missus had too soft a heart to shoo him aside." She slipped her fingers through Chetfield's hair. "Just like you, Master."

Seeing her touch him turned Keelan's stomach, but he forced himself to remain where he was, watching, waiting, and for a moment he almost thought he saw the baron's features soften. Then Roland's voice broke the spell.

"What the hell's he doing here?"

"Worried for my well-being, Mr. Roland?" Chetfield asked, "or for my fortune?"

"I don't trust him."

"Trust him?" Chetfield said, and laughed. "I daresay I don't trust anyone." His gaze shifted to the girl, and he smiled. "Except our Charity, of course."

Her expression was solemn. "I'm sorry to bother you, me lord. But Cook says to tell you dinner will be served in half an hour."

"Thank you, my dear," said Chetfield, and turned his gaze on Roland. "And what of you? Do you bear a message from the house servants as well?"

The bastard turned his malevolent gaze on Keelan, then: "It'll keep."

Worry prickled Keelan's scalp, but Chetfield only nodded. "Very well."

"We'll get gone. You stay abed for a spell," Charity said and rose to her feet. Chetfield held her hand, his dapper, lacy sleeve snowy white against her fingers for a moment before he let go.

Keelan steeled himself for the ordeal of rising, but the old man turned toward him. "You will stay, Mr. MacLeod."

With one more withering glance, Roland followed the maid from the room.

Keelan could feel the old man's attention turn back toward him. "So you are indeed a thief *and* a healer," he said.

Thoughts tumbled wildly in Keelan's mind. His hands trembled against the blanket beneath him, but he remained as he was. Indeed, he was frozen by the unearthly thoughts that raced through his mind. Thoughts of trophies stolen from his victims. But had he taken other things as well? Things that could not be kept in a box, safely hidden away. "Some would disagree on the healer part," he said.

Chetfield's expression changed not a whit. His eyes were narrowed and steady. "So you are from the Highlands."

"Finegand," he said. "Near the grand Glen Shee."

A pause again as he considered. "Did your people ever dwell in London?"

"Me mum's uncle bought a bullock there when I was but a wee lad. Said the place smelled of goat piss."

Chetfield's eyes gleamed. "And what of your father?"

"As I've said—"

"You are fatherless, I know, but your dear mother must have given you some idea."

"In fact, she did na."

"No explanation at all?"

He remained silent a moment, then: "On the contrary," he lied, "she said she had conceived while remaining untouched."

The gray brows rose. "A virgin birth."

"I hear it has happened afore."

Chetfield laughed. "That, my dear boy, is called heresy. Indeed, in my day, she would have been burned for less. And you with her."

"Your day?" Keelan asked evenly, though he shivered with rage and premonition.

"Such antiquated ideas there were back then. Still . . ." His eyes gleamed. "Mothers must sometimes be punished."

Keelan's stomach twisted. "Oh?"

Chetfield smiled and tilted his head. "And how are you feeling this afternoon, if I may ask."

"Have ye seen horse dung after a rainstorm?"

"Ahh, no Celtic stoicism for you, I see. I like that. Indeed, I like you." He smiled. "But if you cross me . . ." His expression turned cold and sharp. "The pain you feel now will multiply tenfold and it shall go on forever."

Keelan kept his tone steady. "Forever be a long while."

"You've no idea."

"I shall not forget," Keelan vowed.

Their gazes met and held. "Good," Chetfield said finally, and nodded. "Now do your magic again."

Some minutes later, Keelan rose shakily to his feet. The staff rested against the wall, solid and deadly. But it would do no good to retrieve it. That much he knew, though he dare not consider how.

The house was quiet. Exhaustion felt heavy across his back as he trudged toward his own bed.

". . . but I fear I can't."

Charity's words snagged his attention. They came from behind the closed door to his left, but it was Roland's voice that chilled his blood.

"Perhaps you could for the Highlander though, aye, Cherie?" The bastard's voice was low and gritty. Keelan stepped closer to the door, every fiber trembling with fatigue, every nerve cranked tight.

"What?" asked Charity. "Angel?" she said,

and laughed. "Naw. I mean . . ." He could hear the shrug in her tone. "He's a nice enough bloke, I suspect, but I ain't gonna be wasting no porridge on him."

"What?"

She laughed again, then quickly tapped across the floor. "Once when I was a girl, a dove flew smack into our cottage window. Knocked itself clean senseless. I learned me lesson then, I did."

There was a long pause, then, "'Tis fortunate you've a pretty face, Cherie, for you're dense as a stone."

"That's what me father said when I wouldn't let him give the bird to his hounds. *Charity luv,* he said, *if you didn't cry so pretty, me dogs would be fat as corn-fed hogs.*"

"I'm getting tired of waiting."

"Yeah, I got tired too, feeding it porridge from me own spoon, morning, noon, and night. And keeping the dogs off'n it day after day weren't no chocolate truffle neither."

Outside the door, Keelan fisted his hands against his thighs.

"Then one day I took it out from its little cage and up it flew. Never caught so much as a glimpse of the blessed thing after that."

Footsteps again, heavier this time. "I can make you fly, girl."

179

She laughed, moved away. "Fly! Goodness, Mr. Roland, it sounds terrifying. I never said I wanted to fly. Said the dove flew."

"Can you be so damned daft?" he gritted.

Her gasp tore through Keelan's soul. Without thought, without intention, he stepped through the door. The two stood near the corner. Surrounded by plants, the bastard was holding her arm. She was leaning back, eyes wide, face pale against the greenery.

Rage was like a fire in Keelan's murky soul, but he kept his expression bland. "The master said I'd find ye here."

Roland's face contorted. "What the hell are you about?" he hissed.

"Said I should give you a message."

The bastard stepped forward, fists clenched, teeth bared, waves of hate flowing off him like water. "I'll give you a message you'll not soon—"

"Says ye should na dally where ye are na wanted lest ye find yerself alone in the dark just as Mead did."

Roland stopped dead in his tracks.

"Meself, I dunna ken what he meant," Keelan said, but it was a lie. He knew much more than he had ever wished to know. A hundred haphazard scraps of the past. "Mayhap ye should ask him."

Reaching out, Roland curled his fist into Keelan's shirtfront. "I think you'd be less irritating without a tongue, Highlander."

The waves of hatred were as strong as a wind, beating Keelan down, but there was an image in his mind now, sharp as etched stone. "And that ye can keep the crown."

"What?" The bastard's word was no more than a hiss.

"The coin ye took from his coat. Ye can keep it."

The fist against Keelan's throat shook, then: "Touch her and I'll rip out your balls with my bare hands," he snarled and then he was gone, striding out of sight and slamming the door behind him.

Keelan's head swam. He pressed his back against the wall, feeling the cool plaster through his shirt, searching for his balance amid the confusing tumble of his thoughts.

"Mr. Angel." Charity rushed to his side. Her hand was warm and soft against his arm. "Are you all right?"

No, dammit! He was a fooking witch!

"You poor thing, what be you doing in the conservatory? You must have worn yerself clean out. Come along now." She was tugging at his arm. "We'll get you off to bed." Her arm was steady about his waist, her tone chipper in his ear. "There now, just a bit further."

"He didn't hurt ye?" His own voice sounded distant, foggier than the image of Roland dipping into Chetfield's pocket.

"Mr. Roland?" She turned wide eyes on him. "Naw. Of course not. He wouldn't hurt a flea."

"Lass—"

"Don't talk now. Save your strength. We're almost there. And you been too hard on yerself. Still . . ." Her bonny face was set in a sudden frown. "I'm glad you showed up when you did. 'Cuz nice as Mr. Roland is, I just didn't have no more time to chat. Cook's gonna be needing help getting supper to table."

Chapter 15

The house was as quiet as a grave. The library was dark but for Keelan's single candle. He'd been loath to light it, but the moon was hidden this night, lost beneath a ragged layer of wispy clouds, and he could wait no longer. The fragile flame flickered in an unseen draft. Perhaps there were ghosts in this place. It seemed likely. Nothing else was as it should be.

His mind scrambled over a thousand facts, even as he searched the books. Maybe his father's treasure had not been a priceless jewel or precious metal as Keelan had once assumed. Mayhap it was something less tangible. Knowledge or truth. Sir Stanton would have found his son's sudden obsession with either quite amusing.

Keelan flipped through a small book of poetry, mind racing, trying to make sense of things, to find logic. True, Crevan House was a strange place, but surely his wild thoughts were only that. Nothing but crazy imaginings brought on by pain and terror. Chetfield was cruel, aye, but there was no true reason to believe there was more to it than that.

Skimming the bookshelves, he glanced about the room. Shadows darkened the corners like lingering spirits, bent and hidden. But 'twas naught more than an overactive imagination. Naught but—

"Keelan," a voice murmured.

He swung about. The book flew from his hand. His candle flickered on a shadow and sputtered out. "Who's there?" His whisper sounded raspy in the darkness. Memories quivered in his mind. Memories of his father's laughter. His father's voice, so clear after a hundred wayward years.

"Da?" he said.

"Come hither."

"Who are ye?" He breathed the words and took a faltering step toward the shadows.

"I knew you would come," whispered the voice.

Recognition dawned, sharp with anger. "Chetfield!" Keelan rasped, and lunged forward, ready to kill, to avenge, but his feet struck an obstacle and he fell. His knees hit the floor. He jerked his head up, searching wildly, but the shadow was gone, the room silent.

"I'm going mad." His voice sounded shaky in the stillness, but then he saw the book. A narrow, leather-bound volume, spurring memories from a century past. His fingers quaked as he picked it up. No one stopped him as he turned away. No shadows haunted. No voices spoke. He rose shakily to his feet and left the library.

His bedchamber door was silent as he opened it. Lambkin bleated softly but did not rise. Keelan lay wooden beside the little body, his father's journal clutched in his hand, and dared not close his eyes for an eternity. But the dreams came nevertheless, haunting, ravaging, undenied.

His father's face, alight as he faced the endless sea, awed as he opened an ancient trunk, horrified as he faced his dearest friend . . . Kirksted, enraged, gleeful, standing over him, raising a staff, striking, bludgeoning, until Hallaway's body lay lifeless and broken.

Joy illuminated Kirksted's face, but his features changed, shifting eerily through the decades, turning slowly into a man of business, a landed gentleman, a baron. Until it was Chetfield who smiled down at his gory victim. But 'twas a girl that cowered beneath him now. A girl with blood in her bonny brown curls and terror in her wide amber eyes.

"Nay!" Keelan rasped, and awoke with a start.

Charity gasped and leaned away.

"Lass!" His breath came hard.

She was seated beside him on his bed.

"I was but passing your door and heard you talking to yourself. Are you well?" She gave him a tremulous smile, eyes wide in a face too perfect to be real.

Narrowing his gaze, holding his breath, he reached out and touched her arm. It felt soft but solid beneath his fingertips. "Ye're real," he mumbled, and she smiled.

"Did you think otherwise, luv?"

He strove for lucidness, but it was misty in his mind, shadowed and peopled by a hundred souls long dead. "History would suggest it."

She gave her head an inquisitive tilt, but he was disinclined to tell her of her unknown nocturnal visits. So perhaps he wasn't entirely mad.

"What be ye doing out of bed, lass?" he asked, and strove to push the horrid images from his mind.

Her smile faded into the etchings of a frown. "Something woke me."

He tensed. Had she heard him in the library?

Or had he dreamed that too? "What was it?"

"I'm not certain. When I went to take a look there was no one about." She shuddered a little. "Felt strangish though. As if there was . . ." She paused. "Ghosts or the like."

And then he felt it. His father's journal, lying against his ribs, nestled beneath Lambkin's forelegs. 'Twas unopened, but there was no reason to read the text, for it had come to life in his soul.

"I know it sounds silly. But this spooky old house, it is ever creaking and groaning as if it's got secrets to tell."

He felt tired. Exhausted and beaten and old. "What secrets do ye suppose?" he asked.

She shrugged, gave him a tender smile. "If'n I knew, they wouldn't be secrets, I suspect."

He drew a long breath, watching her face, unscathed, so beautiful it made his soul ache. No fear shone in her eyes. Only kindness. But the dreams . . . He shut them away, not knowing. "Speak to me, lass," he pleaded.

"What do you wish to hear?"

He watched her, the light in her merry eyes, the quirk of her lively mouth. "I but long to hear yer voice."

"Sure." She laughed. "Me and me lovely cockney tones."

"They be bonny to me own ears. Did yer mum have the same accent?"

A shadow flickered across her face and was gone. "Naw. She spoke proper. But me father and me Grimmy, they spoke as bad as me."

"Grimmy?"

"Me father's father. He used to feed me cherry tarts till I was stuffed to me ears."

"How old was he?"

"I don't rightly know. But he helped the Lord God name the beasts of the field." She smiled. "Or so he said. I used to believe it too. Me cousin Lily had her a good laugh about that."

"Ye've a host of family memories." His own burned inside his mind.

"And what of you, Angel? What memories have kept you dreaming this night?"

Dark images nagged him, trying to snag his attention, to reel him in, pull him into their dark depths, but he fought the undertow. For a short time he would live in the present. "Nothing pleasant enough to recall."

She gave him a teasing smile. "Not about me then."

Her gown was powder blue accented with narrow black stripes and a dark ribbon tied beneath her bonny breasts. It was a simple garment, but its humble state did nothing to detract from her feminine beauty, her earthy charm.

"Ye should na be here, lass."

"I thought mayhap you were in need of a friend," she said and touched his hand tentatively.

Well, he was that, he thought, and felt the skin beneath her fingertips come alive with pleasure. He cleared his throat, tried to do the same with his racing imagination. But life was so short. Short and uncertain. "I'm quite certain the bast—Roland," he corrected, "would be unhappy if he knew of your whereabouts."

"You're most probably right," she said, and lightly brushed the hair from his brow. "But Roland doesn't please me, now do he?"

Mayhap it was the sheer shock of her words that galvanized his body. But perhaps not, for there was something about her shy advances, her feather-soft voice that called to every part of him. She was comely and funny. Graceful and kind. Goodness itself wrapped in a tender package that made him long to be that which he was not, which he never would be.

"Lass . . ." He lowered his gaze lest he become lost in her eyes. "I verra much appreciate yer—"

"Truth to tell I was happy you happened along when you did today. Mr. Roland . . ." She traced his vein with one slim finger. "He was acting strangish. Angry almost," she added.

Keelan forced himself to remain silent, to refrain from commenting on the rage he'd felt roiling off the bastard.

She eased her finger on a meandering course up his wrist. "But I didn't do nothing to make him mad. Course . . ." She shrugged, causing her bosom to swell slightly over the crest of her simple gown. "I think . . ." She caught her lip between square little teeth and glanced down at their hands. "Perhaps he knows how I feel. Perhaps he knows that I . . ." Her eyes struck him suddenly, like the kiss of a warm spring breeze. "That I'm sweet on you," she said, and catching her breath, she kissed him abruptly.

Her lips were a balm against his, a sweet infusion of stark feelings.

"Lass—"

"I know," she whispered. Her lips were trembling. The feel of her breath against his cheek was nearly his undoing. "I know I shouldn't be here." She searched his eyes, waiting for him to argue or agree.

He managed to do neither, for he was immobilized, stuck in place lest he move and find himself unable to stop, to draw back, to save himself or her.

"I know nothing about you." She touched the

backs of her nails to his cheek and skimmed them gently toward his ear. Her fingers felt like warm sparks of magic against his scalp, scraping back his hair, waking every slumbering sense. "You could be wed to another for all I know."

Her lips were moving. And though he knew it was suicidal, he could seem to think of nothing but how right they had felt against his.

"Mr. Angel?"

He tightened his fists against the rumpled bedsheets and raised his gaze to hers. "What's that?"

Her eyes were as big as oceans. "Are you married?" she whispered.

And here it was, a means of escape. But God help him, he had no desire to flee. No strength even to try.

"Nay," he rasped.

Her lips quivered. He felt his soul quake in unison.

"Promised?" she asked.

He managed to shake his head.

She caught her lip between her teeth, sky-wide eyes troubled, voice soft. "Is it that you don't find me attractive then?"

Were there tears in her eyes? Was she about to cry? He scrunched the bedsheet into his palms.

"Mr. Angel . . ."

"Nay, lass, nay. Any man would find ye bonny beyond words."

"Any man but yourself?"

"I assure ye, 'tis na the case."

She frowned. "Life's a whistle," she said, and traced an invisible pattern on his naked chest. He shivered like a wet cur. "There have been gents." She paused, cheeks flushing prettily. "More than a few gents . . ." She could no longer hold his gaze. "What have thought me comely. Monied, some of them was. And landed." She smoothed her palm over his nipple and watched it pop back on alert. He gritted his teeth and stayed very still. "But I never . . ." She flickered her gaze to his and away. "I was never . . . tempted, if you take me meaning."

Her hand was skimming lower. His muscles cranked tight beneath her innocent fingers. He steeled himself against her silken effects, but holy heaven, he was not equipped to withstand temptation. Nay, he was ever one to fall right in.

"But with you . . ." She slipped her finger over his navel. "I find meself imagining all manner of things I should not."

"What things?" His voice sounded hoarse.

"Yourself," she breathed, leaning closer. "In the altogether."

His breath caught in his throat. Her cheeks

were bright as a berry beneath her down-swept lashes.

"Do you think me terrible?" she whispered, and skittered her fingers along the edge of the blanket.

He sucked air between his teeth. "Terrible alluring," he hissed, and grabbed her hand.

"What's that?" She rushed her gaze to his.

"Ye are beauty itself, lass," he said, holding her fingers tight in his own. "Beauty and goodness. Any man would be twice blessed to hold ye in his arms."

For a moment she remained perfectly still, then joy shone in her eyes. She rose slowly to her feet and put her hands to the ribbon beneath her bosom. It fell away.

"Listen, lass . . ." He tried to look aside . . . to think. "I would dearly love to . . ."

But in that moment the garment slipped from her shoulders, revealing the high swell of her breasts. Mary and Joseph!

"To take what ye so kindly offer," he rasped painfully, "but I fear—"

"Then do so," she whispered, and let the gown slip away. It cascaded downward, skimming her luscious breasts, breathing past the scalloped beauty of her hips.

She stood before him then, gloriously naked,

and he could do nothing but draw in the beauty of her. She was perfect, from the tiny mole on her left breast to the crescent scar on her opposite thigh.

"Holy Father," he breathed, and reached for her.

"Am I disturbing your prayers, Mr. MacLeod?" Chetfield asked.

Keelan opened his eyes with a snap. The sun was shining through the east window. The room was empty but for himself and the hideous baron. His mind tumbled in his head, freefalling like loosed goose down as he grappled for reality. He'd been dreaming again. And yet they were unlike any imaginings he'd ever encountered. More real than reality itself.

Chetfield remained as he was, staring, one brow raised.

"Nay, I . . ." Keelan began, but suddenly his mind stumbled to his father's journal. Was it yet hidden beneath the lambkin, or was his life about to end? "'Tis naught but dreams."

"Truly?" The old man settled onto the edge of the mattress. Keelan's breath tangled in his throat. Reality mixed with fantasy, leaving him shaken, uncertain. "Tell me of them."

"I would dearly love to," Keelan lied, "but I fear I can na remember them upon waking."

"They are not about my Cherry then."

"Cherry? Nay. Nay indeed. Never that."

"Good," said Chetfield, and smiled, "for I've no wish to kill you. Not until I have benefited from more of your magical ministrations, leastways."

Chapter 16

"**Y**ou jest," said Charity. Her voice echoed from the vast interior of Crevan's dining chamber.

Keelan stood in the hall, out of sight, silent, listening. Naught but a few days had passed since he had first touched his father's journal. He had read the entries, had turned the pages with hands that shook as he pored over the scratchy words, words that spoke of tides and bearings, of plans and dreams. Words that said naught of betrayal or pain or death at the hands of a cherished friend. 'Twas only the mind-bending dreams that spoke of those things.

"I do not," said Chetfield. "Mr. Cornwell had tied himself to the mast, wearing nothing but a turban and a drunken leer."

Her laughter was magical. "It must have been

ever so exciting sailing in His Majesty's royal fleet," she said.

"Can you keep a secret, sweet Charity?" The old man's tone was conspiratorial.

"A secret?" She whispered the words like an enchanting child.

"I was, in actuality, what one might call a privateer."

Keelan closed his eyes.

"Naw you wasn't," Charity denied. "A privateer, what brought back what was unrightfully took."

He paused a moment. "Just so," Chetfield said, and laughed.

"Coo. Did you ever come across treasure? Rubies and the like? Or was it all stodgy cargo?"

"Have you not heard, Charity, my dear? All that is gold does not glitter."

"Perhaps not," she said. "But the glitter sure makes it more interesting, don't it now? What was the best booty you ever come across?"

"Booty?" He chuckled. "How long have you dreamed of becoming a pirate?"

"Pish. I get seasick in the dogcart on the way to market." She sighed. "But I do think it would be exciting . . . living on the high seas."

"Exciting? Oh indeed it was. Starvation.

Swells so large they block out the sun. Mutiny. Nothing like it."

Charity laughed.

The old man remained silent for a moment. "But nothing is so exhilarating as your smile, my dear."

"Well, it's happy I am to see you feeling yerself, Master."

"At my age, I am lucky indeed to be feeling anything at all. I credit you with that accomplishment."

"Me?"

"You have taken such excellent care of me these past months."

"Go on. 'Twas nothing anyone wouldn't have done in my place."

"I can assure you that is not true."

"Well, I'm happy to do it. But I suspect I'd best be getting back to work now." A chair scraped against the floor. "Or Mrs. Graves will be thinking I fell in a hole or something."

"Tell me, my dear, don't you tire of menial labor?"

"Me?" She laughed. Crockery clattered as she stacked it together. "Sure, sometimes, same as most I suspect, but me mum always said no one was so big nor so small she couldn't carry her own weight."

"A wise woman, your mother, as well as beautiful, I would guess."

"Oh, she was that. Me father always said she—"

"I thought she yet lived."

"Mum?" she said, and laughed. "Indeed she does, but she's the one what always says, enjoy yer pretty whilst you got it, missy. 'Cuz youth don't last more than a wink."

Chetfield was silent a moment, then: "I have been thinking," he said. "As your wise mother implied, youth is indeed fleeting. So perhaps your fair frame could be used for more . . . pleasing endeavors."

Keelan could hear the girl's footfalls clatter merrily around the table. Chetfield's followed.

"Life ain't always 'bout pleasure." Silverware clattered on dishes. "That's what Grimmy used to say. Sometimes—"

"But pleasure can be very pleasant."

The old man's voice had changed. It was deep and slow with suggestion. Keelan raised his fists, then unfurled them slowly and closed his eyes against such foolishness. He was a survivor. Not an idealist. Not his father. Indeed, 'twas far too late for that.

Still, despite the battle that waged in his soul, he could not help but slip from his place against the wall. Soft-stepping farther down the hall, he turned, picked up a louder gait, and shambled through the doorway to the dining room.

"Oh." He halted abruptly, just as intended, but truth to tell, seeing the girl so close to evil all but stopped his heart. "Master Chetfield." He snapped his gaze from the old man's to the girl's. "They said I might find ye here."

Chetfield gave him a predatory smile. "Mr. MacLeod, what a pleasant surprise."

"I like to think I be pleasant," he said, and forced a grin.

"And why is it that you care where I am this evening?"

"Truth to tell, I was worried about ye."

"Worried. Truly?"

"Aye," Keelan said, and laughed. "I've put so much effort into ye, I hate to see ye pass on now. Couple more days under me hands and ye'll be leaping aboot like a schoolboy."

The old man watched him in silence.

Keelan shifted his gaze to the girl's, refusing to fidget. "Sure ye see a difference in him, don't ye, lass?"

Her pretty face was solemn. "I can tell he's feeling spry as a spring gosling." Her eyes were wide and adoring. "You've been grand to us here at Crevan House, Mr. Angel, and for that I'll be forever in your debt."

"Debt! Nay," he said, and took a step back. She might be as sweet as clover honey, but statements like that were likely to get him killed. "Nay. Na a'tall. I'm just using the gifts what God gave me."

She blinked up at him, then blushed and snatched her gaze away, flustered, as if they'd been lovers, as if she too had felt the breathtaking wonders of his skin against hers. "Well . . ." She stepped back. Chetfield dropped his hand from her arm. "I'd best be about helping with that wash."

And then she scurried from the room. The world fell into a grim silence.

"It looks as if you have made a conquest, Mr. MacLeod." Chetfield's tone was low and grim. "I think our Cherry has become quite enamored of you."

Keelan forced a laugh. "'Twould be flattering to think it, sure. But I fear she's na the type to spark me dreams."

A weathered brow rose the slightest degree. "I believe I saw evidence to the contrary some days past."

God save him. "She's a bonny lass, and no mistake, but, well . . . truth to tell . . ." He laughed again. "I'm na so foolish as to go fishing in another man's pond."

Both brows were raised now. "In fact, Mr. Mac-Leod, I think you are just that type of man."

"Well . . ." He nodded amicably. "Mayhap 'tis true, but na when the pond be stocked with sharks and all manner of beasties that are wont to chew the flesh from me living bones."

"Tell me, Mr. MacLeod, might you be referring to me as a shark?"

"Nay. Nay, indeed, I would na—"

"If I did not know better I would almost believe you do not think me good enough for the girl."

"Not good enough?" He shook his head, shutting out the shattering images of his father's battered face, the dimming light in his sky-blue eyes. "Ye're a wealthy man. And a peer of the realm. What lass would na be lucky to spend her days in yer company?"

"Her days?" Chetfield chuckled, his eyes predatory. "Indeed yes, but her nights even more so."

Keelan's stomach pitched.

"Does the idea of our wee Charity in my bed bother you, Mr. MacLeod?"

"Nay. Nay indeed. Whyever would it?"

The old man was watching so closely, Keelan was certain he could feel the thoughts inside his very head. He kept his hands steady, his emotions carefully packed away.

"No reason if you have no designs on her yourself."

"And of course I dunna."

"That is good. Good indeed," Chetfield said, and turning toward the wall where his staff rested, took the misshapen thing in his fist. His hand looked stronger now, steadier. "Because tonight I shall introduce her to wonders she's never seen."

The world turned cold. Keelan searched for some blithe rejoinder, but there was nothing. Only rage and misery and loneliness.

"Nothing to say, Mr. MacLeod?"

"I hear there are many foine sights in Paris."

Chetfield grinned. "I fear I had forgotten how amusing you are. But no, I speak of initiating her into the world of sexual pleasures, Mr. Mac-Leod."

If he rushed the fooker, Keelan thought, he could take him, could beat the life out of him before his beasties arrived.

A glimmer of a smile shone in the old man's eyes. "Have you objections, boy?"

It took all Keelan's strength to pat down the rage, to calm the beast. "Nay, of course not. 'Tis the lassie's choice."

Chetfield laughed, evil personified. "Is it? Since when, I wonder."

Keelan felt nausea curdle his gut, but Chetfield was watching, both hands steady on the head of his staff, eyes narrowed.

"Am I sensing protectiveness, Highlander?" The baron's tone was low, introspective, amused. "From you—a coward and a thief?"

"Damn—" Keelan rasped, but the old man's face was aglow with anticipatory pleasure, and somehow that expression calmed the storm in his raging soul. He forced a laugh. "Damned if you're not right. 'Tis foolishness, of course. Best of luck to ye, Master Chetfield," he said, and sketched a bow.

But in that instant the baron shoved the end of his staff into Keelan's open wound. "After all these years I don't need luck, boy," he snarled. "I need a bloody good fuck."

For a moment Keelan was tempted almost beyond control to take him by the throat, but 'twould do no good. Despite his father's innocuous writings, he knew the truth. Sensed it through the ancient leather, felt it in his quaking soul if not in his stumbling mind. He drew himself up, caught the old man's gaze.

Chetfield scowled, then widened his eyes. "Who are you?" he rasped, but Keelan only pushed the staff aside.

"Naught but a coward," he said, and turned away.

Chapter 17

Was the old man with her now? Would he take her by force? Could any man look into her soul-soft eyes and do her harm?

Lightning speared the sky outside Keelan's window. He lay in the ensuing darkness, sweating, hurting. Memories washed through him like an untamed tide. Memories and passages and voices, warning him to tread softly, to bide his time, to think.

But her innocent amber eyes filled his mind. He sat up suddenly. Beside him, Lambkin raised her head. Lifting the little creature in his arms, he cuddled her absently against his chest.

Charity was not his responsibility. She was a woman grown, here of her own accord. 'Twas not his fault she had come at the outset. Not his fault she would be used and discarded. He would not concern himself with her. God knew he had problems of his own.

Memories came again, sharp as spears in his mind. He pushed them back, knowing better than to dwell on them. Knowing the consequences. Pain. Endless pain. He lay back down, muscles burning, mind on fire. The lamb crowded close, curly coat rough against his arm.

Truth be told, he had no reason to believe Charity would reject the old man's advances. What Keelan had said was true. There were a host of maids who would gladly welcome the old man to their beds. Surely Keelan was not the sort to blame them, for Chetfield was both rich and powerful. And if that was not enough, the lass seemed fond of the old bastard. Perhaps fond enough to long for his touch.

Keelan found himself pacing again, though he couldn't remember rising. Thunder rumbled in the distance, echoing his tortured thoughts.

"It could na be true," he hissed.

Lambkin watched him, ears droopy beside her soulful face.

"Surely na. He is naught but evil. The devil." He halted, whispering to the lamb. "I think he may actually be Satan himself."

Lambkin blinked.

"But she doesn't believe that, does she now?"

He was pacing rapidly, barely noticing the pain in his ribs. "Most probably because it's insane. Mad as a June hare, I be. Dreams and voices and—" He stopped abruptly, turning toward the lamb. "She thinks him naught but a sweet old man what can do no wrong. Who am I to save her? No great warrior. No hero of yore. No—"

But in that moment Lambkin raised her head and bleated softly, black eyes adoring.

The room fell silent, then: "Verra well then," Keelan said, and suddenly he was in the hall, striding toward her chamber.

She was sweet innocence in a world of harsh evil. A gentle, lovely soul who did not deserve to be hurt.

The stairs groaned beneath his feet. Her door was closed. He could hear nothing. Did that mean she was yet safe? He moved closer, pressed his ear to the portal. No sound disturbed the night. He wiped his palms on his breeches.

Lambkin was wrong; he was no hero. But he would warn the maid. That much he could do.

The door latch turned softly beneath his fingers, not so much as a sigh of protest. He stepped inside. Lightning flashed, illuminating fragments of the room, a bedpost, the hearth, a scrap of russet carpet, then pitched the chamber back into blackness. Thunder rumbled, muffling the soft fall of his footsteps. His breath came hard in his overtaxed lungs, but he pushed himself forward until he could see a bump beneath the blankets, could distinguish an uncertain shape against the pillow.

Terror struck him like a rusty blade. Terror and pain. Too horrible to speak through. Too terrible to escape, but in that instant a fork of lightning lanced the night. The shadows skittered away, showing the truth. The bed was empty but for the rumpled bedclothes.

"Merciful Father," he whispered. He was shaky with relief, but suddenly a new question haunted him. If she wasn't there, where was she? In the old man's lair?

". . . must be careful," said the baron from the hall.

Keelan froze at the sound. Terror washed him anew.

"You are sweet to worry." Charity's voice was soft but clear in the throbbing quiet of the night. "But you needn't. I feel safe as a cuddled chick here at Crevan House."

"It warms my old heart to hear you say so, my dear." Their footsteps treaded closer. "But who knows what evils lie outside our doors? You must remember that we have not yet determined what injured poor Mr. MacLeod."

They were close now, almost upon him. Keelan glanced wildly about, searching for a place to hide. But there was nothing.

The footsteps drew nearer.

Breathless, Keelan dived behind the filmy grate of the fireplace screen.

"'Tis a dreadful thing," she said. There was a shudder in her voice. Candlelight flickered past the doorframe, bathed the whitewashed walls. Keelan huddled behind his weakling shield. "Have you no idea what might have wounded him so grievous?"

They entered the room. Chetfield shut the door behind him. Candlelight flickered in his eyes as he swept his gaze past the fireplace.

Keelan's breath knotted in his throat, choking him, but Chetfield only stepped away, out of sight.

"Tell me, Cherry, what possessed you to go wandering alone in the dark this night?"

There was a strange tone in the baron's voice. What was it? Suspicion? But nay. Keelan's stomach twisted at the thought. Surely not. Evil itself could not think Charity guilty of anything more heinous than innocence.

"The thunder woke me," she said, "and I could not for the life of me find sleep again." Her voice trailed off, and when she next spoke, she had turned away. "Me father used to say the thunder growls at the rain but that there be no bite to it. Yet I've never liked the sound of it."

"It must get lonely for you . . . so far from home." His footfalls paced across the oaken floorboards and onto the carpet. His walking stick went with him, clicking in unison.

"Lonely?" Her footsteps moved closer. Keelan caught his breath just as she appeared in his narrow line of vision.

"A beautiful girl like you must be accustomed to being surrounded by admirers."

"Me lord," she said, and laughed. "'Tis not nice to go teasing girls like me."

Chetfield stepped into view, catching her with his strange, canine gaze. "Surely you know how lovely you are," he crooned.

"I'm a simple girl," she said, shaking her head. "Nothing special."

"You're wrong there, my dear." His eyes lowered, skimming her rain-soaked form. Her creamy bodice was all but diaphanous now, clinging like lace to her lovely bosom, her narrow waist. "You do special things to me." His dry lips curled up. "Spectacular things. Would you like to see?"

Lightning crackled in the black square of the window. Keelan's heart jumped in his chest.

"Oh!" she gasped, and when Keelan looked

again, she was gone from view. Only Chetfield remained, brows lowering. "Gracious. That was a close one, it was. Frightened me something awful. But like me dear old mum always said, sometimes it takes a good fright to make ye know you're alive."

"I am very much alive." Chetfield was closing in on her again. Keelan could tell by the hushed tone of his voice.

"Of course you are, Master. You're going to live for a good long time yet."

He chuckled. "Yes, I am. But there is living and then there is living. Don't you agree?"

"Well, me father used to say—"

"I can offer you much."

"You've already given me more than I could ask for. I don't need much by way of—"

"More than you can guess with your simple mind."

"What's that?"

He was crowding her now. Keelan could hear it in the tension of her voice, could feel it, though he couldn't see them.

"I am a very wealthy man, little Charity."

"Master Chetfield, I don't mean to seem ungrateful, but I don't know if me mum would approve of me being in me bedchamber alone with you."

"And powerful. If I wished . . ." He paused. "I could make your life quite miserable. Or . . . I could make it extremely pleasant."

Keelan could hear her soft breathing now and tightened his hands to fists.

"Which would you prefer, sweet Charity?" he crooned.

"I like pleasant," she murmured.

"Good. That is good. For what I have planned will feel pleasant indeed."

"Master Chetfield . . ." she began, but the old man hushed her.

Keelan squeezed his eyes closed.

"Master Chetfield, I don't think—"

"Good." His voice was melodious. "Do not think. Just act."

"Please, Master—"

But suddenly she moaned. From pleasure or fear, Keelan would never know, for he could bear it no longer. Driven from his hiding place, he leapt to his feet . . . and stopped.

Lightning crackled. White light sprang across the room, illuminating Chetfield, unconscious on the floor.

Chapter 18

The girl was gone.

Keelan stared, mind stumbling blindly. Chetfield was down. Why? But suddenly he felt a fist in his hair, sharp-edged steel against his throat.

"What the devil are you doing here?" hissed a voice.

"I—"

"Answer me." The grip tightened painfully against his scalp.

"I . . . Charity?" he guessed. Her voice seemed strange. Not to mention the knife she held at his throat. "Is that ye, lass?"

"What do you know?"

Not much apparently. "What happened to Chetfield?"

She nicked his throat, drawing blood. "I asked why you are here."

"I was—"

"And who the hell are you?"

He shook his head, trying to clear it. "Tell me the truth," he said, words slow as he tried to wrestle through the fog in his mind. "Be I sleeping again?"

She stabbed the tip of the knife a little deeper. A droplet of blood flowed down his chest, warm and sticky.

"Does that feel like a dream?" she asked.

He shifted backward the slightest degree. Her breasts felt soft and warm against his back. "A wee bit."

Pain pricked his neck. Another droplet followed its mates. "How about that?"

He tilted his chin up, mind scrambled. "Not so pleasant as some."

"Tell me who you are."

He opened his mouth.

She gave the knife a nudge. "And no lies."

"Me mum called me Angel, but—"

Chetfield moaned. Fear tightened Keelan's gut, but he kept his tone bland.

"Might I inquire what be happening here?"

She tightened her fist in his hair. "I don't want to have to kill you."

"Good. Excellent. Neither—"

"But I will. Swear to God I will if you cause

me trouble," she whispered, and glanced toward the door. "Follow me, and you'll wish you were dead," she warned, but he laughed.

The sound echoed with madness. "I already am, lass."

"What?" Her attention snapped back to him.

Chetfield moaned.

"He's waking up."

"Dammit!" she swore, and suddenly pain exploded in his skull.

Keelan felt himself falling. Felt his knees strike the carpet. His hands grazed Chetfield's downed form. He rolled to the side. The girl moved away from him, slanted and distorted as she grabbed something from the floor. The door opened, and then she was gone.

The ceiling wavered. Time trembled. Chetfield groaned, drawing Keelan's attention. He was lying face down, but his arm was moving, sweeping slowly across the floor. Lightning flashed, illuminating the crawling blue veins in the baron's outstretched hand. The skin looked parchment-thin, the fingers bent and gnarled.

"Where is it?" The words were a deep hiss of evil.

Terror brought Keelan to his senses with a jolt.

Chetfield's eyes blazed as he raised himself

to hands and knees. He turned back, searching, then shifted his attention to Keelan. Lightning crackled across the sky, setting the golden eyes aglow. "You bloody, thieving Scot, what have you done?" he shrieked and lunged.

Keelan jerked, skittered backward on hands and feet, but Chetfield was already racing toward him, poker in hand. It rushed past Keelan's head. He rolled sideways, staggered to his feet, weaving drunkenly and spinning away.

Pain sliced across his back, but the door was in sight. He staggered toward it. It opened beneath his hand. He stumbled out, Chetfield behind him. The hallway stretched out forever. Then, Frankie! Only a few yards away.

"Kill him!" Chetfield growled.

Keelan turned to sprint toward safety, but in that moment he heard a plaintive mew of sound. The world seemed to shift into strange, slow motion. He turned back in a gray haze. Lambkin was trotting toward him, little ears bobbing. Frank turned his massive head, glanced down, and suddenly the universe shifted back into gear.

"Holy fook!" Keelan swore, and lunging forward, snatched up the lamb. Frankie's grasping hand closed over his shirt. Buttons popped, but Keelan was still moving, scrambling forward on knees and one hand. The stairs appeared out of nowhere. He tried to run down them, but his legs tangled with his chest, and suddenly he was tumbling head over heels with Lambkin hugged tight to his body.

He hit the bottom with a jolt. The world spun away into oblivion, leaving him in its rocking wake.

But footsteps were thundering down upon him. He found his feet. The world tilted, throwing him off course, but he bore down on the front door. It was there. Just to the left. It opened with a snap. A giant loomed in the center.

Keelan jolted right, rolling on a wave of pain and terror.

"Catch him!" Chetfield screamed.

But Keelan was running, stumbling toward his room, slamming the door behind him, propping a chair beneath the latch.

"Bring him to me!" The world shuddered with the command. Something heavy struck the far side of the door. The house threatened to collapse. But Keelan was already moving, racing dizzily across the floor, ripping up the window, falling outside.

For a moment the world went black, but Lambkin's nose on his face brought him to. Something crashed inside the room. Snatching up the lamb, he stumbled into the darkness, leg throbbing, lungs screaming as he glanced behind. Chetfield was framed in the window.

"Come back here, boy."

Keelan jerked toward the woods.

Chetfield hissed. Someone shrieked in pain. But it wasn't Keelan. And that was enough. The stable loomed before him. He rushed inside. Death leapt from the shadows. He jumped back. The hounds lunged again, but their tethers held. A horse nickered from a nearby box. Keelan fumbled against the wall, feeling for a bridle, but a noise from outside distracted him. They were coming, expecting him to take a steed.

Leaving the door open behind him, he searched frantically for another escape. Lightning split the sky, spilling through a high, open window. Hugging Lambkin to his chest, Keelan scrambled up a ladder, across ragged floorboards, and through the shuttered opening. The night beyond the barn was only marginally lighter than the interior of his skull. He crept carefully through it. Behind him, voices shouted. A door slammed against the barn. He steadied his heart. They were there, inside the stable. He was safe for the moment, for the giants were behind him, vainly searching—

A noise rustled to his right. He jerked in that

direction. A pale image flashed through the night and was gone. Another followed, indistinguishable, and yet Keelan knew. Roland! And suddenly like a beacon in his mind, he saw Charity's face, smile broken, eyes raw with pain.

Rage roared like a blaze inside him.

He raced forward, stumbling on a root, falling, mind spinning with uncertainty. What the hell was he doing? She had struck him. Why? It made no sense. Unless she was not what she seemed. Unless she had come for the same reason as he. Had gotten what she'd wanted, snatched it from under his very nose.

Unless she'd been fooling him from the start. Fooling them all.

Arm curled about Lambkin, Keelan slipped into the woods after Roland. The pace was fast, but the bastard wore white. It was not difficult to follow, only to keep up. Keelan's ribs throbbed with the effort, but he dare not slow his pace. The terrain slanted downward. Branches slapped his face. Lightning cracked the sky. Air rasped in his lungs. And suddenly his cover was gone. The land was open, shorn short. Sheep were scattering in every direction. Up ahead, Roland was half crouched beside a tumble-down shelter.

Painful memories stabbed through Keelan.

He stumbled back into the cover of the trees, but the bastard's voice was clear.

"Come on out, girl. I won't hurt you."

The tone was wheedling, twisting Keelan's stomach. His legs were shaking, his strength draining away. Shushing the lamb, he set her carefully on her feet and crept to the edge of the woods.

"I've got no quarrel with you," Roland continued. He was inching around the building, then crept from sight. Finally, able to wait no longer, Keelan rushed through the darkness past the opposite side of the building. From that vantage point, he watched the bastard emerge from the other side and glance about.

"So there you are," said Roland, and straightened.

Chapter 19

Charity remained where she was. Thunder rumbled in the distance. The rain had stopped—rain that blurred vision and erased tracks. Dammit!

"What are you doing, Cherie girl?" Roland asked, tone wheedling.

She set her attitude carefully to match. "I didn't do nothing wrong." Her own voice sounded as if she might cry, making her wonder if she could manage tears.

"Then why are you hiding?" he asked.

"Master Chetfield ..." She was crouched against a tree. A branch was jabbing her in the back, but she remained exactly as she was, her hands curled tight around the bottom of Chetfield's staff. "I never seen him like that before. He was out of his mind with rage."

"Was he now?" Roland took a few steps

forward. She tightened her grip and waited.

"Aye." She sniffled. But tears wouldn't come. Damn the luck! Months of pretending, years of scheming, shot to hell. "I don't know what set him off. I was just . . . I couldn't sleep is all. So I took me a bit of a stroll outside. 'Twas there that he found me. I didn't think nothing of it. Thought perhaps he couldn't sleep neither what with the pain in his hip and all, but then he . . ." She let her words tremble to a halt.

"What did he do?"

"He touched me," she whispered.

She could hear the chuckle in Roland's voice though he tried to hide it. "Did he now?"

"I didn't mean to 'it him but I was—"

"You hit him?" He did laugh now.

"It ain't proper. I know I don't speak real pretty nor nothing but that don't mean I don't have no principles. Me mum raised me right, she did."

"Of course she did." He laughed again, quietly. Evil personified. Crouched in the underbrush, Charity stifled a shiver. "It's shameful what he did. But he's an old man. Sometimes he forgets himself."

"Does he?" She tried to remember the path south of the shanty, but it was dark, and she'd been running. Running until her legs gave out. But they damned well better gain their strength back soon. "I've not thought so in the past." She wiped her nose with the back of her left hand and kept her right where it was, hidden in her skirt and bracken. "He's always been so kind to me."

"Well, you're a pretty girl, Cherie. And the man's not dead . . ." He chuckled. "Not yet anyhow."

What the hell did that mean? Did Roland have plans of his own? Probably. Who didn't? And what of Angel? What the devil had he been doing in her room? "Maybe I been taking me place at Crevan 'Ouse for granted. Maybe I ain't been working 'ard enough."

"Well, we don't want you working too hard. It might wear you out for more important things."

She glanced to her right. Where was that damned path?

"Come on out of there now. We'll go back. Explain everything to Chetfield. I'm sure once he realizes he frightened you, he'll make amends."

"I don't want to go back." She made her tone petulant and allowed herself one quick glance to the left. The terrain was fairly steep there, but maybe she could use that to her advantage.

"No?" He was close now. Within five paces. It was almost time. "Then I'll take you somewhere else. Somewhere safe."

"You'd do that for me?"

"Of course I would. I'm not a barbarian."

"But won't Master Chetfield be angry when I ain't in the kitchen in the morning?"

"Not so angry as he'll be when you're not in his bed."

"What's that?"

He chuckled. "Nothing, Cherie luv. I know a place where you can stay while Chetfield calms himself. You can rest for a while. Decide what you want to do." He closed the gap.

She remained where she was, drawing back just a little, like a frightened child or an animal that's been cornered. In a way she was both, had been for many years. "Where's that?"

"Don't you trust me?"

She paused for a second. "You always been good to me."

"Then come on out of there."

Her heart was pounding against her ribs. Her hand ached against the wooden staff. "You ain't gonna hurt me?"

"Hurt you?" He was grinning. "No. Of course not."

"All right then," she said, and rising to her feet, swung the staff with all her might.

But Roland's instincts were strong. He lunged sideways. The metal knob grazed his shoulder.

He fell back with a curse, but she was already running, scrambling up the slope, staff in hand.

"Damn you," he snarled.

Close. So close, but she didn't turn back. Didn't dare.

His fingers grazed her leg. She shrieked and kept running, but a hand closed over her ankle.

She kicked with all her strength and felt her foot strike flesh.

He grunted. His grip loosened. She scrambled upward again, but he yanked her back. Her chest hit the ground. The air left her lungs in a hard gasp, and suddenly he was straddling her. She rolled over, kicking and cursing, but he was already on top of her, crushing her down.

"A spitfire," he panted. "I like that even better than the milksop you been pretending to be."

"Get off me!" she snarled, but fear was crowding in, crushing her lungs.

"Oh, I'll get off, sweet thing, when I'm done."

"I'm not who you think I am," she rasped.

He laughed, teeth gritted so close to her face that she could smell the hot stench of his breath. "I figured that much out for myself, luv."

"My real name's Lady Dorenton. I'm a baroness."

"Really?" he said, and grabbing both wrists in one hand, tore her gown down the front.

She couldn't stop the scream. His breath felt hot against her breasts.

"I've never had a baroness before."

"Please." She couldn't stop the plea either, though she gritted her teeth against it. "Don't do this."

"Had a preacher's daughter once though." He bit her nipple. She shrieked, hating herself for the weakness. "She was a scrapper too. For a while. Then she went all still. Come to find out she was dead before I finished up. Guess the joke was on me."

She felt sick to her stomach. "I've got money," she rasped. "I'll pay you."

"Never mind, Cherie girl, I'll fuck you for free," he said, and reached between their bodies for his pants.

For a moment he lifted his weight from her. She brought her knee up with a snap, but he was quick and jerked aside. Her knee grazed his thigh, and then he hit her. Lightning exploded in her head, but she still struggled.

He was spreading her legs, pushing between them. She felt the heat of his member press against her as he reared above her.

"You're going to enjoy this," he gritted, and then, suddenly, something swung from the sky.

There was a crack. His eyes went wide, limned

with white. His lips parted, and then he fell, toppling over sideways.

She scrambled backward on hands and feet. Angel stood over her, legs spread, tree limb in hand.

"He was right," he said. "It was fun."

Chapter 20

Something whizzed through Keelan's hair. He jerked backward. Air rushed past his ear.

"What the devil are ye—"

She came at him like a whirlwind. The staff caught him in the ribs. He hissed in pain, gritting his teeth, doubling over.

By the time he managed to glance up, there was little to see but her backside disappearing up the hill. He cursed and stumbled after her, crouching, babying his ribs, trying to breathe.

Jesus, Mary, and Joseph, for a nearly raped, half-dressed serving wench, she could run like a racehorse. And he was already winded, confused, hurting like hell. But his anger was foremost. He bottled it up, letting it drive him up the hill. She was already out of sight when he reached the top. He clung to the twisted trunk of an elder, panting, holding his side, wondering if his innards were still in place.

If lightning hadn't crackled overhead at that precise moment, he would have died wondering, for 'twas then that Charity struck again. The staff swung toward him. He jerked back. It scraped across his left ear. Her aim was improving, but rage propelled him sideways ... toward her now, not away. He caught her about the waist, plowing her under. She went down hard, fighting like a caged cat. Arms, legs, claws, teeth.

He rasped in pain as her fingers found a dozen raw places at once, then realized belatedly that she was slipping away. Snagging the hem of her gown, he reeled her back in, grabbed her leg, and yanked her downhill.

"Not so bloody ... ach ... fook it!" he swore as her heel struck his shoulder. The old burn hurt like the devil, but he dragged himself over her, pressing her into the forest floor. "Not so fast!"

She was breathing hard. He was panting like a retriever. And even in the darkness he could see the spitting anger on her face. But there were more interesting things.

Breasts, for instance. Peeking between her shattered gown, pale as winter in the moonlight but for that tiny mole. The mole he'd seen in his dreams. His breath left him again. Her body went still beneath him.

"Go ahead then." Her voice was little more than a raspy whisper. "Have done with it."

He glanced up. Her eyes were closed, squeezed shut, her face turned away. In a waning flash of lightning, a tear glistened on her cheek. Her lips trembled.

He shifted uncomfortably. "What the devil's wrong with ye?"

"Better you than him," she whispered.

"What the hell are ye talking aboot?"

"Me innocence." She opened her eyes. Her voice trembled with agony. "'Tis all I have left. But if I'm to lose it . . ." She sobbed a little. Her bare breasts trembled against his chest. He eased off half an inch. "Better to someone like yourself." Her voice was almost lost in a rumble of thunder. "Someone handsome." She swallowed.

God, she looked small. Small and broken. No wonder she had fought like a wild beastie.

"Someone I thought I could care about," she murmured.

He opened his mouth, then noticed the narrow strap that crossed her chest and attached to a pale reticule close to her hip. Damned thing probably housed a cannon. Remembered pain reverberated in his skull. He shook his head. "Holy fook, ye're amazing."

She sniffled. "I don't know what you mean."

"Who the bloody hell are ye?" he asked, and suddenly she was crying full out, her shoulders heaving, her face turned away.

"I'm just a girl. A simple maid with nothing to call me own except—"

But lightning flashed, illuminating the staff that lay not five inches from her arm. The head of it was as big as Keelan's fist. An ungainly, tarnished lump of—

"Gold," he breathed, staring transfixed. "'Tis gold."

He could actually hear her breath stop in her throat.

"Holy God!" He should have seen it before, should have known all along. The old man never let the thing out of his sight. Not until he had tried to seduce her, at any rate. "'Tis solid, bloody gold."

She wriggled wildly beneath him, almost breaking free. By the time he had her back under control, she was all but spitting.

"It's mine," she snarled.

Gritting his teeth against a score of searing aches, he shifted his gaze to hers. "What happened to the sweet, little, simple maid, lass?" he asked. "The one what was crying?"

"Get the hell off me," she hissed, and pushed at him with elbows and knees.

Every muscle groaned, but Keelan spread himself flat atop her, holding her down. "How long have you been planning this wee little trick, lassie?"

"I don't know what the devil you're—" she began, but suddenly her eyes went wide. "What was that?" she gasped.

He jerked, but realized in that split second that she was already reaching for the staff. "Clever minx," he said, tightening his fingers on her arms. "But I'm na so daft as I look."

"'Twould be all but impossible," she rasped, pushing at him again.

He subdued her as best he could, gritting against the pain until she lay still once more. "Tell me, lass, have ye ever told the truth in the whole of yer life?"

She remained silent.

"I'll take that as a no then," he said, and she smiled, tilting her head the slightest degree.

"Someone truly is coming," she murmured.

"Really?"

"Yes."

"Forgive me, lass, but I dunna think ye'd be so

calm if ye expected Chetfield to come charging from the bushes at any blessed moment."

Her body felt soft beneath his, almost relaxed. "He *is* going to be rather angry."

"You think so?" he asked.

She was still smiling. "Until I explain that it was you that took the staff."

He studied her from mere inches away. "Are you even human?"

She laughed, but the sound was cut short by the snap of a twig. Keelan jerked his attention to the rear. He could see nothing, but he felt it. Felt something.

"Shh," he said, but when he turned back to her, he saw that her eyes were wide, her lips pale. "Someone's coming," he mouthed.

"That's what I said," she hissed.

"Shh," he repeated, wincing as he levered himself to his feet and pulled her up after. She rose, jerked away, grabbed the staff.

A noise scraped in the darkness, something almost recognizable.

"Dogs!" she rasped.

"Run!" he said, but she was way ahead of him, racing through the darkness.

He sprinted after her. A branch cut his face. He slapped it aside. Up ahead, she fell to her knees, then stumbled to her feet with a curse. The sound of tearing fabric ripped the night, and then she was running again, drawers flashing, leaving a ragged circle of torn skirts behind her.

The land dipped dramatically into the darkness, nearly pitching Keelan onto his face, but he found his balance and scrambled downward, slowing his slide with branches and roots. He hit the bottom with a jolt that slammed pain from his knees to his shoulder blades. Water splashed onto his legs. A bog. Dammit! But there was nothing for it. The maid was slogging straight through, and she had the staff. He plowed in. Mud sucked at his feet, pulling him down. It took all his strength to make it through, to drag himself up the far slope. Some yards away, she was panting, face streaked with mud, holding on to a tree, eyes wide as she glanced about.

"What are you doing?" The words hurt his chest. His lungs were burning, his legs shaking. "What are you looking for?" It struck him suddenly that she might have a plan. Merciful God! He wanted a plan.

A noise scraped in the forest behind them. Charity glanced back, eyes wide, then jolted off to the left. There was nothing to do but hold his ribs and stumble after.

Pain was all there was now. Pain and the vision of her bare calves darting through the woods.

Good God, she was all but naked. All but—

His foot struck a hole. Pain shattered his ankle. He hissed as he fell. A dog howled. He rocked back and forth, teeth gritted, watching her. For a moment he saw the pale oval of her face as she turned back. Her steps slowed. Their eyes met. She delayed a moment and then she was gone, turning like a wild goat to scamper up the hill and out of sight.

"Fook—" he began, but a crackle in the underbrush stopped his soliloquy. They were close. Closer than he knew. Reaching blindly to his side, he curled his hand around a branch. It felt hard and firm in his hand, but it would do him no good. He could see his own death in his mind. Still, he would fight. He hobbled to his feet, dragging the branch with him. "Who's there?"

Someone snickered. Branches crackled.

"Come on out then." Good God, he sounded like a warrior and not some barely breathing charlatan with one good ankle and a penchant for lying. "Come and fight me," he yelled.

And Lambkin scampered into view.

The warrior loosened his grip. "Sweet Jesus Lord," breathed the charlatan.

Lambkin bleated. Somewhere in the night a dog bayed.

Keelan gritted his teeth against the pain,

scooped the lamb into his arms, and turned toward the hill. It looked insurmountable, but he shambled up it, the lamb cradled against his chest, branch acting as a staff.

At the top he rested, breathing hard. Which way? He waited. Lightning flared. He scanned the woods below. There. A flash of white, not two furlongs away. He could yet catch her, he thought, but suddenly he recognized the sound of water, realized the truth. She had reached the river. It glistened misty gray, hustling along. And then he saw the bobbling little boat she'd pushed into the current.

Holy God, she *did* have a plan, but suddenly the night was shattered with noise.

"Loose them!" Chetfield boomed, and instantly hounds howled and bayed and snarled.

Keelan sprinted downhill. His ankle almost gave way, but he rushed on. He could see Charity now, throwing a rope onto the craft. Almost there. He was almost upon her. A howl split the night. He glanced over his shoulder. A wolfhound topped the hill, running full out, tongue lolling.

Terror ripped through him like a blade.

He sped up, lungs tearing in twain. Twenty feet from the water now, but the girl was casting off. "Wait!" he rasped.

The hound was on his heels. He could hear it panting. Ten feet to go. He knew the moment the dog sprang, felt it in his soul. There was nothing to do but jump, to leap for his life. The water cracked like ice beneath him. He went under, bobbed to the roiling surface, went under again. Beneath the rushing waves, it was as dark as hell.

He tumbled in the black current and was suddenly shot into the air. Lambkin bleated, hooves paddling. Keelan twisted about, searching frantically for the boat. There! Just to his right, Charity's eyes as wide as the sea. "Help me," he rasped and grasped for the gunwale. But he was rolled under again. His head struck granite. Pain greeted him, but it was the blackness that overwhelmed him. Cold and hard and unforgiving, it pulled him inexorably into its grip.

Chapter 21

Keelan awoke to firelight. He opened his eyes slowly. Beyond the crackling flames, the world was as dark as sin. He glanced about. Where was he? Out of the elements. That much was certain. A cave, perhaps.

His chest ached. He rolled to his side, and stopped abruptly, for there, in front of his very eyes, was a woman. And, great God in heaven, she was naked. The merest sight of her soothed the ripping pain. She stood facing away from him. Her hair was wet and curled down her back in glistening tendrils. The firelight caressed her shoulders, turning them to molten gold. She was mesmerizing. The length of her endless legs, the swell of her butter-pale buttocks, the curve of her waist.

And then she turned with breathtaking slowness. Firelight kissed the swell of her breast, shadowed the shallow divots between her ribs.

Keelan's body tightened as she faced him, full frontal, baring every luscious inch. Her belly was flat and firm, the hair between her thighs downy soft, her nipples so luscious and bright that—

But suddenly the world lurched and tilted. He felt himself falling an instant before he struck the water. The cold shocked him to the bone, freezing his heart, stalling his lungs. But in a moment, his instincts were kicked into scrambling lucidness. He was paddling before he was fully conscious, striving for something he couldn't quite see, couldn't imagine.

Coherency washed him in measured beats, like the pounding of his heart. He wasn't drowning. He realized with flooding relief that he was lying on his belly. He stopped his kicking, coughed, rolled over. A boat bobbed restlessly in the nearby reeds. Beside him, in the softening darkness, Lambkin bleated. Keelan shifted his gaze, letting his mind take in these new, confusing circumstances. A body lay beside him, wet, breathing hard, half dressed—Charity, bodice torn down the midline. He recognized her breasts from his dreams. They were naked, heaving, tiny raindrops beading near the ripe nipples. The sight made him feel strangely thirsty and absolutely transfixed.

She caught him with her sultry eyes, and for a

moment she looked breathless, almost euphoric, as if she too had felt the magic of the dream. But in an instant her expression hardened, and she scowled. Keelan steeled himself for the disappointment of clothing, but there was little with which to cover herself, thus she tugged her sodden sleeves toward her shoulders, grabbed the staff, and pushed herself to her feet. A nipple popped out. Her legs were bare to the knees, the rest covered by fabric as sheer as a dragonfly's wing. He watched her turn away. The view was no less inspiring from behind.

But the truth of the situation dawned on him with blinding accuracy. She and the staff were leaving him behind.

Standing up was a lifetime in hell. Every muscle screamed, but he managed to limp after her, mind bumbling weakly.

Lambkin trotted up behind. The country close at hand was open and rolling, but that gave him no clues as to their whereabouts. Still, the landscape seemed oddly familiar. The world was turning gray, chasing back the blackness, but his mind remained strangely foggy.

He remembered the wolfhounds closing in. Remembered his jolting panic, his leap, the knife-cold cut of the water, her face as she watched him go under. Then nothing.

He shivered. "Where be ye going?" he asked, though it seemed fairly obvious, even in his current state, that she was heading for a copse of trees some distance uphill.

She kept walking, but her pale shoulders were slumped, her steps dragging. Had she saved him? Had she pulled him from the gaping jaws of death?

"Lass."

She didn't stop. The rain was steady now, a drizzling coldness that chilled on contact.

"Ye must get dry. Rest."

She turned slowly. He could feel her fatigue like a weight on his own shoulders. "It's a bit late for you to lose your mind now, isn't it, Scotsman?"

He considered her words. Thunder rumbled in the distance.

"What the hell are you talking aboot?"

"Do you see a palace nearby in which to warm myself? Or is it a mere cottage in your mind's wild imagination?"

"Nay," he said, and his dreams flashed back to him. "'Tis naught but a cave." He wasn't sure from whence the words came, but his fuzzy thoughts were not ready to question. "Yonder." He nodded toward the east, where the land roughened into broken hillocks.

Morning was becoming more aggressive. He could almost see her expression now, but there was no real need. There would be curiosity melded with distrust. Well, join the fooking club.

"So you've been here before?" she asked.

Who the hell could answer that? Certainly not he. His mind felt as if it had been dunked too long in the brine and worn raw. He didn't try to answer, but turned left and shuffled uphill. He was almost too tired to care if she followed him, and was somewhat surprised when he realized she had.

The copse consisted of poplar and fragrant yew. Up against a rocky embankment, thorny blackthorn battled with bracken fern. Pushing aside the unfurling fronds, Keelan gazed into the blackness of a cave. He could not see the depth of it, and yet, in some inexplicable way long denied, he knew. Knew the cavern would measure no more than thirty feet in length. Knew it would be uninhabited. Knew it would be safe . . . at least in a physical sense. Memories drove him past the rocky doorway, or perhaps it was the wind, biting cold and hard against his shivering back. Inside, it smelled of damp earth and pungent pine.

The remains of a fire lay on the rocky floor. A noise rustled at the entrance of the cave. He glanced up. Lambkin toddled in. Charity followed. Backlit by the weakling morning light, she looked small and pale, her arms scratched and bleeding, her legs smeared with mud, her breasts just peeking . . . He turned away, immediately hard, absently gathering wood to steady his mind, to keep his hands busy. What sort of cruel magic made him hard for her? She had lied to him, struck him. Good Lord, she'd left him to die!

"What do you hope to gain?" She remained near the doorway, silhouetted against the misty gray morn. Her voice was unwavering.

He glanced up, only to find that her breasts were all but bare. Holy fook. He shifted slightly, trying to ease the chafing. "Mayhap ye should cover yerself." The unfamiliar words grated against his throat, against his very temperament.

She took a step toward him. Outside, the wind was rising with the sun. He sensed her shiver, but when he glanced up, she stilled the motion and raised her chin.

"Have you an agreement with Chetfield?" she asked, circling a little as she drew the saturated reticule over her head. "Or do you simply hope he will compensate you when you turn me over to him?"

Keelan wasn't sure what surprised him more, her perfect dialect or her assumption that he was somehow in league with the old man he hated with painful ferocity. He arranged the kindling before glancing up again, a scathing rejoinder ready, but she was still mostly naked.

The words died on his lips, shriveled to nothingness. He turned back to the wood, mind blank.

"Who are you? How do you enter my—" She stopped herself, took a breath. "Who are you?" she asked again.

He shrugged, irritated by his own foolish weakness, and remembered her pathetic words after Roland's attack. "Just a simple lad." He tried to emulate her earlier statement but found it impossible to dredge up the tears. If she didn't cover herself soon, though, he'd be crying like a spanked babe. Still, he wiped away an imaginary tear with the back of his finger and managed a sniffle. "Me innocence be all I have left."

She stared at him a moment, then snorted. "It was very nearly effective, you know," she said, fishing a curved piece of steel from her reticule and tossing it to him.

He raised his brows and gratefully struck it with the flint. Sparks scattered. "Ye've an overactive imagination," he said. But she was right, of course. The sight of her sadness had nearly caused him to loose her, had almost turned him aside. Which, of course, would have given her every opportunity to crack his head open like a ripe melon. The surprising realization that he was a dolt did little to improve his mood. "I knew what ye were aboot from the verra—" he began, but when he glanced up, she was just stepping out of the remains of her gown. Her back was one long sweep of satiny skin, and through her short, saturated pantaloons, her ass looked as tight and luscious as a plum.

The flint clattered to the floor.

She turned her head, scowling over her shoulder. "I'm assuming you've seen a naked woman before, Highlander."

He gathered his wits with fumbling difficulty. "Dozens," he said, collecting some tinder and striking the steel again. His brow felt damp and warm. What he said was true, of course, but for the past hundred years or so, most of his naked companions had been confined to his lurid dreams. And recently they had all been she. Only the dreams couldn't do her justice. His brain was starting to simmer, but he refused to look up. Still, he could see her perfectly in his mind's eye. She was sculpted like a revered statue, every curve as smooth and firm as marble. "Mayhap scores." He tried repeatedly to strike a spark. He was champion at starting fires, the best of all the boys at school, but his fingers seemed strangely numb today. 'Twas just the cold, of course. Although his mind didn't feel all that much more capable. Still, he rambled on, words accented by the sound of flint on metal. "Once, while in Versailles, I was with three lassies all—"

A noise distracted him. He glanced up. She had turned around. The world stood still. Her breasts were small and firm, round and pale and topped with a heavenly bright cap of red. Somewhere in his soggy mind he wondered why he had ever preferred buxom women. Shortsighted of him really. Stupid. Just plain ruddy daft.

"Close your mouth," she said. "And move back."

He couldn't.

"Or don't," she said, and shrugged. He watched the movement, mesmerized.

It was then that he realized a flame was smoking between his legs.

"Fook!" He skittered backward.

She stretched her hands toward the fire, though the flame was naught but a tiny orange tongue.

He realized then that her lips were tinged blue. There was a bruise on her upper arm, big as his fist, and her ribs were scraped raw. He turned his attention to the infant flame, mind churning.

"How did you get me out of the water?"

She didn't answer. He glanced up. She was shivering again, but adroitly turned the movement into a shrug.

"You caught hold of the side. I couldn't get shed of you."

"I dunna remember it quite thus."

She shrugged, unconcerned. "'Tis no more than I deserve, I suspect. I should have thought to stash an oar. But my reticule was too small."

He watched her, waiting for an explanation, but she only smiled, the expression as perfect as sunlight, amazing in its innocence.

"Oars tend to stop the most determined of men, no matter how hard their heads might be."

He snorted and turned to the flame again. Seconds ticked by. The fire flickered higher. Lambkin pressed close to Keelan's side, seeking warmth.

"And what of the lamb?" he asked. "Might she have caught hold too?"

A muscle danced irritably in her cheek. Her dimples winked perversely as she struggled with the chill. "You dragged the damned thing in with you."

"Over the gunwale while soaking wet and unconscious?"

"Would you rather believe I was too concerned with your welfare to let you drown?"

"That would indeed be more pleasant," he admitted.

"Believe this," she said. "If I'd had an oar, you'd be bobbing downstream like a bloated bullock by now."

"And the lamb?"

"Mutton's not my favorite, but . . ." She shrugged. Lambkin looked from one to the other, wet ears drooping.

"You'd eat Lambkin?" The idea was revolting, almost cannibalistic. Of course the idea of his own bloated carcass floating toward sea wasn't all that appealing either.

"Right now I'd eat *you*," she said.

"Well . . ." he admitted, looking straight at her. "I've had me thoughts about ye too."

For a moment he almost thought she blushed, but then she snorted and turned away. Her buttocks bunched and separated as she squatted to lift her tattered garment, and for a moment he was afforded a glimpse of heaven.

"That wasn't me," she said and rising, held her torn bodice in front of the weakling fire.

He stared at her. Not that he had a choice.

"The girl you thought about . . . that wasn't me," she explained.

"Who then?"

"A maid I met once. Very sweet, but not terribly bright. I believe her name was Charity?" She said it with her former accent.

He stared at the dark, tiny circle on her left breast, then turned back to the fire. 'Twas the hardest thing he had ever done. "She had yer mole."

Surprised, she covered the pigment with her hand, but he could see all in his mind's playful eye.

"Na to mention yer scar."

She narrowed her eyes.

"Right thigh," he said, nursing the blaze. "A hand's breadth from yer hip."

She glanced down, but the mark was hidden beneath her drying drawers.

"I realized you weren't what you seemed," she said. "But I didn't expect you to be peeking in my window."

"Should have," he murmured. "But it didn't seem right. Na with a sweet lass such as yerself."

"That was the other girl too," she said. "The one who wouldn't kill you if you turned your back."

"So the other maid be the one with the scruples."

"But no brain."

"Aye well," he said, and nodded as he glanced up again. "A conscience can come in handy, I suspect. But it canna compare to yer stunning lack of modesty."

Chapter 22

Charity laughed. She couldn't help it, for honesty seemed so out of place here, unlikely and unexpected, as if he were truly the gentle shepherd whose soft burr whispered from her dreams.

Angel. She could not set aside the name, though in the harsh light of reality she knew it could not be his. Still, it had suited him, back at Crevan House. Back in hell. He had seemed like a ray of sunlight in the midst of darkness. Like kindness personified, cuddling the scrawny lamb to his side, giving her that heart-shattering grin, part rogue, part motherless lad. But that was all past now. He was not what he seemed. And the dreams . . . The lurid images that left her damp and desperate, they were not for him, but for a gentle, oddly old-fashioned lad who did not exist.

He shifted his heaven-blue gaze back to the fire. "How did you learn of the treasure?" he asked.

"What treasure is that?"

He glanced up. Emotion sparked in his eyes as he drank her in. She almost blushed again, but now for her ridiculous modesty. She was not a timid woman, but there was something dangerous here.

"The staff," he said. "I thought at first that it was naught but a walking stick with a hunk of lead on the up end."

"What makes you think differently now?"

He snorted. "Call me numskulled, lass. But mayhap 'tis the fact that ye took that and naught else when ye hammered out Chetfield and took off like an Irish Thoroughbred."

She shrugged. The firelight danced dully on the head of the staff. How many nights had she lain awake trying to ferret out the mysteries of it? Of Chetfield. But she hadn't planned for the Highlander. Couldn't have foreseen him. "Perhaps I simply have a fondness for walking sticks."

He nodded in agreement. "Aye, of course. Ye've a strange longing for canes and the like. Thus ye risk yer life with a mob of murderous thugs in the hopes of adding to yer collection."

253

"Call me eccentric."

He poked the fire. It flared, tossing light across his beautiful features—broad cheekbones, dark skin, generous mouth. There was hardly a scar to be seen. If she believed in white magic, she would think it had a hand there. But there was only evil. Only the dark sort.

"Ye could have been killed, lass," he rumbled. "Or worse."

"Worse?" She forced a laugh. "Truly, Scotsman, what's worse than death?"

His gaze settled on her, making her heart race. "Torture's not as enjoyable as ye might think."

She remembered the sight of his wounds on the morning after his arrival. She had known what to expect even before she opened the stable door, had known by the gleam in Roland's predatory eye. Her stomach had roiled, only to have the sickness multiply a thousand times at sight of the Highlander's sweet, ravaged face. "No one made you come to Crevan House," she said.

"So you knew all along."

She gave him a blank stare. It had been honed to perfection long before she dared venture into Chetfield's dark shadow. "Knew what?"

If her naïve act angered him, he did not show it. In fact, he smiled a little, one corner of his lovely mouth lifting. "Ye knew 'twas the old man and his ugly bastards that had beat me to the verra door of death, despite yer wide-eyed concern."

"Of course I knew." Guilt she'd thought long dead flared up, spurring anger in its wake. All had been going well until he'd shown up bludgeoned on her doorstep. No one had yet been hurt. She'd not been discovered, though she had spent countless breathless hours searching the estate, dredging up every secret, every hideous truth. Her carefully laid plans had been moving along just so. And they hadn't involved him stepping half-naked into her heated dreams, blue eyes laughing as he brought her to life night after restless night. Neither had they entailed a skittering trip cross-country with no food and less hope. The boat had been naught but a precaution, if worse came to worst. But she had seen him behind her fireplace screen and knew his life would be forfeit if she did not act.

She almost closed her eyes to the overpowering memories; for a moment she had thought him lost, drowned beneath the darkling waves. "Surely you didn't think even Charity was so daft as to believe you had truly been set upon by some unknown beast."

Something flared in his eyes, a smattering of the gentleness she had seen in Angel's. But she would not be so foolish as to believe it again. "Not so daft as kindly," he murmured.

She refused to acknowledge his regretful tone. "Kindly will get you dead, Highlander. Don't you know that?"

"Aye," he said. "In fact I do. I but thought you too softhearted to agree."

She laughed. "Softheaded, you mean."

He poked at the logs. "Tell me, lass, what has made you so cold?"

"I think it is the fact that I've been all but bare-assed in the rain while I—"

"I did not mean it quite so literal."

She inhaled carefully, calmed herself, pushed the terrifying memories behind her. "I like to breathe, Scotsman. I see to myself and expect others to do the same."

"Then why did ye try to convince me to leave?"

He was watching her, eyes steady. She fought to hold contact, though there was nowhere safe to look. Even his neck was appealing. And his arms. And his back. And . . . Lord help her.

"What are you talking about?" she asked, tone marvelously steady.

"Ye tried to get me gone. Indeed . . ." He

paused, thinking. "Methinks 'tis why ye kissed me. So that he would send me away."

Well, he had those damned eyes, didn't he? Those damned soulful eyes that could make her want to laugh or cry at a moment's notice. "Perhaps I was trying to get you killed instead."

"Or mayhap ye truly are drawn to me."

"Well . . ." Her heart was thrumming madly, her breath short in her chest, but she skimmed her gaze insolently down his rain-soaked form. "You *are* well hung, Highlander."

He glanced up, eyes flashing. "What?"

"I said . . ." She smiled, paused. If only she had been so convincing on stage. But theater had only been a tool, a way to learn, to delve for secrets long hidden. "That's horse dung, Highlander. Have you seen that hunk of gold? I wasn't about to share it with the likes of a wayward Scot."

He was staring at her as if he might well be going mad. As if she had tortured his dreams just as he had hers. She would have laughed at the idea if she hadn't been so damned tired. But her back ached and her feet throbbed.

"So ye knew all along I was after the treasure?" he asked.

"No one could be as appeal . . . as . . . *appall-*

ingly naïve as you seemed." Dear God help her. "Besides, I've always been the suspicious sort."

He grinned, probably knowing things he should not know—that she had imagined him in her bed a dozen times, had felt his fingers like cool magic against her feverish skin.

"Suspicious? Ye, lass? I would na have thought it."

She gave him a dismissive shrug.

"Then ye must na be the sweet maid, but the other."

She didn't bother to glance at her bare breasts, but they should go far to prove she was not the innocent fool he had once thought her to be. Nor was she the child left to cry, broken and alone, at her mother's grave site. She was a woman of cunning and strength, a force to be reckoned with. "A fine guess."

"And what might your name be?"

"Some have called me Guinevere." In fact, she had played that part at Drury Lane. But she would never be the actress her mother was. That rare, shining jewel that drew men like drones to her side. All manner of men.

He canted his head at her, thick lashes cast low over quicksilver eyes. "What of yer da then? What did he call ye?"

Anger flared in her soul, but she was far too accomplished to let it slip past her veneer. "You may address me as Charity."

The fire crackled in the ensuing silence, then: "I wish to know what yer sire called ye, lass, na what the ghoul called ye." He had placed his arm over Lambkin's back and absently stroked the animal's little shoulder. She felt strangely weak at the sight.

She was silent for a moment, then: "They both called me Charity, for that was my given name."

"Ye mean to say there was one thing ye did na lie aboot."

"That and the fact that you're an idiot."

"Ye did na say I was an idiot. Indeed, ye kissed me."

"That was because Roland was about to enter the room, and I was hoping he would toss you from the window."

"How verra charitable of you," he said, and grinned. "But regardless, it's happy I am to meet ye, Charity lass."

"Really?" She cleared her throat and turned away from his smile, hoping to find something less dangerous, something to do with her hands. "I would have thought after the beatings . . ." She found a log, strode to it, and tugged it near the fire. "And the burns . . ." She glanced toward him. He was staring at her nether parts. It made her feel marginally better, safer. "And the near drowning . . . meeting me wouldn't be all that wondrous."

"Well . . ." He shrugged. The hint of a grin peeked forth. "Ye dunna wear an abundance of clothes."

No, he was not the guileless soul she had once thought him to be, but he had a rare ability to smile in the darkest of hours. "Which of course makes the beatings well worthwhile," she said.

He opened his mouth as if to argue, then: "Aye."

"Men," she mused, seating herself on the log and letting her knees fall open a fraction of an inch, "are strange."

He stared. "Have ye known a good many of them then, lass?"

Why did he ask? Did he care? Did he hope— But she locked away her girlish thoughts and scowled at the remains of her severed gown. A four-inch strip had been torn from the center.

"Men," he said. "Have ye known many?"

She had known him, in her dreams, in her heart. And she was a fool. "It's mine," she said finally, and reaching down, untied the lace from the gathered bottom of her drawers before pulling it free. "The staff." She caught his gaze with her own. "It's mine. And it shall remain so." Bending, she snagged the simple reticule close and drew out her knife.

Angel raised his brows, but she only used the tip to poke tiny holes in the fabric of her bodice.

"Because ye stole it first?" he asked.

Memories assailed her. Sharp and ugly. But she would not share the truth, for she had a mission and she would not fail. Not even for an angel that made her jaded heart soar. Certainly not for him. "'Tis as good a reason as any," she said, setting the blade aside and shoving the lace diagonally from one hole to the next.

He nodded, touched his fingers to his scalp, and winced.

"Does your head hurt?"

He grinned, that glimpse of angelic devil so close to the surface. "Everything hurts, lass."

She shrugged, unconcerned, though even now, even knowing he hoped to take her one treasure, she longed to touch him, to slip her fingers into his hair and soothe his aches. "Perhaps you hit your pate while falling from the boat."

His eyes glistened. He was no fool. No one to be trifled with. "I think I may have been pushed."

She shrugged, shoved back the memories. He'd

been unconscious when they'd reached shore. Unconscious, maybe dead, causing her stomach to twist in knots with her heart. Not knowing whether he was the silver-eyed lad who whispered from her dreams or a dark-haired devil come to foil her plans, to ruin her life. She had, in fact, considered sending him downstream alone and wondered now if she should have done so. He knew things. What things, she was not certain. But more than he admitted, that much was sure.

"Where'd you hear of it?" she asked.

"The treasure?" He glanced up. She knew what he saw, tight breasts and a tighter waist. For a moment his breath seemed to stop. But he didn't try to pretend otherwise. "It's something of a legend," he said, and stroked the lamb. "People talk."

No they didn't. Few remembered there had ever been a treasure taken from the depths far off the coast of Madeira. Fewer still knew of Chetfield, of his treachery. Of his evil. "What people?" she asked.

"Are you wondering who else you have to worry aboot?"

"Perhaps I should stock up on oars."

He chuckled. His teeth gleamed in the firelight. His dark hair glistened. Sometime during their journey, he had bound it behind his neck with a strip of fabric, and for a moment she couldn't look away.

"It's mine," she said, lifting her arms and carefully slipping the newly repaired garment over her head. The drawer lace crisscrossed crazily between her breasts. She pulled it tight and tied it with a scowl. Two inches of flesh remained visible between the gown's edges.

The Highlander shifted uncomfortably. She caught his gaze.

"Mayhap we could share," he said, returning to their conversation, but his voice sounded hoarse.

She smiled at the sound. "Perhaps you don't know me."

"Mayhap I'd like to," he countered, and pushed himself to his feet.

Their gazes locked. Her breathing escalated beneath his regard, and for a moment she almost forgot about the staff, about her mother, about Chetfield, but he passed her by. "Ye stay," he said to the lamb, and stepped out into the rain.

Charity watched him go, then hurried to the mouth of the cave and glanced outside. He was already disappearing through the underbrush. For a moment she considered slipping off in the opposite direction, but even as she thought of it, her knees trembled with fatigue. Yet she would not be caught unawares, would not allow him to snatch her treasure while she slept. Retrieving the staff, she glanced outside once more, then slipped along the rock wall to hide it beneath a dozen years of fallen leaves. Only a few minutes had passed when she carried a plain, knobby-ended stick into the cave and piled a trio of logs near the doorway. Then, after placing the would-be staff in the distant shadows where a casual glance might suggest it was the treasure for which many had died, she pulled the strap of her reticule back over her head and curled up near Lambkin.

But dreams came despite her fatigue. Angel, kissing her, teasing her, laughing as he raced past, a dark-haired child giggling madly on his shoulders.

A noise woke her with a start.

"Fie me," he complained in his unique, anti-quated manner, stumbling over the pile in the doorway. "Are ye trying to kill me, lass?"

She shoved the dreams away, focusing on re-ality. "Yes," she said, and yawned.

He gave her a look as he passed her by. The fire had burned down.

She scowled and scrubbed at her face, trying

264

to wake up, but just then she noticed the pot he carried.

Her hands stopped of their own accord. Her heart might have done the same. "What's that?"

"This?" He lifted the lid from the kettle, and then she smelled the stew. The scent of it tickled her nostrils, teased her shaky senses. And though it might have been wise to act nonchalant, she was not quite up to the task. "I think I may have underestimated you, Scotsman," she said.

"Keelan," he said.

"What's that?"

"Me name."

She nodded. "So your mother didn't truly call you Angel." She drew a deep waft of the stew, feeling faint. "You probably didn't even have a mother. Were probably spawned—"

"She had eyes as dark as midnight," he said, but his smile was gone, replaced by a solemn tenderness she could not mock. "And when she laughed . . ." He held her in his gaze . . . in his power. "The world was happy."

"I'm sorry." She could not stop the words, though she tried, and then he smiled, blessing her with that softest of gifts.

"In truth, she called me Ange," he said, then cleared his throat and looked away. Were there tears in his eyes? But no. 'Twas an act. Surely she knew a fine performance when she saw one. "I fear ye'll have to eat out of the pot. The butterer caught a glimpse of me afore I could filch his master's crockery."

She glanced away, trying to find her bearings. "Butterer?"

"One who butters," he explained. "But mayhap he was a cupbearer."

She must have loved him madly, this woman with the midnight eyes. "You're telling me you stole this from some fine lord?"

"Hunting party," he said, and glanced up. "Mayhap ye thought I've been out slaving over a hot stove?" He grinned, but the expression was somehow lost in retrospection. "After melting the iron and hammering out the kettle, of course."

She couldn't quit watching him.

"There's na a great deal left, but 'tis still warm." His voice was gruff. What had happened to her, the mother who loved him? "Sit down."

She did so.

He handed over the pot. A wooden spoon protruded past the rim. She lifted it and ate, letting the sustenance clear her head. They each had a role to play. The victor would be the one who played his or her part the best.

"My compliments to the butterer," she said finally.

He was watching her, admiration unhidden in his dark-fringed eyes.

"It's not polite to stare," she said, and stifled the shiver that snaked up her spine.

He shrugged. "Some might say it's na polite to run aboot in the altogether either, as wee Charity so charmingly put it."

"Does my lack of modesty bother you?" she asked, and tried to scrape out a bit more stew. There seemed to be an infinitesimal amount stuck to the bottom.

"Me? Na a'tall."

"Good, then I shall remain like this and hope to keep you distracted until I can knock you on the head again."

He grinned, stealing her foolish breath. "And after I slaved over that fine meal."

"Don't forget hammering out the kettle."

"Me hands be still sore."

Her mind was working better since the meal, tripping along, trying to determine who he might be. How he figured into the scheme of things. "So who told you about the staff?"

"'Twas a man named Thom," he said. "We met in a wee pub in Carlisle. He was fond of his drink."

"He knew Chetfield," she guessed.

"Said he'd inherited a treasure."

"Did he?" If so, he was wrong. The staff had not changed hands, not in well over a century.

"Aye."

"Is this someone I should be concerned with?"

"He didn't seem to know what the treasure was exactly, just something Chetfield's father's father had taken from the deep many long years past. Something beyond precious. Mayhap even magical." He was studying her. Why? "Still, if the staff were me own to worry on, I would na invite him to tea."

"The staff isn't yours," she reminded him, "and I don't drink tea."

He shrugged as if to say she was perfectly safe then, but what was he truly thinking?

"So you traveled all this way from Carlisle on the slim chance that this Thom fellow was correct and that Chetfield still owned the treasure?"

He shrugged. "I am naught but a bold gambler."

"Then why haven't you tried to take it from me yet?"

"The staff?" He grinned. "I saw you brain Chetfield, lass. Scared the life out of me."

Maybe she would have believed that at one time. "I'm beginning to think you don't scare easily, Highlander."

"Ye jest," he said, eyes laughing. "Me knees be shaking even now. But truth be told, I expect ye to be me best defense once the nasty bastards show up."

"My turn to be flattered. How far behind us do you think they—" she began, but suddenly he held up his hand for silence and jerked toward the mouth of the cave.

"Not far at all," said Chetfield and stepped into view.

Chapter 23

"Holy—" Keelan rasped, but suddenly he was grabbed from behind and jerked backward. A knife pricked his neck and Charity's voice hissed near his ear.

"One step closer and I swear to God I'll kill him."

Caution or shock kept him perfectly immobile.

For a moment Chetfield stood just as still. Then he spoke. "'Tis a pity, but I fear our little Charity has gone quite mad, Mr. Roland."

There was a rustling of underbrush and then the bastard stepped into view. Keelan felt the maid's attention flicker to him. "I'm as sane as Sunday, Chetfield." The knife felt perfectly steady against his neck. Perhaps he should have thought to take it from her when she'd been repairing her bodice, but he'd been rather distracted.

"Then why, my dear, do you imagine I would care if you killed a wayward Scot who has been nothing but trouble since the day I set eyes on him?"

"He took the staff," she snarled.

Keelan cranked his eyes toward her. Was she mad? he wondered, but she only tightened her grip in his hair.

Chetfield tilted his head. "Are you telling me that young MacLeod here stole the staff you stole from me?"

She yanked his head back with a growl. It hurt like hell. "'E said 'e loved me."

Chetfield's lips smirked up even as he narrowed his eyes. "Did he indeed?"

"We've been planning this for months." Her accent was back. "Him and me. I didn't want to do it, but he could sweet-talk a toadie. Said all I had to do was make you trust me. Then we'd snatch the thing and hock it in London town. Make us a fortune, live happily ever after. Wouldn't be no trouble."

"But . . ." Chetfield suggested.

"He took it whilst I was sleeping. Put a worthless branch in its place." She jerked her head toward the back of the cave. "Thinking I wouldn't look too close, I suspect. Thinking he could buy hisself some time."

"As much as I'd like to believe you, my dear, that seems a bit far-fetched. Why would he come back if that were the case?"

She laughed. It sounded as crazy as Keelan felt. "Sex, Master Chetfield. One more good bump. I'm damned good at it, you know." She snarled, her lips close to Keelan's ear. "Thought you could have me one more time before you took off with the spoils, didn't you?" she asked, and drew blood at his neck. "Didn't you?" she repeated.

"Well, lass . . ." His throat felt dry. His thoughts were buzzing like bumblebees in his head. But it was die trying . . . or just die. "If ye did na want to be swived, ye should na strut aboot with yer bosoms hanging out and—"

"Me bosoms . . ." She ground them into his back. ". . . brought you back though, didn't they?"

Holy God, he didn't know the rules to this game. Couldn't keep up with the twists and turns. "I did na take the staff, Master Chetfield. Dunna believe—"

"He's lying," she growled, and urged forth another droplet of blood.

Keelan gritted his teeth. "Verra well then, aye, I took it. But think on it, luv," he rasped. "I could have run off and left ye to die. Yet I could na bear to leave you here alone in the midst of nothing."

"Not with me bosoms hanging out at any rate," she snarled. "Ye're no better than the others. No better than a damned rat. I should have knowed—"

"As interesting as this is," Chetfield interrupted, "I'm wondering what your plans are now, my dear."

"Me plans?" She darted her gaze from one to the other. "I plan to get out of here alive."

"But my men, which I've felt the need to gather, are likely getting bored holding the hounds at bay. And I fear you hurt Mr. Roland's feelings when you kneed him in the groin."

"Well that's too bad, ain't it now. I'm leaving," she hissed, "and I'm taking him . . ." She pricked Keelan's neck again. He closed his eyes and hoped to hell this one was a dream. ". . . with me till I comes to the river."

"The river?"

"That's right." Her tone was taut. "I got me a little vessel there. Once I'm free on the water, you can have the rodent, here. But if you try to rush me, I'll kill him."

"She's lying," Roland murmured.

But Chetfield shook his head. "A woman scorned," he said, then: "What about the staff?"

"If you can bang it out of the Scotsman here, it's all yours. And good riddance to it. I don't want nothing to do with any of you."

"But that hardly seems fair after all the work you went to," Chetfield said. "Why not turn the Scotsman loose now? We'll convince him to tell us where he hid the thing, and compensate you for your efforts."

For a second she seemed to hesitate, but then she laughed. "You think I'm stupid, don't you? You think I'm bloody daft. But I ain't." She nudged Keelan forward. "We're going now. Out that way right there." She nodded toward the opening. "And if you give me a peep of trouble he's gonna die."

"But think of it, my dear. If you kill him, you'll still be here with us."

The blade trembled against Keelan's neck, but for the life of him he couldn't determine if her terror was real or pretend. "He said he loved me," she sniffled, and once again let his blood flow down his chest. "I'm carrying his baby right now."

Keelan cranked his eyes toward her. She didn't even pause.

"Only I just found out he's married to some tart in Edinburgh. Believe me," she said through gritted teeth. "I'll kill him if it makes sense or no."

They were looking into her eyes. Chetfield nodded. "Very well, my dear. You have a free course to the river."

"Tell yer animals outside."

"What's that?" Chetfield's tone was melodious.

"Yer bloody big beasts," she said, her voice grating in his ear. "They're waiting right round the corner."

"You're wrong, my—"

"Call them off," she rasped.

Anger suffused Chetfield's face, but he spoke in a moment. "Frankie," he said, barely raising his voice. "Bear. Miss Charity will be coming out in a moment. You'll not hurt her."

"Nor the shit-head here neither," she added, nudging Keelan. "He's mine till the river."

Chetfield's eerie eyes gleamed dangerously. "Likewise," he added, "you will give Mr. MacLeod free passage."

"Tell them to back away," Charity ordered. "All of them."

"Step away now." Chetfield's voice was grim.

They heard heavy footsteps rustling through the underbrush.

"Way back," Charity said, "where I can see them."

He gave the order. Half a dozen men could

be seen in the narrow opening. Frankie held two wolfhounds at bay. They slavered, hackles raised. Charity nudged Keelan forward. He moved on stiff knees. Lambkin trotted after them. Outside it was still drizzling, cold and cheerless.

Horses stood some distance off to their right, hips cocked, half dozing in the misty rain. But Charity was pulling him back along the stony embankment, heading downhill. Chetfield followed them out, moving carefully, but Keelan felt the girl's attention slip sideways for a moment, then back.

"You're not going to try to cheat us out of our goods, are you, my dear?" asked the old man.

"You can have him," she said, "soon as I—" but suddenly the knife disappeared from Keelan's neck. She bent down and yanked something from the bracken. And then she was running, sprinting past him full-bore.

It took Keelan a moment to realize she was racing toward the horses, longer still to understand she had the staff.

"Run!" she shrieked.

Terror stabbed him like a spur. Lambkin bleated. He leapt forward, snatching her up at a run. Chetfield yelled something indiscernible, but the words mattered little.

A dog bayed.

The nearest horse snorted and plunged at its reins, but Charity was already scrambling aboard. And then she was flying, driving the beast straight toward Keelan. The animal bore down on him. He leapt aside at the last second, rolling wildly. Directly behind him, someone screamed as he was plowed under, but Keelan never identified his pursuer. Charity was thundering away. The three remaining mounts were pulling at their tethers. He grabbed the gray's reins and jumped for a stirrup just as it broke free. But something grabbed his leg as he threw himself into the saddle.

He cursed and kicked. Someone growled back. The bay broke loose and slammed into the gray, who lurched left. Keelan held on. His attacker fell with a yelp, and then he was flying, racing after the girl, Lambkin's ears blown back in the force of the wind.

Branches whipped past Keelan's face. They careened up a hill, then down, heading for the river. Charity was nowhere in sight, but Keelan let the gray have its head. They hit the water full tilt. On the far side, hoofprints charged through the mud and up the incline. He pushed his mount in that direction as water rushed around the animal's hocks, but something snagged his mind. A damned premonition maybe, but he had no time to deny it. Yanking one rein tight, he pulled the gray to a halt. And there, a furlong or two downstream, he saw a fleeting glimpse of something. Whirling the gelding toward it, he pushed it back into a gallop. Rocks slipped beneath the animal's plowing hooves, but Keelan dare not look down. She had been here. His scalp tingled with the knowledge. But where was she now? And what should he do? Leave the horse and search on foot? Move on or—

"It's about damned time," she said, and stepped out from behind a boulder.

Keelan wrestled the steed to a jolting halt and stared at her. She was covered in mud. Her face was speckled with it, the sweet curves of her breasts freckled. But she held the staff firmly in her hand.

Chapter 24

The sun sank deep in a crimson sky.

Fatigue rode Keelan like a demon. He had given the girl Chetfield's old tunic sometime back, saying it was for chivalry's sake, but it was more for his own peace of mind. Her impromptu moorings hadn't held her bodice in place as well as she might have hoped, thus he had covered her in gray muslin from shoulder to knee. Still, the feel of her back against his bare skin was almost more than he could bear.

By the time they reached Ramston, Keelan was at wit's end. By the time they reached the Fox and Hounds, his hands were shaking. If pressed, he was prepared to blame it on fatigue.

They had gathered something of a crowd, but Charity rode straight as a ramrod despite her bare legs and tousled hair. Even Lambkin, whose head poked inquisitively from a giant saddlebag, did nothing to ruffle her haughty demeanor.

An innkeeper bustled out of his establishment, eyes as round as his belly, already talking as Keelan shoved Lambkin deeper into the bag. "I fear we've no room—"

"My good sir," Charity interrupted, tone arrogant, "I am Lady Tempton. As you may have guessed, we were set upon by miscreants. My manservant . . ." She glanced imperiously over her shoulder.

"Was lost," Keelan said, kicking his mind into gear before he was relegated back to rodent status. Slipping from the gelding's haunches, he tried to match the girl's noble demeanor. "A terrible thing. Terrible. Poor Davey." He would never obtain the lassie's sterling ability to lie, but he would give it a mighty effort. "He was like a brother. Upon a time we would—"

She toed him in the ribs with the tip of her tattered shoe. He gritted his teeth and tried not to glower.

"We realize how we must look to decent, God-fearing folk such as yourself," she said, "but we cannot turn back. My dearest father, the Duke of Bant, is at death's very door, and—" Her soliloquy was stopped by a quiet deluge of tears.

Keelan glanced up, impressed as hell. 'Twas all but impossible to keep pace.

"There, there, my dear," said the innkeeper, hobbling forward and patting her knee. It was bare. She glanced at him from the corner of a sloppy eye.

"I do not mean to seem indelicate," he said, and cleared his throat, though his tone was just as nasal when he spoke again. "But I've heard tales before, only to be left with no coin while my guests slip away in the night."

She straightened in the saddle, pushing her breasts out against old Chetfield's damnably lucky shirt. "Do I look like some vagabond—"

"We shall sell the horse," Keelan interrupted, doing his best to hush his wild Celtic burr. "In the morning. And give you a goodly share."

The innkeeper narrowed his eyes. "But what of the lady's father?"

Damn! He'd forgotten entirely about the poor Duke of . . . whatever. Fook it! He was too tired to remember the angles.

"We shall be forced to procure another means of travel," Charity said. "As I do not believe in incurring debt."

The fat man eyed them carefully, then: "Very well," he said finally.

Some minutes later they were ushered into

the inn. The stairs were almost more than Keelan could manage, but he followed the girl's backside up the steps to their rented chamber.

The room was nothing special, or would not have been, had it not been for the bed. It called to him like a siren song, but Charity reached it first. Seated on the mattress, she pulled off the filthy tunic and tossed it to the floor just as Keelan lifted Lambkin from the bag. Breasts all but bare, she scowled at him.

He stared dazedly back, but before he made any sort of move, she had turned her back to him and fallen asleep, staff clutched in one grubby hand.

A dozen possible scenarios kept him awake far longer than he would have thought possible, but finally he set the lamb between them, dropped onto his side of bed, and fell soundly into sleep.

He awoke to waning daylight, but as far as he could tell she had not yet moved. Her lashes made dark crescents over her pale cheeks, and her hand was still curled firmly over the staff.

Thus Keelan lifted the sleepy lamb from her warm cradle, hid her in her leather pouch, and wandered groggily down the stairs. The air outside was cool and rain-washed. Leaving Lambkin to graze on a patch of sweet clover that grew between the inn and the smithy's shop, he secured a simple meal of bread and honey, then settled beside the little ewe. From this vantage point, he could watch the window of the chamber where the girl slept. Behind him, a dark-haired fellow with forearms like country hams pounded nails into a gray cob's near fore.

Keelan sat quietly, remembering the hours just past. Surprisingly, he had dreamed, but not of evil times long past. Instead he had imaged Toft standing at his bedside, looking down, watching him sleep. Or had it been a dream a'tall? If the old man had used his eerie gifts to arrive there in the flesh, he could have at least left a bottle and a loaf. Although a score of battle-ready soldiers would have been even better.

Near the smithy, a tall boy of ten or so watched from the shade of a spreading walnut tree. His auburn hair poked out at odd angles above evergreen eyes, and his dark, hand-me-down garments looked stark and baggy against his pale skin.

Dipping into the saddlebags taken from the gray, Keelan brought out the only thing of value that had been found there—a hand-carved wooden flute. It was a quick conversation after that.

Five minutes later, Keelan draped his newly purchased garments over his arm. After setting a meal on a simple wooden board, he bore it and Lambkin back up the slanted stairs.

Upon reaching the top, he pushed the door open and stepped inside. Charity turned toward him as he entered, eyes half mast and red lips swollen. The drawer lace, he couldn't help but notice, had completely abandoned its post, tearing through the last remnants of her bodice.

Keelan's throat felt dry. Other parts weren't so arid. "You sleep like the dead," he said, and set Lambkin on the floor.

She sat up, tugging the bedsheet over her breasts. "That for me?" she asked, eyeing him sleepily.

A thousand bawdy replies rumbled through Keelan's mind, but he merely handed over the tray.

The sheet slipped a hair as she settled the tray onto her lap and broke off a hunk of dark bread. Keelan watched as she drizzled on honey and licked her lips. He cleared his throat and turned toward the window. It had been far safer outside on the patch of sweet clover. "I found ye some clothes."

She gave him a glance out of dark, bedroom eyes, lips quirking. "Because you can't keep yourself from me much longer?"

He clenched his jaw, grinned, and sat down on the room's only chair. "Because some think it improper to go aboot naked as a new-birthed bairn."

She washed the bread down with a mug of cider and glanced at the breeches that hung over his arm. "Seems rather a small village to be stealing some poor gaffer's only garments."

He snorted and shifted uncomfortably in his chair, hoping she wouldn't notice. "Mayhap 'tis some bonny maid's husband's."

Taking the breeches from his arm, she held them up for inspection. "About my size, is he?" she asked.

He shrugged, nonplussed. "Mayhap she desired something on a grander scale."

"You're not exactly a brute, Highlander."

"I wasn't talking aboot me height, lass."

"Still trying to impress me? Even after I've seen you . . . fully exposed?"

"Ye're na me type, lass, or I would have been even more imposing."

She laughed.

He gritted his teeth. "We should be off."

"Should we?" Something flashed in her eyes. The realization that he had no idea what it was disconcerted him. "I was thinking this might be the best place for us till daylight."

Certain of Keelan's body parts agreed. But what of the ramifications of spending the night in such close quarters? Seeing her. Hearing her. Keelan had never been good at resisting temptation. Hell, maybe he'd never tried. But he could not trust this girl. Not as far as he could spit, and this once, this singular time, he must not fail, for his plans had changed, had morphed into something far different than he had intended. "I dunna think so, lass."

She stared at him a moment, then canted her head as if in sympathy. "So that's it," she said.

"What's it?"

"You don't trust yourself with me."

"Are ye daft?" he snorted, sounding winded. "'Tis ye I canna trust. I had to do the entirety of me business dealings below yon window for fear ye might flee at any given moment. Damned bright-eyed lad all but robbed me blind in exchange for his breeches and a wee bit of his time."

She laughed and set the tray beside the staff, then rose to her feet. The sheet fell aside, baring all, or enough to make him feel faint.

"Tell me, Highlander, what would you pay for a bit of *my* time?" she asked.

Fook it all, his hands were shaking again. "Not as much as I paid the lad for his breeches," he said.

"So you don't find me attractive?" She stretched her arms above her head, pulling her breasts taut between the ragged edges of her bodice.

Merciful Mary! "'Tis yer bloodthirsty nature I find somewhat less than appealing," he said, but the truth was less intelligent, for just then he thought it might be well worth death to lie with her just once.

"You're afraid of me then?" she asked.

"I'm na a complete fool." In fact, he actually was. His windpipe seemed to be seizing up at the sight of her.

She laughed and turned away as if to contest his statement. "Then it won't bother you if I bathe?"

"On the contrary, me nose would welcome the change."

She gave him a smile over her shoulder, then, bending at the waist, fed the remainder of her bread to the lambkin. Her buttocks pressed against the fragile fabric of her simple undergarment. "Have we any soap?" she asked.

He cleared his throat, tried to do the same with his mind. Impossible. "Mayhap," he said, and pretended to search. A bar of soap lay on a worn towel near the basin. He picked it up and turned, only to see her just shedding her drawers. He felt his chin hit his cock.

"Scotsman?" she asked, and pivoted toward him.

"Holy God."

"What's that?" she asked, but he was already recovering, getting his wind, steadying his heart.

"Tell me, lass," he said, and managed, just barely, to fumble the soap into her hands. "What has given you such a fook— refreshing lack of modesty?"

"Maybe it was my profession."

"Which was what?"

She poured water from a chipped pitcher into a basin, dunked the soap, and began washing her hands. "An opera dancer," she said.

"I dunna ken what that is."

"Some say it's a whore."

He nodded numbly, picked up Lambkin, and held her on his throbbing lap.

"But prostitution . . . it's quite a worthy profession really."

Good God. And all this time he'd been keeping himself from her, thinking she was pure, unsullied. Or maybe it was because Chetfield would have killed him. Either way, it seemed like a horrid waste of time now. "I would never have guessed it. Not back at Crevan House."

She rubbed her arms, working up a feeble

lather. He could just see the curve of her left breast past the snowy sweep of her back. "I have the theater to thank for that."

Lambkin curled up on his lap. "So ye were an actress . . . also?"

She laughed. "I was an actress."

He felt breathless. "I'm na sure how Myrtle fits into the image," he said.

She narrowed her eyes for a moment, then laughed. "Myrtle. Mother's milch cow. You've a good memory, Highlander. But I fear I lied. Mother was also a thespian by trade."

What the hell was a thespian? His head was spinning. His wick was more focused. "And yer da? He approved of yer . . . way of life?"

"I didn't actually know my father." She kept her back to him when she said the words. Though it wasn't as if he would have learned anything from her expression even under the best of circumstances. "So what of you, Scotsman? Were you born with a silver spoon?"

"Do I look the gentleman to ye?"

She glanced over her shoulder at him. "A bit."

"I thought ye quite astute until this moment, lass."

She watched him, eyes narrowed. "If not, then why your aversion to . . . the fashionable impure."

"Is that a whore also?"

"Where have you been, Highlander? Certainly not among the improper beau monde."

"I've been busy the last few . . ." Centuries. ". . . years. And I did na say I had an aversion."

She laughed. "I've been walking about all but naked for days. Yet you've barely glanced at me."

"Mayhap I have an aversion to being killed whilst I take me pleasure."

"Ahh. A practical man."

"I like to think so. But I'm flattered that ye are so verra attracted to me own humble self that ye would feel the need to disrobe at every opportunity. Especially considering yer vast amount of experience."

She smiled. "How sweetly naïve of you."

"Are ye saying ye dunna want me, lass?"

She dried her arms, breasts bobbing. "That is, in fact, what I am saying."

"Then why are ye forever strutting aboot . . ." He indicated her with a sweep of his hand. ". . . as ye do?"

"I don't like to see men think too hard."

He raised a brow.

"Admit it, Highlander. You've thought of little else since I removed my first layer some days ago. Regardless of the fact that there were more than a few who hoped to see you dead."

He considered denying it, but 'twould do little good. "What was your price?" His voice sounded dry, unused.

She glanced at him over her shoulder.

He felt flushed, untried, shaken. "For . . . dancing," he said.

Her smile was goodness personified. She must have been peerless on the stage. "You can't afford me, Angel."

"I have a gold bobbed staff."

"No you don't."

The room was quiet. Good God, she was beautiful, stealing his breath, depleting his dubious good sense. "When this is through ye'll na need to sell yerself again."

She caught him from the corner of her eye and slipped her arms into the boy's tunic he'd brought for her. "Maybe I liked it."

He stared.

"It gives people pleasure. What could be more rewarding?"

"Cleaning slop buckets?"

She smiled, turned toward him, and let her gaze slip down his body to his crotch. He remained very still.

"So you still don't want me?"

"Mayhap ye've forgot that ye tried to kill me."

She laughed and sauntered toward him. "I shall make you a proposition." Facing him, she slipped a knee between his legs and nudged them apart. The tunic fell open. One tremendously lucky button caressed her nipple. "If you cannot resist me . . ."

He was sweating like a butcher. "Methinks I've already proved I can, lass."

She raised a brow and lifted Lambkin from his lap, setting her atop the bed. "Surely you're not naïve enough to think I've tried to tempt you?"

"Ye're naked," he croaked.

"Silly Scotsman." She slipped her calf up his thigh. "As I was saying . . . if, after an hour's time, you cannot resist me, then the staff is mine."

"I fear ye've lost yer mind, lassie."

"Not that confident?"

"Na that daft. Na daft enough to trust ye, leastways."

"That is yet to be seen," she said, and sat down on his lap, her bottom warm and soft against his thigh.

He opened his mouth. Maybe planning to object. Maybe hoping to breathe past his lolling tongue. Either way, she interrupted.

"The greater share then," she said, and skimmed her fingers up his cheek.

"What's that?" he rasped.

"If you cannot say no to me I get the larger portion of the spoils."

He remained silent, pretending to think. "And what if ye canna say no to me, lass?"

She laughed and skimmed her knuckles across his lips. "Then it doesn't matter, Scotsman, for the world is about to end."

"Ye are amusing," he said, and refused to shiver.

"And alluring," she added.

He didn't bother to disagree. He was, after all, still trying to convince her he wasn't daft. "Same round aboot."

"What's that?"

"If ye canna resist me," he growled, "I get the lion's share."

Chapter 25

Leaning forward, she kissed him on the lips, mouth open, fingers slipping through his hair.

"A subtle lass," he breathed, eyes shining like midnight stars.

She smiled, because this once, against all good sense, she would allow herself to touch him. Maybe to purge him from her dreams, from her mind. But maybe, in truth, simply because she could not resist. He had captured her heart weeks ago, and now she could not free it, no matter what he was. "In my immensely vast experience, subtlety is wasted on men."

"Mayhap I be a different kind of man."

She licked her lips.

He watched the motion . . . and moaned. The sound soared through her heart like loosed doves, and she smiled.

"Tell me, lass." He was still watching her mouth. "How did ye become so cruel?"

"Maybe it was my tragic childhood."

"Was it?"

"No."

"So ye were doted on constantly by your beloved mum?"

Memories again. Laughter beside the hearth. Poems and readings and candlelit banquets Then death. Sudden and horrid. But she would not tell him that. "That's right."

He watched her, then reaching up, touched his fingers to her cheek. His skin felt like magic against hers. "Liar," he said.

"And whore," she lied.

"So I've heard, but I've na seen a scrap of proof thus far."

"That's because you're wearing far too many clothes."

He glanced down. He didn't even have a shirt. "Absolutely."

Sinking to her knees, she let her breasts squeeze between his thighs. He closed his eyes and set his jaw. "Tight fit," she murmured.

"'Tis bound to happen when you're as well endowed as I."

"I imagine," she said, and leaning forward, kissed his chest.

He shivered, and for that alone, she loved him. "Do ye? Imagine?"

"Ever since I met you." The truth slipped out, braving a cold reception, but he barely seemed to notice the horrid truth.

"'Twas probably the bloodied eye. I'm certain it was terrible becoming."

She remained silent for a moment, forcing herself to be still, to fight past the memories. He was not the first person to suffer, after all. Nor was she to blame. Nevertheless, she could not resist touching the wound on his arm with careful fingertips, feeling the warmth of skin against skin. "I'm sorry," she whispered.

He sighed, his expression unusually somber. "Mayhap I deserved it, lass, since I planned to take his treasure for me own."

She smoothed her hand gently down the corded muscle of his arm. "I can hardly blame you, since I was there for the same purpose." 'Twas true, in an odd, twisted sort of way.

"Aye well . . ." He sighed and smiled with his breathtaking eyes. "Me mum taught me better."

"Perhaps you believe my own mother insisted that I sleep with men for money?"

His gaze caressed her. "How old were ye when she passed, lass?"

She drew away a bit. "What makes you think she is gone?"

He was leaning back in the chair. "I see it in ye," he said, "a sadness. Little matter what she was or was na, ye were yet a lass when she was taken from ye and ye cherished her."

She did not want his pity. Nor would she give him the truth, for soon she must leave him and take his dreams with her. "You're wrong," she said, and trailed her fingers down his midline.

"Oh?" The muscles were taut beneath her hand. He let his eyes fall closed for a moment, but forced them open, teeth gritted in concentration. "Where does she live?"

"In Chiswick."

"All alone is she?"

"Not at all. She has a cat." She skimmed her fingers sideways, between the lovely sheets of muscle that spread across his belly. Fascinating. "A one-eared tabby. Ugly as sin. Hates the sight of me. Spits every time—"

He caught her hand. Their eyes met. "Ye lie, lass."

She raised her brows, and he brought her hand slowly to his mouth. Straightening her fingers, he kissed her palm. Languid feelings flowed like mulled wine, but she kept her tone even. "What makes you think so?"

"Na one could hate ye."

"You only say that because I'm naked."

He smiled against her palm, watched her from beneath his lashes.

"'Tis na true. 'Tis also because ye said I was hung like a horse."

She laughed, breathless. "So you heard that."

He swept his thumb in an arc across her life line and kissed her wrist. Her pulse beat like a throbbing drum against his lips. "What's his name?"

"Whose . . ." Dear God, that felt good. "Whose name?"

"The ugly-as-sin cat," he said, and skimmed his fingers up her arm. Sparkling sensations followed his progress. Amazing really. She had heard of such things. Had heard, but never believed. Never let herself take such a risk, for she had a mission and would not be distracted.

"Lass?"

"Riley." She said the name a bit too fast, cleared her throat, tore her gaze from his progress and tried again. "Riley."

"Ahh." He nodded, kissed the crease of her arm. "Good name, lass, considering ye made it up in the heat of the moment."

"There is no heat," she breathed.

He chuckled against her skin.

She forced a smile. "I am being entirely honest," she said, and slid her hand up his thigh. "You should try it sometime."

"Verra well then, lass. Here's a wee bit of truth for ye. Me own mum died many long years back."

It was a game, all a game, she told herself, and yet she felt something in him. Something she had sensed from the first—a boy, bereft and broken, longing madly for love. "I'm sorry."

"Are ye?" he asked, holding her gaze like a fragile sparrow.

"Of course." Indeed, she felt a blink away from tears, from drawing him into her arms, into her heart, from confessing all. "For it gives you the advantage in this little contest."

"Is that what this is?"

"Certainly," she said, and ran her fingers up his chest. The muscles there quivered in her wake. "A game of chance."

"Then I shall tell ye this too. She died saving me."

Her hand stopped of its own accord. Her heart cracked. For she knew loneliness. Knew it. Hated it. And still, though she was no fool, hoped to conquer it. "From what?"

"Greed," he said. A muscle jerked in his jaw.

"Whose?"

"If I told ye that, lass, I fear I would be showing me hand."

"So that's why you're here," she said, and then, because she could no longer resist, kissed the corner of his lovely mouth. "Because of guilt."

Surprise sparked in his eyes. "The guilt is na mine own."

"No. It is not," she said, certain suddenly that it was true. "And yet you are here with me because of it."

His eyes spoke volumes, but his lips quirked into a roguish smile. "I am here with ye, lass, because ye are all but naked," he said.

She teased him through her lashes and kissed his hard pectoral.

He gritted his teeth. "And for revenge."

She paused, drew back slightly, breath held. "What?"

He stiffened, paused. "Do ye disremember? Ye left me to die, lass."

"I didn't think you would hold such a small offense against me," she said, and brushed her fingers lovingly across his nipple.

The muscles in his thighs jerked against her.

"Chetfield," she said suddenly, and drew back, staring at him. "You want revenge against Chetfield."

His breathing was labored, but in a moment he shook his head, denying.

"What did he do?" she asked, and pressed her breasts against his fevered abdomen. He let his eyes fall closed.

"Ye canna read me mind, lass," he said. "Ye are entirely wrong."

"I only meant . . . There is nothing that is beneath him. No one too kind to wound. I can assure you of that much."

He stared at her, expression shadowed, eyes filled with a dread so deep it sucked her in. "Tell me he did na harm ye, lass."

His dark emotion all but stopped her heart. For there was caring there; there was fear, real and undeniable. For her. Something twisted in her chest. "No," she said, "Not me."

She knew the moment she said the words that they should not be loosed but 'twas too late to draw them back.

"Yer mother," he whispered. "He forced . . ." And then he stopped, his expression a sea of sorrow. "Fie, lass, does he know?"

She was careful, controlled, lest she spill the truth and the thousand awful secrets that lived with it. "Know what?"

A tic jumped in his jaw. Dread shone in his eyes. "Does he ken that ye be his daughter?"

She forced a laugh. "Good gracious, Highlander, I think my nudity has driven you quite mad," she said, and slipped her hand toward the fasteners on his trousers, but he caught her fingers.

"Does he?" The easy smile was gone from his lips. Her stomach felt sour. Memories were crowding in, prodding, torturing.

"Apparently he can't see the familial resemblance." She closed her heart to the horrid, unbelievable truth, but the words came out all the same. "He has my moth . . . *mouth*. Did you not notice?"

"Ahh lass, 'tis so terrible sorry I be." His words were a tender burr against her senses, weakening her, softening her. "So terrible sorry. But 'twas surely best that he did not nurture ye."

She laughed, but the sound was off. "Believe me, I wish I had never heard his name."

He nodded, touched her face. She closed her eyes to the caress. "So ye've come to get a bit of what should be rightfully yours."

She didn't argue. 'Twas safest that way, though she'd come for far more.

"You know the worst of it then." Her throat felt tight, unwilling to loose the words. "I was sired by the devil."

"Lucky lass," he murmured.

She raised her eyes to his.

"There be no pressure then. No reason to be good. To be better. While I—" He gritted his teeth.

"You what?" Her fingers played a little sonnet on his side.

"I was born to an angel. An angel and her hero." There was tragedy in his eyes. "Only the hero died, and the treasure could not save me. Only she could. Only her death. And mine."

There was a riddle here. Almost solved. So close. "Your what?" she asked, but he drew himself from his trance and smiled.

"Ye will never win the bet with talk, lass."

She touched his face. "Your what?" she whispered.

Subterfuge fell away. His eyes looked as old as time. "My death," he said.

Another kink in the riddle. "You don't seem dead."

"But I was," he breathed. "Afore you."

Chapter 26

"**E**xplain," Charity whispered.

Keelan watched her. She was too lovely, too wounded. He could resist neither her body nor her questions. "There was trouble," he said. "In London." He cleared his throat and took the plunge. "Indeed, they thought her a witch." She said nothing. He drew a careful breath. "As I see it now, these many years after, she was certain me life would be forfeit because of it." He shrugged. The movement felt stiff and ungainly, shooting pain through his chest, through his heart. "Therefore she killed me herself. But only for a spell."

"I don't—" she began, but then her eyes widened. "She knew potions."

"Aye. I was so deep asleep that they thought me dead. All but me aunt, me mother's sister. I am told she knew the truth and carried me body back to the Highlands where she yet lived."

"And you remained there for—"

"Above the earth," he hurried to say. "Na ghoulish grave for me."

"Still—"

"Toft . . . an old man . . . me aunt's . . . relation . . . he looked after me, I suppose ye could say, until I wakened."

There was a long pause. "And your mother?"

"Witchcraft was an unforgivable sin." He fought back the memories.

Her face was stricken. "They killed her," she whispered.

He said nothing.

"But . . ." She scowled. "They don't burn witches. Not since—" Her words stopped. Her eyes widened. "When were you born?"

He remained silent. Few knew the truth. So few.

"What year?" she asked, palm warm as sunlight on his chest.

The sensation of skin against skin was beyond compare. "I be older than I appear, lass. Indeed, some call me well preserved."

She was watching him, breath held, lips parted. "Did you know him then?"

"Who?"

"Chetfield. Did you know him as a child?"

She thought him Chetfield's contemporary. But she did not know the truth, that the old man had lived even longer than he, stealing lives not his own. Stealing his father's very breath. "I am becoming bored, lass," he said, and slipping a hand behind her neck, he kissed her with fierce longing. Wanting, nay, *needing,* to forget the past and lose himself in her arms.

Her lips were bright, her eyes dark when he pulled back.

She leaned forward, her luscious mouth inches from his. "Did you know him?"

"Nay, lass, I did na," he lied.

She kissed the hollow of his throat where his heart beat like magic. "So what, then, brought you to Crevan House?"

"As I said, old Thom told me of a treasure."

"And you came for that alone?" she asked, breathing the words against his skin.

He closed his eyes. "'Tis a chunk of gold the size of me head."

"Still . . ." She kissed a wound on his chest, so feather-soft, 'twas little more than a dream. "It seems rather mercenary of you."

"And this from the lass what tried to brain me with it."

"I have rights," she said.

"Because he is yer sire."

"But I'm willing to seduce you for it," she said, slipping her hands down his body. Opening his breeches, she wrapped her hand around him. "Concede," she said, "and I won't humiliate you with this loss."

He gripped the chair with all his feeble strength. "I've been humiliated afore, lass. It's na so verra bad."

"Really?" she said, and lapped her tongue across his engorged head.

"Mary and . . ." His body jerked. His breathing was ragged. "I rather liked it."

"Humiliation?"

"That too."

She rose to her feet, straddling him, nestling him against the core of her being. "Very well then, make love to me, Scotsman."

He managed to smile, though his brow was beaded with sweat. "Nay."

She returned his grin and rocked gently against him. Ecstasy screamed his name. "Stubborn," she whispered, and arched her smooth, ballerina's back. One nipple peeked past the edge of his shirt like a mischievous fairy. She rocked again. He gripped the chair with both hands. "You can't win this one, Highlander."

"I believe ye're wrong," he said, and in that moment her other nipple popped into view. It might have been then that he began chanting Christ's name.

"Concede," she said, and eased back between his legs to the floor.

"Nay." He gritted the word even as she drew his swollen head into her mouth.

He arched against the beautiful pain of it, but she had already withdrawn. Instead she lapped her tongue up his body as she slid higher.

"Concede," she demanded, but he could take no more.

Capturing her wrists, he eased her onto the mattress and kicked free of his clothes. Her tunic fell away, baring all. His thigh nestled against her hot core.

"Ye fight dirty, for such a sweet, young lass," he rasped.

"I'm not sweet, Highlander."

"Oh?" he said, and lowered his lips to hers. Moving slowly, he kissed her, then slid his tongue along the crease of her mouth. Lifting his head slightly, he smiled at her. "Like honey on me lips."

"You're wrong." The words were breathy.

"Truly?" He canted his head and narrowed his eyes. "And where do you keep your sourness?" Bending again, he kissed the corner of her mouth. Her lips parted the slightest degree. He dipped his tongue inside. "Not here," he whispered, and moved back. She licked her lips. He smiled and kissed her chin. It was peaked and adorable. "Or here?"

Easing lower, he skimmed his lips down her neck and up the curve of her breast. Slower now. Concentrating, until he reached the crest and breathed on the nipple. It was as upright as a sapling. She moaned, wriggling beneath him, and that alone was nearly his undoing. But he kept himself still, gazing, soaking her in, for never would there be another moment like this. Nay, for when she knew his true intentions, she would hate him, would do all she could to stop him. But he could not be moved, for this once he had a goal, a purpose greater than himself.

She was quiet now, still, waiting. He leaned closer and kissed the ruddy circle that surrounded the crest of her breast. She breathed something under her breath, and he laughed.

"You can't win this," she snarled, but there was a fine sheen of sweat on her porcelain skin. "You might just as well—" she began, but he kissed her nipple.

She jerked like a marionette. Keelan lifted his head to watch her. She was arched against the mattress, pressed hard into the pillow as her dark hair sprayed like a dark mist across the cotton fabric.

"No sourness there," he murmured, brushing the words against the inside curve of her breast.

"Give up, Scotsman," she growled, and he laughed.

Perhaps it was that sound that brought out her fighting spirit, that made her prop herself on her elbows and glare at him, dark eyes spitting challenge.

"You think I want you?" she asked.

He glanced at the straining nipple so close to his mouth, then kissed it again.

She sucked air through her teeth and bucked against him.

"I believe there be a wee bit of a chance, luv, but who could blame ye?" he asked, and pressed a thigh more firmly to her heat.

She stiffened against him. "Such a great lover, are you?" she rasped.

"I was thinking of me adorable bloodied eye. But in truth, ye'll have to be the judge, lass," he said, and nudged his thigh closer still. She was wet with fever. "Ye, with all yer own vast experience."

"I'm afraid you're going to have to ask someone else," she said.

"Funny thing. I dunna want another," he said, and kissed her again.

She shrieked something high and soft and jerked beneath him.

"Fook it, lass!" he said, overcome by her beauty, her passion as he slid up the length of her sweat-slick form. "Could it be that ye dunna ken how bonny ye are?"

"No." She was breathing through her mouth now, eyes wild, hair mussed. "It couldn't," she said. "For men have been telling me such for as long as I can recall."

"Men are na always so complimentary to whores, lass."

"Maybe I'm a different kind of whore."

He kissed her mouth. She kissed him back, hard and fierce.

"I've known me share of ladies of the night, lass."

"I never doubted," she said, and rocked her body against his thigh.

He moaned at the wet squeeze of heat against him. "There be some talented lassies, that be true."

"Glad to hear you speak well of my contemporaries," she said, and rocked against him. Her nipple brushed his.

He sucked air through his teeth and tried to remember his train of thought. "They generally be less than enthusiastic."

She pressed her body against his chest. "There's a good deal at stake here, Scotsman."

"So . . ." He drew a careful breath. "Ye become wet at the thought of coin, do ye?"

She drew up her legs and pressed against his heat. "Take me," she whispered.

"Be this a dream?" he murmured.

"If I say it is, will you concede?" she asked, and slipped up the length of his shaft.

Sweet Mary, if there was naught but money at stake, he would not hesitate a moment, but would lose himself in her a thousand times, would take her into his life, into his trust, into his heart.

Gritting his teeth against the burning temptation, he eased himself down, stretching full length atop her. His balls slipped against her moist heat.

"How long has it been for ye, lass?"

She wriggled a little beneath him. "The lads at Crevan kept me well entertained."

"I did na think a murdering little bastard would be yer type," he said, and slipped the head of his cock against her entry.

She closed her eyes, breathing hard. "Bear was really quite gentle." Bending her legs, she wrapped them around his back. It felt hopelessly right. Wondrously compelling. "Considering his size." She rocked against him. "Concede."

He gritted his teeth and swore. "Ye're lying."

"He's big as a bull."

"But only half as smart. Give up and keep yer dignity."

"Can't keep what you've never had." She tilted up, opening like a flower. "I didn't swive his brain."

He held himself absolutely still. "Ye did na bed him a'tall. Say ye want it."

"Never," she rasped, and kissed him.

He kissed her back. Teeth clashed against teeth. "Give in."

"You first."

"I've never yet lost a wager."

"It's good to try new things," she whispered.

They were at an impasse, breathing hard, quaking with desire, slick with sweat.

"Together." He whispered the word.

She held perfectly still. "What?"

"We might concede together."

She opened her mouth, eyes bedroom dark. "Yes," she breathed.

"Yes," he agreed, and sank into her.

She was as soft and tight as a velvet glove, gripping him, driving him. He rolled over, putting her on top, seeking her pleasure. She looked dazed, lost in her own world. Grasping her hips, he pressed into her. She gasped and took up the motion, riding hard. There was nothing but pleasure now. Nothing but the sound of her breath, the feel of her skin, pulling him higher, lifting him toward ecstasy.

"Sweet Mary, I canna wait." He gripped her thighs. She grabbed his straining biceps and threw back her head.

Her breasts thrust between the edges of his shirt. He exploded within her.

She came an instant later, shrieking softly before falling against his chest.

He was breathing hard, heart galloping, trying to survive the ecstatic agony. "You flatter me, lass," he gasped.

She barely managed to shake her head in confusion.

His chest ached with his efforts to breathe. "Ye flatter me with yer little squeal of pleasure."

Her own air came no easier. "I didn't squeal."

"Ye—" he began, but suddenly he realized the truth.

The noise had come from the stairway.

Chapter 27

They froze. The inn was absolutely silent. No reason to think there was trouble. No reason whatsoever.

"They're coming," he whispered, and somehow she knew it was true.

She nodded jerkily. And then they were scrambling, throwing on clothes, grabbing possessions. They glanced at the door, turned in unison toward the window.

"Go," he whispered, snatching the chair from the floor and propping it against the door.

She swung the window open. It creaked. They froze, staring at each other, hearts pounding. The door latch groaned rustily. They shot their attention in that direction, but he was already pushing her through the opening.

It was as black as sin outside their window. She searched for purchase with her fumbling toes. A crack. Too small. Vines. They gave way beneath her weight.

The chair rattled against the door, but did not give.

"Chetfield," Keelan hissed.

And then toeholds no longer mattered. She scrambled downward, praying and gasping. Something bumped. She glanced up in time to see Keelan turn slowly toward the door.

"Come on," she rasped, but he moved away, out of sight. Beneath her shivering foot a vine pulled free from the wall. She stifled a gasp, searching desperately for another toehold. There, there. She crept lower. Almost to the street.

"Lord Tempton."

She heard the nasal voice from above, stifled through the door and her own terror.

"I need a word with you, sir. I fear there's been a bit of trouble."

She froze, listening. Not Chetfield's voice at all. The innkeeper's. Wasn't it?

Another vine gave way. She scrambled to the earth, legs shaking, breathing hard, trying to hear.

"I thought I might find you here."

She spun about and he was there. The nightmare made flesh. "Roland!"

He appeared as a shadow in the darkness, stepping forward. "We've been looking for you."

She tightened her grip on the staff and shimmied away, skirting the wall. Where were the others? Upstairs? Outside the door? Or was it truly the landlord who'd spoken?

"You're not scared of me, are you, girl?"

Her head was spinning, grappling for ideas. "You weren't very . . . y' weren't very nice back at Crevan."

"No." He chuckled. "I apologize for that, but Lord Chetfield was distraught. I was only trying to detain you."

"You weren't trying to . . . to . . ."

He shook his head. "Of course not, Cherie. I wouldn't do that to a sweet maid like yourself, but I was too rough. My apologies. I wasn't myself."

"Who was you?"

His teeth gleamed in the darkness. "I was a fool." He took a step forward. She forced herself to stand her ground, lifted her chin.

"Truth is . . ." She made her voice tremble. It wasn't difficult. "I'm glad you're here."

"Are you?"

She nodded upward. "The Scotsman, he took me hostage."

"I thought you two were friends. That you'd been planning this theft."

Dammit! She'd lost track of her lies. "He made me say them things . . . back at the cave. It was his plan, should we be found. Said he'd kill me if'n I didn't play along. I tried to get away. Thought I was free and clear once I got on that horse. But he found me again. Threatened me with . . . with horrible things."

Roland tsked as he took another step. "Well then, I'll make sure he suffers for that. Not to mention the rap on my head." His eyes gleamed. "Chetfield's a mite put out, you see. What with his staff gone missing and all."

Her stomach cramped up hard. Her fingers trembled on the lumpy gold. "I was out of me mind with fear. Grabbed the first thing what came to hand."

"Of course you did."

"Didn't know it was important to him."

"How could you?" He grinned. "You're little more than a half-wit."

Where was Bear? And what of the others? "It's true I ain't never been too smart. Me mum—"

A noise rustled in the bushes. She shot her gaze toward it, and suddenly Roland was on her, fingers tight on her throat.

318

She stumbled sideways, clawing at his hand. Her shoulder struck the wall. His grip tightened, squeezing off her air, crushing her windpipe.

"Damned lying bitch," he snarled.

She tried to break his grip, but her knees were giving way. Terror tore at her insides. But her mind was still kicking.

Jerking her gaze to the side, she snarled, "Hit him!"

Roland twisted sideways. A moment's reprieve. She brought her knee up with all the strength she could muster, driving it between his legs, but her aim was off. The blow caught his thigh, knocked him backward. She scrambled away, but he was already following. His fingers tangled in her hair. She screamed as she tumbled backward. Straddling her head, he pulled a knife from his coat. His eyes gleamed.

But something streaked down from above, knocking him away.

Charity scrambled to her feet, poised to flee, but Roland lay still. Only Keelan remained, just clambering to his feet, Lambkin tucked into the leather pack tied across his back.

"How—" she began, but he grabbed her hand and pulled her along. And then they were running, racing down a rutted alley. A dog snapped at Keelan's pants leg, but he shook it off. An opening appeared on their right. Charity sped down it. Stone walls lay on both sides. She stumbled over unseen objects. The shadows were as black as sin, but she dared not slow down. Dared not fall behind. But suddenly she realized she was alone.

She turned, panting, searching the darkness. Keelan was there, twenty feet back, on the ground.

She rushed to him, grabbed his arm. "Get up!"

"Me ankle—"

"Spread out," rasped a voice. Chetfield. At the mouth of the alley.

She felt Keelan stiffen beneath her fingers. He pushed her away. She shot her attention toward the faint light at the opposite end of the lane.

"Lass," Keelan whispered, "ye must—"

"Lie down," she ordered.

He shook his head, but she was already on the ground, stretching out in the deepest shadows that lay along the wall. She pulled him down with her, yet he was visible, the bare skin of his back, the lamb's pearly head. Hands shaking, she unbuttoned her tunic, pushed Lambkin to the side, and crept over the top of them, spreading the dark fabric over all.

Footfalls shuffled nearer.

"Where are the others?" Chetfield asked.

"Link is searching the stable." An unknown voice, dark and low. "Cleve—"

"They're gone." Frankie's voice was an eerie rumble in the darkness. "Disappeared. Like magic. We shoulda never—"

"Quiet," Chetfield hissed. The world went silent. Charity could feel him drawing nearer. She closed her eyes, held her breath, felt her heart pound like thunder against Keelan's back.

They passed by, footfalls shuffling in the darkness.

She remained as she was, frozen, barely breathing, until Keelan nudged her off. She managed to rise to a crouch then, peering into the blackness. But the trio was gone from sight. Even so, her knees barely straightened when Keelan pulled her to her feet. They kept to the deepest shadows, slinking forward. Almost there now. The head of the alley loomed. She could feel Keelan's hand on her back, urging her forward. She turned the corner, ready to bolt, and bumped into Bear.

"Hey." He grabbed her arm in a meaty fist, imprisoning her, freezing her.

But in that instant Keelan thrust Lambkin into his face. She bleated. The giant stumbled back. Charity leapt away, but the others had heard and were already dashing noisily back down the alley toward them.

It was naught but a footrace then, darting from shadow to shadow, shivering in holes, racing through forests. It was blackness and terror and pain, until morning found them curled amid the bracken in a dew-covered dale.

Charity awoke first. She glanced about, assessing, remembering. A hundred errant memories stormed through her mind. Keelan lay behind her, arm warm against her ribs. So right. So good. But things were not what they seemed. They were on diverging paths, and she dare not deviate from hers, not on pain of death. She was not safe. Would never be. Not as long as Chetfield walked the earth. Neither would anyone in her company be exempt from the old man's awful vengeance.

She turned toward the Scotsman. He opened his eyes, as silvery blue as a mountain stream, and for a moment she was struck dumb by the beauty of him, by the gut-wrenching intensity of her feelings, the horrible longing to touch him, to lay her head against his heart, to tell him the truth. But the truth would not save him. Only action would see him safe, only the fulfillment of the promise she'd made to her mother, to herself.

"I'm flattered," she said finally. "Truly I am, but I'm not that sort."

He watched her, face sleepy, disheveled hair barely caught behind his corded neck. "What the devil are ye talking aboot?"

She tilted her head and filled her eyes with sympathy. "You're in love with me."

"What?" He sat up, scrubbed his face. Lambkin wandered up, still chewing, a buttercup thrust at a jaunty angle from her tiny mouth.

"You're an attractive man . . . for a Scot," she said. "And I'll admit I'll not soon forget our night together, but . . ." She rose to her feet and brushed off her breeches. "I don't take partners."

"Partners!" He rose with her but more slowly, favoring his ankle, his back. "I never suggested pairing up with ye."

Tilting her head, she gave him a pitying glance from the corner of her eye and walked away, heading south.

"It was naught more than a bit of sport," he said.

"Then why did you save my life?"

"I never—"

"Jumping from a window." She shook her head. "'Tis said love can make the greatest coward brave."

"Be ye calling me a coward?"

"No." She stopped, eyes wide as she glanced back over her shoulder. "I'm calling you brave," she said, and continued on. "But I have no time for a husband."

"Husband!" he hissed. "I fell from the damned window."

"And coincidentally crushed Roland. Of course." She laughed. "But regardless, I think we should hasten to London and sell the staff. I'll take my sixty percent and we can—"

She heard his footfalls stop.

"What's that?"

She turned, stared at him. "Surely you don't think you won that wager."

"Ye agreed to concede together."

She gave him a look. "I said we could consider conceding together. I would have explained further, but you seemed in a terrible rush to . . . Well, you know," she said, and turned away.

He hurried after her.

"If I recall correctly, ye were in a bit of a hurry yerself, lass."

"I didn't mean to sully your reputation as a lover," she said. "Indeed, should someone ask, I will say you were quite good."

He opened his mouth to object, but she strode away, keeping a careful distance between them.

* * *

The weather turned cool that night, but they did not dare risk a fire. Keelan sat some yards away with his back to a tree, knees bent. Lambkin lay with her head on his lap. His shirt had been left at the inn. Charity could see a broad patch of lean, tight-packed muscle, and just the suggestion of a wound. She could touch that muscle, could kiss that wound. Of course, Lambkin would have to be convinced to give up her spot on his crotch. The idea of fighting the little creature for his attention made her feel fidgety and ridiculous.

"Steak," she said. "I'm going to have a pound of steak for every meal once I sell the staff."

Keelan turned toward her, magic eyes shining in the darkness. "Ye mean once *we* sell it, sure."

She shrugged. "What will you do with your share, Highlander?"

He glanced down, stroked the lamb's ears. "Mayhap I'll buy meself a fine town house in Mayfair."

"Mayfair?" She said the word with surprise. The world was her stage. "Whatever will you do with Lambkin in Mayfair?"

Keelan rose restlessly to his feet. The lamb did the same, gazing up at him. "Might ye be thinking I'll be building me life around her?"

The little animal pressed her body lovingly against his leg.

"It seems quite likely, actually."

"Well, ye dunna know me well, lass."

"Don't I?" Probably not. Still, despite it all, she would like to. But he would not forgive her, not when she'd done what she must. "Because it seems fairly clear that you'd . . ." She paused, playing her part and drawing her name in the dirt with a broken twig.

"What?"

"Nothing. Perhaps we should be off. How far to the nearest port?"

"What were ye aboot to say?"

She shrugged as if loath to speak. "I only thought that it seems fairly obvious you'd give your life for us."

He scoffed. "For you?"

"And the lamb," she hurried to add. "I mean, don't misunderstand, Highlander, there's nothing wrong with that. It's simply that . . . I'm not that sort."

He tilted his head, watching her. "I ken the truth, lass," he said finally. "There be little need to pretend."

"Oh? And what truth is that?"

"'Tis ye that be in love with me."

And wasn't that a fine joke at her expense? There was a time, not so long ago, when she could have had her pick of husbands. But that was before she'd learned the entirety of the terrible truth—that some bastards don't die. They simply took what belonged to others, their dreams, their futures, their essence. She hid a shudder. "What an interesting theory."

He smiled. "When I fell in the alley, ye stretched atop me, hiding me from Chetfield."

"But of course I did, for if they had found you, they would surely have found me as well."

"Is that what ye tell yerself, lass?"

"I never lie."

He snorted. "Ye do nothing but lie."

"True," she said, and laughed.

He opened his mouth to object, but she continued on. "I've been thinking."

"God save me."

"I believe it would be best if I went alone to sell the staff." She was building a world. Brick by brick, constructing a universe he would believe. What would happen when it all tumbled down? When the staff was gone? When he hated her?

His expression was blank. She hurried on. "Not as I am, of course. I will transform myself into a lady. A baroness perhaps. From Coventry. Lady Boughton."

"Ye truly believe I would trust ye alone with the staff."

"Not me. The baroness."

"I may actually trust her less."

"Think of it . . ." She gestured at him with an open hand. "A ragged Scotsman selling a thing of such value in London. 'Twould never be believable. A constable would be on you before you got through their front doors."

"While ye . . ."

"While the Lady Boughton . . ." She batted her eyes at him. "Will be more than welcome in La Bijou."

"La Bijou?"

"A little shop on Bond Street. I stole a snuff-box from there once." In fact, she had not. But she had sold one there, had taken the money to buy information, little pieces of history that trailed back a hundred-plus years.

"And tell me, lass, how do ye hope to transform yerself into this lady of such sterling quality?"

"Well, I will need a good night's sleep first, certainly. Do you suppose you could choose an inn where Chetfield won't break down the door and try to kill us?"

He gave her a grim smile. "Some folk be a mite chary aboot being cheated out of their fee, lass, and I have no coin. How do you plan to pay for the room?"

She scrunched her face, then brightened. "I could seduce the innkeeper."

His expression darkened, but he turned away. "Then mayhap we will na have to pay extra," he said.

And she laughed.

By midday they had reached a hustling little river. Lambkin grazed contentedly as they rested their backs against smooth-barked ash trees and watched the glistening waves hurry by.

"A boat would be helpful," Charity said, thankful for the moment's reprieve.

"If ye're wishing," Keelan countered, leaning his dark head against the silvery bark, "ye might hope for a fine meal and a feather bed."

"My apologies," she said, and opening the reticule that still slanted across her chest, she pulled out a cloth bundle. "No bed, but I do have these." Untying the cloth, she revealed two biscuits and a pair of plums.

He stared at her. "Ye had food all along?"

She handed him half the meal. "I like to be prepared."

"What else do ye have in there? A hot bath and a pint of ale?"

She shrugged and took a bite of fruit. "Of course. But I'm waiting until evening to enjoy them."

"Merciful Mother," he said, and ate the biscuit. It was stale and hard—ambrosia to taste buds that had all but given up.

By dusk they'd been walking for an eternity. Keelan's ankle throbbed with a life of its own.

"How far do you think until we reach Felixstowe?" Charity asked. They had carefully avoided Falkenham and the other hamlets that dotted their path to the port.

Keelan shook his head. "I fear I've lost track—" he began, but just then they topped the crest of a hill. Below them, the river took a leisurely bend. A simple raft was moored in the quiet bay, and some furlongs away, a small hunting lodge was nestled, snug and happy, in a copse of horse chestnuts. Its lone window was broken and its mortar crumbling. Never was there a lovelier sight.

"Ain't life a whistle," Charity cooed. With one glance at each other, they hustled down the hill to the cottage. A song thrush sang in the treetops, but all else was quiet. Settling Lambkin in a patch of wild grasses, Keelan knocked on the slanted door. When no one answered, he called hello and stepped inside. Cobwebs stretched across the corners of the single room, and dust lay in a sheer sheet upon the tilted tabletop and rough-hewn floors.

"Feels like 'ome," Charity said, adopting her old accent and brushing past him. A white cloth bag hung from a hook in the ceiling. She took it down and glanced inside, then looked up, eyes gleaming.

"Supper," she said, and handed him a dusty pitcher. "You fetch water. I'll start a fire."

By the time Keelan reentered the little cottage, she was feeding scraps of kindling to a small flame that licked at the blackened stone.

He set the water beside her on the floor. "We will need to gain passage to London," he said. "Thus I've been thinking—there be those what believe I'm a healer. I could—"

"Why make it more difficult than it has to be?" she asked. Dipping her hand into her reticule, she pulled out a small leather pouch and tossed it to him. It thudded quietly against his palm.

"What's this then?" Loosing the strings, he opened the bag, dumped the contents into his hand, and stared dumbly. "Ye had coin all along?"

"My mother said never to leave home without a bit of jingle in your pocket."

"Where the bloody hell did ye get it?"

Pouring water into a smoke-blackened kettle, she hung it on the metal arm anchored in the fireplace and swung it back over the fire. "My mother?" she asked.

"The coin!"

"Oh." She nodded, dumped a bit of the remaining water into a wooden basin, and washed her hands. "I stole it from the inn's other guests while you were sleeping." Drying her hands on her tunic, she found a wooden spoon on a nearby shelf and stirred the wheat meal. "You sleep like the dead. But you already know that, don't you?" she said, and laughed.

"Ye were sneaking aboot in the middle of the night! Risking yer life?"

She shrugged. "I'm a thief, Highlander. 'Tis what I do."

He watched her, mind churning. Mayhap she truly was Chetfield's daughter as she claimed, but he could see none of him in her. No evil. No cruelty. Oh aye, she would fight if cornered, but if truth be told, she could have left him to drown long ago. Could have had the staff to herself. "Is it?" he asked.

"Yes," she said, and taking the two steps between them, gave him an openmouthed kiss.

His legs threatened to buckle.

"Sit down and eat," she said and glancing over her shoulder, looked him up and down. "Before you fall over."

They ate in silence, Keelan's head spinning. The meal was dry and dissatisfying, but it filled his belly.

"I'll clean the pot," she said. "You'd best see to your little one."

He didn't respond, but retrieved the pitcher and stepped outside. Lambkin trotted up, little hooves clicking on the irregular cobblestones that made a meandering course to the door. Twilight had settled in, night fast on its heels. Keelan made his way into the woods to find a private spot, then washed up and returned to the cottage with the lamb under his arm.

"So your baby is safe?" Charity asked. She was turning down the blankets on a saggy mattress perched on tight-stretched ropes beneath rough-cut planks.

"She is na me babe."

She laughed as she smoothed out the sheets. "There is wheat meal left if you'd like to give her a bit."

Fetching the bag, Keelan sat down on the room's only chair. Lambkin hustled across the irregular floor, little ears bobbing. In a moment she was nibbling meal from his hand with velvety lips. He scratched her back as she ate. "Tell me, lass . . ." With the kiss behind him, his mind had churned slowly back into action. "How long have ye known yer father's identity?"

"For some years," she said. "So your beloved is doing well?"

Lambkin glanced up, adoring eyes soft in the flickering firelight. "She be na me beloved." He scooped out another handful of grain. "Did yer mother tell ye his name?" he asked.

She didn't answer.

"Lass," he began, and turned.

But she was naked. Just crawling into bed, her ass looked as tight and round as a cherry. The air left his lungs like the whoosh of a bellows.

She turned to glance over her shoulder, then slipped between the covers. "This isn't going to be a problem for you, is it, Highlander?"

"Fook!" he said, and wished he were still dead.

Chapter 28

Lambkin licked the last of the grain from his hand, then turned and trotted toward the bed. Lying on her side, Charity lifted her onto the mattress. The blankets dipped nearly to her ruddy nipples.

"Aren't you tired?"

"Nay."

She settled Lambkin on the far side of her. "Truly?" she asked, and yawned. "We've been walking for hours. I would think you'd be—"

"What be ye aboot, lass?"

She smiled lazily and sat up. The blankets dropped lower. His gaze did the same. His breath caught in his chest.

"I promise I can resist your advances if that's your concern," she said.

"Resist . . ." He snorted and cleared his head,

but she was so naked. "'Twas *ye* who couldn't resist *me*, if ye'll remember."

"I remember quite well," she said, and glanced up through her lashes.

Her eyes were as innocent as a babe's. But her breasts . . .

He was surprised to find himself pacing. "I've na wish to be killed in me sleep, ye ken."

She blinked. "You think I'm going to try to kill you?" Her tone was astounded.

He stopped. "I dunna ken what the devil to think. Things are na what they seem. That much I know."

"What things?"

He shook his head. "Why did ye come here?"

"For the staff, same as you," she said. "'Tis priceless."

He waited, breath held. "So ye plan to sell it."

Her eyes were steady. "Don't you?"

A hundred secrets flashed through his mind. "'Tis why I first came here."

"We are in agreement then," she said, and smiling, patted the mattress. "For twenty percent more I'll let you share my bed."

"*Yer* bed."

"What's a whore without a bed?"

He narrowed his eyes, remembering with lurid accuracy their one night together. "I've been wanting to talk to ye aboot that, lass."

"Talk?" Reaching up, she pulled the blankets aside, slowly revealing the swell of her breasts, the curve of her waist, the flare of her hips. "Is that truly what you wish to do?"

He held himself perfectly still. "I dunna think ye are . . . what ye say ye are, lass."

She gave him an amused glance. "And that after I offered to give myself to you for a price."

Pacing to the saggy mattress, he sat upon the edge. "Ye are bonny, lass, whatever else ye may be."

She smiled. "Not to mention skilled," she said, and leaning forward, kissed him gently.

He tried to resist, to keep his head, but . . . "Ten percent," he said, knowing it was all a twisted lie. But where did the bends fall exactly?

She cupped his cheek in a gentle hand. Her lips were magic against the corner of his mouth. "Eighteen," she whispered.

"Twelve."

"You are quite well built," she said, and slipped her fingers, soft as a dream, over the crest of his chest. "For a Scot."

He tensed against her velvet touch. Firelight flickered on her impish face. "And ye are quite bonny," he said, trying to remember to breathe, "for a . . . woman."

"I see you've inherited the famous silver tongue of your ancestors," she said, and rippled the flats of her nails down his abdomen.

"Good Lord, woman," he hissed, "I'm blessed to remain conscious where you're concerned."

"Flattery, Scotsman?"

He winced. "I fear it might be honesty."

Her expression softened. Her sunrise lips quirked. "Seventeen percent then."

Reaching out, he slipped his hand behind her neck, feeling the silky luxury of her hair against his fingers. He tilted his head, holding her gaze.

"Fifteen," he whispered.

"Done," she murmured.

He leaned in breathlessly.

"But stay on your side of the bed."

He stopped. "What?"

"I said you could share my bed, Scotsman. Not my body."

"Ye jest." The words were a croak.

She stared at him, brows raised haughtily, then: "In fact I do," she said, and kissed him.

Time stood still then. She was soft and smooth, her skin like magic beneath his fingers, her voice downy soft against his ear. Every word was a caress, every move a symphony.

He stretched out beside her, skimming his hand down every blessed hollow, every stunning crest. Her fingers were a solemn blessing against his skin, touching, healing.

Entering her was ecstasy. They moved slowly, catching the rhythm, riding the wave. She tilted her head into the pillow beneath her and wrapped her legs around his bunched buttocks.

He quivered at the utopia. Breathing quickened, muscles quivered. Sweat slicked her body, shining like dew on her polished skin. Her fingers were claws against his back now as she pulled him closer, closed around him. Each breath was a gasp, each moment a dream until she arched sharply against him. With a shudder of ecstasy, he collapsed, rolling beside her, taking her in his arms.

Skin against skin, they lay together, hair entwined, hearts surrendered until sleep took them on feathery wings.

Keelan opened his eyes. Dawn was just gracing the world. He turned his head, blurrily searching his dreams for reality. Charity. He remembered every minute of the night just past, every inch of her skin against his, and turned, but the pillow beside him was empty.

She was gone. Far gone, and Chetfield was coming. He knew it, felt it in the core of his being, perhaps had felt it for hours. She had lied to him, lain with him, and fled. Yet he could feel naught but relief, for she was safe. Something in him cried for the joy of it.

From outside the simple cottage came the faint rustle of footsteps. Keelan sat up just before the door burst open.

Roland leapt inside, scanned the single room, and grinned. Chetfield entered next, his movements graceful, his expression unruffled. "Mr. McLeod," he said, "I've missed you."

Keelan exhaled carefully, let his muscles relax. Beside him, little Lambkin shivered. He placed a quieting hand on her back.

Behind Roland, a half-dozen men blocked the doorway.

Chetfield's eerie gaze roamed the narrow space. "It warms my heart to see you again, boy, but our little Charity seems to be conspicuously lacking."

"Aye." He breathed the word like a prayer. "She does that." With any luck she had reached Felixstowe by now. If he were truly blessed, she had already secured a ship, but regardless, he would delay the old man as long as possible, lead him astray, buy her every moment possible. For he loved her. The simple truth struck him softly. He loved her. 'Twas as uncomplicated as that. In the end, it mattered naught whether she was whore or virgin, thief or saint. She was his beloved, would be so until his last breath was drawn.

"And the staff with her," Chetfield said.

"'Tis sorry I was to see it go," Keelan replied, rising slowly to his feet and pulling on his borrowed breeches. The world felt strangely disconnected, as if he were not quite a part of it. As if he too had reached the port and was even now sailing toward a new life. A life of peace.

"You shall tell me where to find her, Mr. Mac-Leod," Chetfield said, and Keelan turned toward him. Reality sifted in like dust motes in the sunlight. And in his mind's eye he saw her, standing at the prow of a ship, bonny hair blowing, eyes shining like heaven's stars as she raised the staff above the curling waters. The waves reached for it, calling it down. She opened her hands, and then it fell, tumbling through sky and sea until it sliced into the living ocean, sinking, turning, claimed by the dark depths that had spewed it forth.

She had come to steal the staff, aye. But not for herself. He smiled, for he knew the truth, knew what he must do. Delay. Fight. Die. 'Twas as simple as that.

"I would tell ye gladly," Keelan said, and faced the old man, eye to eye, unbeaten, unafraid. This once he would not fail. "But I fear I canna."

"Oh?" Chetfield's eyes gleamed gold and predatory. "And why is that, Mr. MacLeod?"

"Because ye are evil itself," Keelan said, and charged forward. The old man went down hard. Keelan scrambled for the door. Behind him, Chetfield shrieked. Roland cursed. Keelan flew toward the window, dived through the opening, rolled to his feet.

A fist caught him square in the face.

He stumbled. His back struck the wall. He tried to recover, to escape, but a score of hands were on him, dragging him to his feet.

And suddenly Chetfield was there, wavering in front of his eyes.

"Mr. MacLeod."

He fought his way through the smoky mists.

"Where's the girl?"

Keelan smiled. The blood tasted warm and metallic in his mouth. "She's gone," he said. Safe. Too smart for them. Too smart for them all.

"Oh? And the staff, where might that be?"

"I sold it. To a fellow in Falkenham. A merchant, he was."

"So you stole it from the girl." The old man tsked and stepped forward. "And disposed of it. Not very gentlemanly of you."

His head was reeling. He braced his legs against the motion, holding on. A score of men were spread across the moor, watching. "I'm na much of a gentleman."

"You didn't kill her, I hope."

His head bobbled on his neck. "She was verra still when she struck the water. 'Twas a shame, for she was a bonny lass, and a scrapper." His voice sounded wispy.

The old man chuckled. "She was that. Our little Charity. Who would have thought we had a thief in our midst, aye?"

"Life's a whistle."

"Isn't it? Where did you leave her?" Chetfield asked, and stepped forward.

"In the river where—"

The fist felt like a hammer against Keelan's ear. His head wobbled back.

"You see, Mr. MacLeod, I don't think you harmed our little Charity at all. I believe, in fact, that she played you for a fool, took the staff, and left you to my men's tender mercies. So I shall ask you again. Where—"

"Holy Christ!" Keelan rasped and jerked, for suddenly the truth flashed in his mind's eye and he saw it all, the horror, the honor, the courage of the girl he would cherish for all time. "I see it now. Ye killed her mother."

The giant hands holding him shook.

Chetfield scowled. "Mr. Roland, restrain our Scottish friend if you please. You others may rest for a time." The brutes backed off, eyes wary.

"So I killed someone?" Chetfield asked. "'Tis entirely possible. Might you know her name?"

The images rolled out in Keelan's mind, leaving him breathless, horrified, aching. "She was an actress. A great beauty." She smiled coquettishly from his thoughts. "Ye learned she'd had yer child. And ye wanted it."

"Victoria," Chetfield rasped. "Of course. The girl has her mother's smile. I first saw her on the stage at Covent Garden. Glorious. Mesmerizing." He refocused, narrowed his eyes. "But in the end, she was spiteful. Hid the brat. Hid her from her lawful father. My only blood kin."

And he'd bludgeoned her to death for her kindness. Keelan winced at the images. "She knew." A small girl sobbed in his mind, rocking inconsolably over her mother's flaccid hand. A young woman vowed vengeance, searched for answers, planned with careful precision. "Learned the truth." He turned his gaze to Chetfield. "Figured out the truth. The mystery of the staff. You were never meant to have it, old man. 'Twas a piece of the sea. The depths have called it home."

"So you know its history, do you, boy?" he asked.

Memories flared in Keelan's mind. A thousand misty, sleepless nights. All come to this end despite his larcenous plans. "I know you're the devil."

"The devil!" He laughed. "So dramatic."

"Ye took his voice," Keelan said. The memories were a burning ache in his mind. "But ye could na take his courage."

"Who are you?" Chetfield hissed.

He could not straighten, but he lifted his head, caught the old man's eye. "I be Keelan of the ancient Forbes. Iona's Angel. Hallaway's heir."

"You lie!" The words were a rasp of anger.

"You killed me da."

The old man was quiet, stunned to silence, but then he laughed. "Did I? 'Twas so long ago I barely remember. But yes, I do recall now. He was crippled after I left him at sea. Crippled and broken. And your mother . . ." He tsked. "She was burned to death if I remember correctly. A witch, they said. And I see now that it was true, for here you are after all these years. I assume it was she who preserved you? Who kept you alive?"

Keelan said nothing, only watched, listened, prayed.

"And now here we are, having come full circle. I hold the father's son in the palm of my hand. The son, trying vainly to protect the woman he loves."

"Ye think I love her?"

"In fact, I do."

"She tried to kill me," he said, and smiled at the thought.

"Where is she?"

"I dunna ken. I left—"

The pain struck him like a slice of death. He gritted his teeth, holding back the scream.

"You know where she is."

"I swear, she be gone from this—"

Pain again, so sharp it crushed his lungs.

"Very noble of you, Keelan of the ancient Forbes. Very chivalrous. But you are not the man your father was. And the girl is nothing like your lovely mother."

Blood dripped from his mouth, hot as lava on his chest.

"Your mother," Chetfield said, "the witch."

"She hurt na one." The words were no more than a whisper sifted through pain.

"You jest. She kept me from my treasure. Just as you are doing now. We took it from the sea, your father and I together, took it from a sunken ship. The *Red Dragon*." He smiled, remembering.

346

"There were rumors of mutiny, of blood running like water. A bad omen, 'twas said. But your father was determined. I was his loyal first mate, you know. Always faithful. Asked for naught, until I saw that one thing . . . that solitary prize, the staff. Humble really. Simple. Just an object of metal and wood. But he was greedy." His eyes gleamed with remembered avarice. "Said we must give it to the Crown. But I knew his true intent." His lips parted. He glanced up, imagining something that was not there. "Have you seen a ship ablaze, boy? 'Tis a glorious thing. A beautiful sight. Firelight dancing like molten gold on the open sea." His gaze shifted to Keelan's face again. He smiled. "I took the staff, all the coin I could manage, and left the others to die. Returned to London to tell them all of the *Intrepid*'s brave crew. How valiantly they had succumbed to the unquenchable blaze. How narrowly I had escaped at the last moment. But your father . . ." He shook his head. "He was a stubborn man. All but dead when he reached his wife's tender arms. But perhaps even then she could have healed him with her witchy ways. I told him how thrilled I was that he had survived, of course. I told him of my own harried escape, but he saw the staff and I knew. Knew there was nothing else I could do."

"Ye killed him."

He nodded rhythmically. "With the staff. But you figured that out, didn't you, boy. You know it gave me life. His life. His voice." He laughed, a poor imitation of the man Keelan had loved. "I knew the moment I saw it that it was special, that it had powers untold. Powers taken from the dark depths. But to give me another's years . . ." He shook his head. "That was entirely unexpected. I had to try it again. Sometimes with beasts." He lifted a graceful hand to indicate the golden sheen of his eyes. "Sometimes with those who displease me." He shrugged. "So you see why I, quite literally, cannot live without it."

Keelan shook his head. Unconsciousness wavered nearer. But that was just as well. For he could spill no truths then. She was safe. He smiled. Blood dripped from his lips. "You'll na find it. Na again."

"You think not?"

"Ye're beaten, Kirksted. Beaten at yer own bloody game."

"You're wrong, Scotsman."

He shook his head. She was safe. "Ye will die."

"You're wrong!" he roared. Maybe it was Chetfield. Maybe it was inside his head. But the old man was swinging for him. He thought himself past caring, yet his body could not give up.

He tried to shift away, but agony exploded like fireworks, knocking him back. The world spun. He was dragged up, legs dangling beneath him.

"Look at me! Look at me!" Chetfield snarled.

He tried. But the world was hazy and dim, the ground shifting erratically.

"Look at me, you sniveling cur, or I'll kill you now."

Relief washed through him. Death. Silence. He would not betray her. After all these years, in this final, sterling moment, he would prove himself. "Please," he begged, knowing his plea would do naught but raise the bloodlust in Chetfield's damned soul. Words were hard to form through broken lips, but this was his last ploy, his final hope, and he dared not fail. "Don't kill me. She is dead. The staff is gone. There is naught I can do to bring them back."

Chetfield drew himself up. "Then there is little reason to let you live, is there, Scotsman?" he said, and raised his cane.

"I am here."

Keelan seemed to hear her voice through the roiling mists in his mind, heard it, recognized it, loved it with a terrible passion that seared his soul.

"Nay, lass." He raised his head, frantically searching the nearby forest. "Go back."

"He's mad," someone whispered, but in that instant she stepped from the woods, dressed all in black, dark eyes solemn in her beloved face.

"Release him," she said.

Keelan tried to gain his feet, but others had joined Roland, holding him down. He felt terror burn his throat like bile, felt tears scorch his face. "Nay, lass, please."

Their eyes met. "Life's a whistle, Highlander," she said, then: "You will turn him free, old man, and I will tell you where I've hidden it."

"But my dear . . ." Chetfield began. They were only yards apart. "Now that you're here, I believe I can force you to tell me whatever I wish," He nodded toward Roland.

She raised her hand. It was fisted around the handle of a knife. "If they come within twenty feet of me, I'll put this blade through my heart," she said. "I swear on my mother's grave, I will."

Chetfield stared at her. "Very well then. I shall release him."

"Nay," Keelan croaked. His ear was plugged with blood. The world seemed strangely distant. "I'll na go."

"Place him on the raft," she said, nodding toward the river.

Keelan shook his head. The earth wavered.

He staggered. "I'll na—" They were dragging him toward the water. It chuckled in his mind, laughing at his weakness, at his failings. He fought against them, but it was futile. Their feet splashed into the waves. He planted his own against the stones, wrestling, cursing. The vessel rocked and sank beneath his weight. They pushed onto the rotting wood. His legs folded beneath him.

"Tie him there," she ordered.

"So Charity, my dear." Chetfield's voice was convivial. "Tell me, do you hope to save him or torture him?"

She said nothing, but even from where he sat, he could see the tears glistening like diamonds on her bonny cheek.

"So it's true," Chetfield mused. "How charming."

Frankie sliced through the raft's tether and wound it about Keelan's wrists.

"Not too tight." Her words were broken.

Keelan cursed, jerking futilely against the restraints, but Frankie was already stepping off the tilting vessel.

"Push it out," she ordered, and they did so, setting it loose on the waves. It dipped and reared.

"Nay!" Keelan shrieked. "Nay, lass!"

"Live long." Her words were whispered, but he heard them.

"Chetfield!" He shrieked the name. "Touch her and ye will die one time for each day ye've lived."

The old man chuckled. "Well, shall we get down to business, my dear? Where is my staff?"

The raft twisted beneath Keelan's writhing form. He craned his neck, needing to see, terrified to see, yanking madly at his bonds. Her words were lost in the rush of the waves, the horror that filled his head, but he could see her, standing proud and alone near the rocky shore.

Her lips moved. She raised her chin. Tendrils of seal-dark hair wisped past her elfish face.

Chetfield stepped forward, but she lifted the knife and set the blade to her chest. The old man held up a placating hand.

She spoke and pointed, raising her arm toward the west. The old man gave her a smile and a nod, and then, as if by magic, the villains parted. She turned toward a saddled steed.

Keelan stared, eyes watering in the wind, breath held as she caught the animal's reins. Almost free. But then Roland lurched forward.

"Lass!" Keelan yelled. The raft swirled sideways. He shoved his feet against the rudder, yanking with all his might. Wood splintered.

He jerked his body free. A shard sliced his wrist, but he was already falling into the water, hands bound. "Dunna die! Dunna. I'm coming." He went under, bobbed up. He tossed his head, trying to see. She was there. On the ground. The bastard was bending over her. "Leave her!" Water filled his nostrils. He kicked madly. A wave rolled him under, tossed him up. Air burst into his lungs, but it didn't matter. Nothing mattered if she was gone. But she was there. Roland stood over her, reached for her. "Nay!" he sobbed, struggling against death. But it had him in its grip now, dragging him down, pulling him under, filling his head.

Blackness swirled amid images. Past, present, future, all garbled into dark, twisting scenes, and suddenly he was yanked into the open air by his wrists. A dark warrior dragged him up beside his destrier's flank.

"Celt!" Keelan's voice was a sob. "He's got her."

"Then take her back," rumbled the warrior, and slicing the rope that held his hand, spilled him to the earth.

Keelan swung his head to the right, searching for her even as his feet touched the ground. The stallion wheeled away. Someone shrieked a warning, but the warrior charged. A villain fell.

Keelan staggered about, and she was there, fighting, scrambling. Roland grabbed her foot.

"Leave her!" Keelan rasped, and leapt forward. There was a knife to her throat. Twenty yards separated them. Too far. Too far.

"Nay!" he screamed, but then a hound snarled and leapt. Roland was torn aside. Charity spilled to the ground. Safe. She was safe and close.

But suddenly Chetfield was there, dragging her up by the hair, arm across her neck, knife to her throat, deadly eyes finding Keelan across the distance.

He stumbled to a halt, legs faltering. "Please." He dropped to his knees.

"Beaten, am I, Highlander?"

He shook his head. "Dunna harm her."

"Go." Her teeth were gritted, her knuckles white as she gripped the old man's arm. "Please, Scotsman. Now's your chance."

"Chance?" Keelan breathed a laugh. Behind him someone screamed and died. "I have na chance, lass. Na without ye."

"Keelan—"

"Cease," Chetfield said, and pricked her neck with his blade. Blood, more precious than gold, slipped down her throat. "Touching as this is, I've a rather pressing appointment with my treasure."

354

Three men were arced out facing the dark Celt. He sliced through the trio and spun about. The Hound snarled and leapt, leaving blood in its wake, but it was a flash of white that drew Keelan's attention—Lambkin galloping from the house. The Hound stopped, bristled.

"No," Charity gasped.

Chetfield shifted his gaze to the right and she struck, driving her elbow into his ribs.

He doubled over. Keelan leapt forward, and in that instant Chetfield loosed her, turned, stabbed. The knife sliced to the hilt between Keelan's ribs.

He was face to face with evil itself. Yet it was almost pain-free. Almost a relief in its shocking brilliance.

"No! No!" Charity screamed the words through a million misty miles.

But the devil was near. "Ye'll na harm her." Keelan snarled the words into the old man's face.

Chetfield twisted the blade, bringing the pain, the mind-blinding agony. "You're wrong again, Highlander."

Keelan staggered, gasping, feet spread, fighting for another few seconds. Just a few. Just enough.

"I'll kill her," the old man hissed.

Rage boiled like tar in Keelan's soul. Reaching up, he grabbed Chetfield by the throat, then slammed his head against the other's. The old man staggered backward. Keelan lurched after. Putting his hand to the hilt of the blade in his side, he jerked it from his ribs. Blood sprayed an arc across Chetfield's face.

"Give up, Scotsman!" Chetfield gasped, but the mocking was gone, replaced by fear, by the sight of his own death in his widening eyes as he stumbled backward.

Keelan shambled on, steps stilted but quickening.

"I can't die," sputtered Chetfield, and in that instant, Keelan struck. The knife seemed to move of its own accord, finding the ancient heart with unerring accuracy.

The old man staggered backward, shock and horror on his face. His knees hit the earth. "I can't . . . die," he repeated, and toppled into the dirt.

Keelan took another step forward. The earth tilted, pitched toward him, struck his face.

He heard Charity scream, felt her hands against his arm, turning him, crying for him.

Life was good. Death wasn't so bad.

He raised his hand to her face. There was blood on his fingers. Sticky. Warm. But she was safe. The Celt would make certain of that. The

Hound would guard her. "Me bonny lass," he said.

"Don't die!" Her words were a sob, her tears felt cool on his face. "Don't you do it, Highlander."

The battle around them was quieter. Lambkin trotted up, huddled against his side. He wrapped his arm about her neck, hugging her close. The world seemed a peaceful place.

A noise shuffled off to his right. Keelan turned his head. Toft stood nearby, seamed face solemn.

"I was wondering when ye would arrive, old man."

Guilt and sorrow melded on the ancient features. "I did na ken ye were on the run until 'twas too late." He shook his head, mouth turned down, eyes bright. "Dunna blame the Hound and the Celt. They came as soon as I told them of yer plight."

"There is na blame," Keelan said, and smiled. "Na more."

The old man nodded, cleared his throat. "Where be the staff?"

"Ye'll have to ask the . . ." he began, but in that instant the Black Celt strode up, sword covered in gore.

Turning, Charity yanked the knife from Chetfield's chest and rose to her feet, bloody blade held before her.

"Stay back!" she hissed. Blood streaked her face, stark and red beneath wild amber eyes. "Touch a hair on his head and I'll kill you. I swear to God."

O'Banyon approached from the left, wearing nothing but a makeshift kilt. The knife shook in Charity's hand, but she stood her ground.

"We've come in peace," said the Irish Hound from amid the broken bodies of the fallen, and lifted his hand for her knife. She raised it defiantly, and he smiled, sharp teeth flashing in the sunlight. "She's too good for the likes of ye, Keelan lad," he said. "But I like her."

She blinked, hope flickering cautiously in her eyes as she shifted them from one to the next. "Save him," she pleaded.

The Celt nodded once, then knelt and lifted Keelan into his arms.

Pain seared him like a hot iron, tearing him limb from limb. "Bloody hell," he rasped, and slipped into unconsciousness.

Chapter 29

She was naked again. Not a stitch of clothes. And it was daylight. The sun shone on her smooth shoulders, her breasts, the long sweep of her waist. Behind her, a waterfall stretched into the sky.

She approached him, hips swaying gently. Naked hips. Holy fook, it was too bad he was dreaming again. Then again, if he was dreaming, he probably wasn't dead.

"You're *not* dead."

"Are ye certain?" He didn't bother to open his eyes.

"And you're not dreaming."

He smiled into his pillow. It smelled of lavender. "Then why is there a waterfall in me bedchamber?"

"Tell me true, is Lady Colline a witch?"

"What?" He opened his eyes with a snap. And she was there . . . naked. So there really was a God.

"Lady Colline," Charity said, and perched herself on the edge of the bed. Her legs were long and smooth . . . and naked.

"Holy fook, lass, I canna take much more of these dreams."

She brushed his hair away from his face. "I told you you're not dreaming."

"Then why are you naked?"

"It was time you woke up."

He stared.

She shrugged. Her breasts jiggled slightly. "Lady Colline feared she had drugged you too deeply. That you would never come to. I told her I had an idea." Leaning over, she kissed him. "I worried," she whispered.

"Aboot me?"

Were there tears in her eyes? "Foolish, I know," she said, and gently moving the blankets aside, she stretched out beside him. Turned out, he was naked too. Naked and ready. Her skin felt smooth and cool as she stretched out against him. Her breasts rubbed his chest. She bent one leg, laying it across his. He stared at the ceiling, trying to tell if there were clouds.

"I'm still dreaming, aren't I?"

"Does this feel like a dream?"

He raised his brows. "Aye."

She chuckled against his shoulder, but the sound was broken. "Tell me you're not going to die."

He slipped a hand over the satin-smooth skin of her hip. It felt like heaven. "I think I may have already."

"I'm sorry, Angel."

"That this be a dream?"

"That I stole the staff from you."

"Ahh." He traced her breast with the backs of his fingers. "Not to worry, luv. All's well, so long as it's safe."

"It's not."

His hand stopped. His gaze caught hers. "Chetfield—"

"Chetfield's dead."

Relief struck him like a wave. "Where's the staff?"

"Here. On the ship."

He thought about that for a moment, felt the dip and weave of the vessel in which he lay. "Where are we bound?"

"I know things about him. Terrible things," she whispered. "He killed my mother."

"I know, lass."

She nodded, unsurprised. Tears dripped onto his shoulder.

"Ye always intended to be rid of it," he guessed.

"As did you."

"Nay." He sighed at his own shortcomings, his own weaknesses. "I have neither yer courage nor yer kindness, lass. I but came to take it. To gain what I could."

"Then you found your father's journal."

Memories sailed in, but weak now, diluted. "He was me da's most trusted friend."

"And my father. Blood of my blood, Angel. Flesh of my—"

"No." He drew her close, sweeping back her hair, loving her with aching intensity. "No, luv. He's nothing. While ye are everything."

"He—"

"Was a monster. But we've bested the beast."

She drew a careful breath. "We must return it to the sea."

"But all that gold . . ."

"Angel . . ."

He smiled. "I jest. We'll throw it back to the deep, luv. 'Twill na be found again."

"Truly?"

"Aye."

"Make love to me," she whispered.

And he smiled.

"So the lad awakes," rumbled a voice.

Keelan scrambled to cover her nudity . . . and awoke with a snap.

"Yes." Charity was sitting primly at the edge of his bed. Fully clothed.

He sat up. The room was dim; the berth rocked gently. Charity smiled. Secrets and dreams flared between them, stealing his breath. Beside him, Lambkin lifted her head from the pillow, black eyes shining, bringing a sliver of normalcy.

"Where am I?"

"Some leagues out to sea," said the Black Celt. "'Tis aboot time ye ceased yer slumber."

Keelan shifted higher against the pillows behind him.

"I'm not dreaming?"

Charity raised a suggestive brow.

"Ye've been doing plenty of that, lad," said Hiltsglen. "O'Banyon's lady feared ye might never come to."

It all seemed vaguely similar to the dream. He glanced at Charity again. She touched his face. Thoughts and dreams flowed between them.

"Lady Colline's on this vessel?" Keelan asked, trying to focus.

"She's been tending you for some days. Ever since the lassie's father tried to kill ye."

"He knows more than you realize," Charity said.

Keelan scowled. "I wish I could say the same."

She laughed and swept the hair back from his brow as an old man stepped through the door.

"Good morning to ye, lad," Toft said, and shambled in, hat in hand. "We worried for ye."

Keelan drew a careful breath, thinking, grappling for footing. "I believe I may owe ye me thanks, gaffer," he said.

"Aye well, one must take care of one's elders," said the old man, and chuckled. "Strange to think I be the youngest man in this room, aye?"

"So you are Keelan's . . . cousin?" Charity asked.

"His mother's sister's son's son," Toft said, "and the Black Celt's grandson many times removed."

"Oh." She sounded a bit dazed, more like the Charity of old, and not the brazen lass who entered his dreams and set the world aright.

"Life be complicated," Toft admitted.

"In yer lineage, mayhap," O'Banyon said.

They glanced up as he stepped through the

door. His incisors still looked strangely sharp. Maybe because he oft spent time roaming the forests in hound form. Life *was* complicated.

"Me lady feared the gift she sent with Toft some weeks past would na be enough to heal ye," said the Irishman. "But I see ye are doing well."

Keelan thought back. "She touched the bottle with her bare hands," he guessed. "Left her healing gift there. Knowing I would na drink it."

"Ye are a stubborn lad," said Toft. "And ye hold a terrible grudge aboot the last potion ye took. Thus she sent the bottle for ye, and the potion inside for Chetfield."

"So it was na me what was healing him."

"Yers be the gift of dreams, lad."

Keelan shook his head. "A poor gift that be. It has caused me naught—" But in his mind, Charity wrapped her legs about his back and squeezed him. He jerked his head back. His breath caught hard in his throat.

It took him several seconds to realize the others were staring at him in perplexed bewilderment. Only the girl's eyes were laughing.

"Be ye ready to be rid of the staff, lad?" rumbled the Black Celt.

Shoving the dream aside for later consideration, Keelan nodded and sat up. He was surprisingly free from pain as he rose to his feet.

O'Banyon's brows ricocheted to the ceiling. Toft cleared his throat.

"'Tis up to ye, of course," rasped the old man. "But ye might wish to don some clothes, lad."

Chapter 30

They were married at Arborhill. The ceremony was small and private. A reception of sorts was served in the dining hall, but the newlyweds slipped away early.

Amid a thousand nodding roses, they stood alone. Keelan wrapped his arms about his bride. She leaned her head back against his shoulder.

"I did na actually think ye would do it," he said.

"Let you stand up naked in front of your forefathers?"

"Ye're cruel, lass," he said then, "how the devil do ye get in me dreams?"

She smiled. "There seems to be a good deal that can't be explained. But I believe you were meant for me, Highlander. It was not some simple coincidence that awakened you from your slumber. You were sent to Crevan House to set things right, for your parents, for my mother . . ." She touched his hand. "For me.

He tightened his grip about her waist. "Thank ye, luv."

"For the dreams?"

He grinned. "That too," he said, "but I've been talking about returning the horrid thing to the depths."

She sighed, face solemn. "It's done no good in this world, Keelan."

"I know, but . . . 'twas *gold.*" He shook his head. "We held it in our hands."

She gripped his arms. "And now we hold each other. 'Tis far better."

He shook his head as if bemused. "I feel I dunna know ye any longer, lass," he said, and she laughed, turning in his arms.

"You've never known me, Highlander."

"But I plan to set that right," he said, and kissed her. The world was right, happy, smiling. "I hope ye dunna mind that we must live here at Arborhill for a time until I come into me own."

"This is a beautiful place," she said. Lambkin wandered up, head tilted at an odd angle. The ribbon tied about her woolly neck was beginning to fray and she staggered a little.

Keelan scowled. "What happened to me Lambkin?"

"I believe I saw O'Banyon's daughter feeding her punch."

"She's intoxicated?"

"I believe so." Bending, Charity picked up the little creature, cuddling her between them before lifting her gaze back to his. "What *is* your own, exactly?" she asked.

"'Twas a time I was quite wealthy, ye ken."

"A hundred and fifty years ago?" she guessed.

"Just aboot that, aye."

"I'm not certain how that's going to help us now."

He nodded. "I'm a fair charlatan," he said. "I could join the Gypsies and tell fortunes."

"A fine idea," she said, "but perhaps we should live on our own estate."

"'Tis a lovely thought," he agreed. Lambkin belched softly. "And I do hate to be the one to remind ye, but we dunna own an estate."

"Chetfield was my father," she said. "And very wealthy. Land, jewels, coin."

"Somehow I dunna think the Crown will accept ye as his rightful heir."

"It's true that I have no proof."

"They're sticklers that way."

"Maybe this will help us then," she said, and dipping into her cleavage, pulled out an ancient coin.

He stared at it. "What's that?"

"I believe it was called a doubloon."

"Ahh. And where did you get it, lass?"

"It was with its mates," she said.

"It has mates?"

"A thousand or so."

He stared. She smiled.

"I didn't spend six months at Crevan House sitting on my thumbs, Highlander."

"I knew I loved ye," he said.

"Prove it," she whispered.

And suddenly . . . they were naked.

Avon Romantic Treasures

Unforgettable, enthralling love stories, sparkling with passion and adventure from Romance's bestselling authors

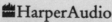

DISCOVER ROMANCE at its
SIZZLING HOT BEST FROM AVON BOOKS